"YOUNG FELLER," SAID BULLEN, SCOWLING, "ARE YOU LOOKIN' FOR TROUBLE?"

Suddenly Dexter laughed. "Why else do you think I've come here, man? Trouble? Of course I want trouble. I expect to have trouble with every meal, every day, until I've gotten back what's mine, the land that belongs to my family!"

He looked Bullen straight in the eye.

"Them that wants trouble, they mostly get it," answered Bullen, sullen and angry.

"Go spread news of *that*," said Dexter. "Go down to the valley and tell your family and your friends that I'm back. And tell them to stand on their guard because I intend to come and take what is my own—and a *hundred* fighting men won't stop me!"

MAX BRAND

Valley Vultures

WARNER BOOKS

A Warner Communications Company

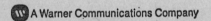

WHEN I first saw "Prince Charlie," I was standing on the veranda of the hotel at Monte Verde. Being new to the West, its ways and its people, naturally I was using my eyes, and yet I did not pick him out from the little crowd which was lounging there. He picked himself out for my attention by what he did, or rather, by what he failed to do.

I had been watching the men with a careful eye, that is to say, I had been looking at them without staring, for I had heard that staring annoyed Westerners, and these fellows had a formidable look, with their rough clothes, their heavy belts, and their holstered guns. However, I managed to survey them all, from their high-heeled boots and their spoon-handled spurs to their wide-brimmed hats. A few men had come down from the mines, and their outfits were different, of course. They wore boots meant for walking, not riding; they had soft, shapeless felt hats; and they affected the heaviest kind of flannel shirts. On the whole, they were noisier than the cow-puncher class, but I could see that both kinds were made of one warp and one woof. They were all big; they were all hard; and they all had in their eyes the look of people who have seen many things that are high and many that are low. It amazes me, as I look back to the time, that I did not select Prince Charlie from the lot of them; but the fact is that I failed to notice him at all until events forced him out from that group as a lighthouse stands out above a harbor.

I had turned from the men, just before the crisis, and was looking down into Dexter Valley, where the blue of the afternoon shadows already had closed over the town of Dexter, though its windows still were blinking like cheerful little fires through the thin mist of color. It was a place to look at and rest the eyes, that valley. It had all that men could want—it had rich bottom lands for the plow, and rolling meadows that receded on either hand, thinly sprinkled with groups of cattle, and all of the upper slopes were darkened by great forests which, at that time, had scarcely been invaded by the woodcutters. It was the sort of a place that one could look at and suddenly feel the greatness of our country. For this was a little kingdom set off by itself, a beautiful, secluded and entire province. The river that went through the midst of it would supply enough electric power for every need—even up to the running of a manufacturing plant, in fact. It was inspiring to look down into that delightful valley. It filled one's heart with satisfaction. I told myself, as I stared at the picture, that I had come out here for my health, but that I would remain to become a rich man!

This thought had barely come home when the crash came. I heard a loud voice bawling out a curse, and I turned to see a man flounder down the steps and tumble in the dust of the roadway. He rolled almost under the heels of a mule team, and the mules showed plenty of interest. They tried to get at him with their hoofs, and with their teeth, but he managed to tumble back to safety.

Instead of sympathizing with his danger, which had brought me to my feet in a sweat, that rough crowd burst into a roar of great-throated laughter until he picked himself up and they saw his face. I could see at a glance that he was well known to them and that they were sorry for their laughter. He did not have to be well known to me to make me feel awe, as he was one of those types that you can pick out at a glance for the prize ring or, better still, rough-and-tumble fighting. He had a face as ugly as a bulldog's, a blunt, wide jaw, and a mere excuse of a nose. Now he was crimson with rage, and he stood at the foot of the steps swaying a little from foot to foot in the very wind and tempest of his passion.

"Who done that? Who tripped me?" he shouted.

No one answered. I don't believe that he had been tripped, for that matter. Who would have had the courage to affront such a fellow intentionally? When he got no reply, he bounded to the top of the steps and struck. I am sure that he did not deliberately select his man. It would have made little difference to him whether he got a big fellow or a small one, but he merely struck out at the nearest face.

The other bystanders scattered back to see the fight, if fight there was to be, and then I had a chance to see the fellow who had been hit. It was Prince Charlie.

Now that I saw him, I marveled that I had not picked hm out before, for he was a man in a million. He was dark enough to be a Mexican, with swarthy skin, silky black hair, and big, shadowy eyes. He was neither tall nor short, but what one might call average height. He was not handsome, either, for he had high cheek bones almost worthy of an Indian, rather a wide mouth, and a nose too aquiline. When I say that it was strange I had not noticed him before, I refer to a nameless air of distinction in which he was clothed, the haughty expression of his mouth, the indifferent calm in his dark eyes, the carriage of his head, and, in spite of the comparative ugliness of his features, a suggestion of infinite care having been lavished upon him, in the making of body and mind. Regardless of his youth, an army might well have picked such a fellow to lead it in battle.

I suppose that he was fully fifty or sixty pounds lighter than the hulking bully who had struck him, but from the first glance I lost my sympathy for the smaller man and gave it to the aggressor.

Something would happen to that fellow, in spite of his size, and I felt my face growing cold with apprehension.

The man who had received the blow neither staggered to one side nor retreated before the other. Instead, he stood fast, and with his eyes fixed gravely upon the big fellow, he moved his hand to the breast pocket of his coat and took out a handkerchief. A small drop of blood had gathered on his lip and trickled down to his chin and this blood, with careful, light touches, he wiped away, then deliberately he moistened his mouth, still watching the stranger.

7

"You're the one that tripped up my heels!" shouted the big man. "I'm gonna bust you in two. I'm gonna crack your head for you. Who are you, anyway?"

His voice was as violent as his words or his blow, but Prince Charlie did not stir, continuing to survey the other with those dark and unfathomable eyes of his.

"I am Charles Dexter," said he, in the most quiet and musical of voices.

"Dexter?" said the big man. "Dexter?"

Then he burst out into a bawling laughter.

"You're one of the Dexters of Dexter Valley, I reckon!" he shouted, and this amused him so much that he rocked with mirth.

That laughter ended, finally, and Prince Charlie said:

"Yes, I'm the last of the Dexters of Dexter Valley."

He was not laughing, you may believe, as he returned this answer, and the last of the big fellow's mirth faded out as though he had had a loaded gun shoved in his face.

He looked about him, and there was wildness in his eyes.

"He says he's a Dexter!" he exclaimed. "A Dexter of Dexter Valley, and everybody knows that there ain't any of 'em left."

"When you come back," said Prince Charlie, "I'll tell you more about myself."

"I ain't goin'," said the other, scowling. "Where would I be goin'?"

"You're going," said Prince Charlie, "to get the gun you forgot to wear, to-day. I'll be waiting here for a longer talk, when you come back."

This he said so calmly that, for a moment, the significance of the thing did not dawn on me. But then I realized that he was inviting the big chap to go get a weapon and come back to pay for the blow with bullets. I was slow in understanding, but the rest of the crowd knew in a second what was meant, and there was a little flash of faces as the men turned their heads and stared at one another.

It was rather a grisly moment. No matter how accustomed these fellows were to guns and the ways of guns, they were not much better prepared than I was for the calm and the quiet of Prince Charlie. The really devilish part of it, as you may imagine, was that he was so sure of himself that he approached a battle for life and death as though he were asking for a drink of water.

The other backed up a little, and his big fists clenched into knobs. His back was rigid, and it wasn't rage that stiffened it, I could guess.

He muttered something, and then went through the screen doors of the hotel, and we could hear his feet trampling up the stairs. Every one waited out there on the veranda, never speaking, except in a tense whisper, now and then, and all nerves were on edge, except those of young Dexter. He remained as calm as you please, and began to walk up and down in front of the door. He was a dapper-looking fellow, dressed in gray flannels, and wearing spats, with a little wild flower in his button hole to set him off, and a bow tie, very neatly done up. By his step, the narrowness of his hips, the solid look of him about the shoulders, I put him down immediately for an athlete, and, I dare say, an athlete he was, and of much training; or else he was born fit and strong, as some men are. Strength seems to be bred into their bones.

I make these remarks now because I never was able to find out anything about his past; I don't think that a single other of the mountain men ever knew, either, except that he was the son of Charles Dexter, Second.

Prince Charlie, while he waited, took out a cigarette case, lighted a cigarette, and went to smoking. He had a rather dreamy look about his eyes, and what would have been sheer bravado in other men was simply natural in him. It happened that he wanted to smoke, and as for the rest of us, our excitement, and our wire-drawn suspense, we meant nothing to him. We simply were not in the picture, so far as he was concerned.

Well, we listened and listened for the step of big Jay Burgess—that was the name of the fighter, I learned afterward—to return. We waited, and we waited in vain, for after a few minutes, a young fellow came around the corner of the veranda and said to some one he knew on the porch: "Jay Burgess has gone nutty. Whatcha think? I seen him lettin' himself down out of his window by a rope!"

Well, that was a sufficient explanation of what Burgess thought of his chances against young Mr. Dexter with guns; every one took in a deep breath, and while they were taking it, a gray flash, like a cat, went by me and jumped to the ground at the end of the veranda. It was Dexter, looking for his mouse; but just then, we heard a sudden rattling of hoofs departing from behind the hotel.

Prince Charlie shrugged his shoulders, and took another breath of cigarette smoke!

CHAPTER II.   CLAUDIA SPEAKS

THAT crowd, as I was saying, was as hardy a lot of Westerners as you could ask for. Even though I was new to the country, I could guess that they were an outstanding lot, and after I had been there for some time, I learned that the men of Monte Verde and Dexter Valley were all made of the same good steel. However, they were fairly staggered by what had happened before their eyes and mine. A Dexter of the Dexter Valley family—that was the first thing that upset them; and the second was the routing of big Jay Burgess. I hardly blamed Jay Burgess, when I had a fair look at young Charles Dexter, but then I could hardly be expected to know much about gun fighting, seeing that I had come to the age of five and forty without ever pulling the trigger of a revolver. Once when I was handling a large crew of roughs building the Chariton Bridge, I had bought a revolver and wore it with a sort of silly ostentation, but I never could have used the thing to any purpose. Gun fights were so far outside of my ken that it could not be wondered at that I blamed no man for avoiding one of them. This Western crowd, however, was a different matter, and I expected to hear from them a good deal of adverse criticism of the cowardice of Burgess. Instead, to my astonishment, not a word was said. There were murmurs, here and there, but that was all.

They seemed to take it rather for granted, so far as I could see, that a man should run when a Dexter was on the firing line opposite!

This little pause after the running away of Burgess did not last very long. The new interest was supplied by a girl who came hastily out through the front screen doors, letting them bang with a great jangling behind her. I had seen her once or twice about the hotel before this. She was Claudia Laffitter, the niece of the proprietress, and even my forty-five years of bachelordom had grown a bit dizzy at the sight of her. She was no perfectly classical beauty, for as a man grows past his childhood, he ceases to look for doll-babies or for clearly cut statues. Instead, we begin to look for a touch of humanity and character, and Claudia Laffitter was full of both. She had the step and the strange carriage of an Indian; she had the brown and rosy face and the bright eye of a boy. She was as straightforward in her ways as any man; and yet that frankness of bearing merely intensified, in my estimation, her real femininity.

Now she walked straight from the door to this stranger who called himself by the name of Dexter.

"You're the fellow who says that he's Charlie Dexter?" she asked of him.

Prince Charlie took off his hat to her, and he bowed a little. There was a sort of Latin grace in his manner which looked very odd out there on the veranda of that little hotel, looking at the great mountains, on one side, and over the huge blue shadow of the valley on the other.

"Yes," said he. "My name is Charles Dexter."

She looked him up and down.

"Come, come!" she said. "There never was a Dexter

as small as you are! I've heard about them all, in the old days. There never was a Dexter who looked like you; and I knew Charlie Dexter when I was a little girl!"

I've spoken of her frankness before, but this was a little more than frank and a good deal of rude. However, there is something about a straight, unshadowed eye and a dauntless bearing that takes the sting out of even such a challenge as she was giving to Prince Charlie.

"You knew me, and I knew you," he said, "when you used to call me Prince Charlie on your good days, and dago on your bad ones. And you were usually rather a bad little girl, Miss Laffitter."

You can imagine the interest which this dialogue was arousing. The men bit their lips with excitement and their eyes kept flashing as they turned from the girl to the stranger and from the stranger back to the doubting face of Claudia. For she was by no means convinced by this last display of intimate knowledge.

"You could have learned about that," she said. "A lot of people knew what we called each other. And—why, Prince Charlie Dexter at twelve was the handsomest lad in the valley, and not two inches shorter then than you are now, ten years later! Do you mean to stand right there before me and tell me that you are Charles Dexter?"

"I stand right here before you," he replied with a smile, "and tell you that I am Charles Dexter."

Suddenly she stamped. Her face reddened, and shone with her doubt and her anger.

"I don't believe a word of it!" she cried.

He only bowed to her again.

"No Dexter has ever looked a bit like you!" she cried.

"No Dexter," said he, "would ever say 'no' to you, Claudia!"

This extreme calmness of his acted as a brake upon her headlong emotion. But, stepping back from him a little, she continued to measure him with her eye, and to shake her head.

She pointed off the end of the veranda.

"If you're the true Charles Dexter," said she, "you have a right to every acre of land in that valley."

He bowed to her, and maintained his smile.

"I have a right to every acre of land in that valley!" he replied.

She stared at him, her lips parted.

"The Livingstons, and the Crowells, and the Dinmonts, and the Bensons, they're no more than interlopers, according to what you say," she declared.

He repeated the names after her:

"The Livingstons, Crowells, Dinmonts, and Bensons; He muttered somethng, and then went through the are no more than interlopers—and murderers, Claudia."

She flinched a little, at the sound of her first name.

I thought, then, that she was going to cry out that she suddenly believed everything that he had been stating and claiming. Instead, she gave her head a violent shake, again.

Then she did a surprising thing—though I don't suppose that it was really surprising in that community of democrats. She turned to all the crowd, and her bright eyes swept across my face, among the rest.

"I'll tell you what, people," said Claudia Laffitter, "we all have a right to question him and we all have a right to make out for sure that he's really a Dexter. Because, if he is, there's going to be something redder than paint running yonder in the valley before long—just as red as it ran ten years ago!"

She looked back to Dexter.

"You know that we have a right to question you?"

"Certainly," said he. "I'd welcome it. I have a decent respect for the opinion of mankind."

He smiled as he quoted this. And with a pang, I was struck by the idea that this youth was entirely too cool, too calm, too much the master of himself and others to be altogether honest. I don't know why one feels that the criminal has an added advantage, but it is true that we have the instinct. Crime makes lying easy. I stared at that boy and told myself that, beyond any question, he had been lying in front of us as fast as a clock ticks, and as steadily.

His assent to the questioning should have pleased her, I suppose, but he was so glib and ready that she frowned more darkly than before.

"Very well," she said, curtly. "We'll get on with the thing. We'll have a little jury to sit on the case. Let me see—who shall we have on it?"

"Hold on, Claudia," said a big, iron-faced fellow with the arms and the shoulders of a gorilla. "Hold on. I dunno that you got a claim to run all of this here affair."

She whirled about on him.

"Why haven't I?" she demanded. "You better believe that I have a right."

"You've got no more right than others," said he. "If our friend here claims that he's Charlie Dexter, you know perfectly well that it's the business of everybody here to get at the truth."

"Was my father Ben Laffitter, or was he not?" asked the girl.

"Of course he was," said the big man.

"Uncle Jed Raymond," she went on, in her clear, strong voice, "answer me this: Did Ben Laffitter die for the Dexters, that night of the betrayal?"

"Aye, honey," said Jed Raymond. "We know how he died. But this job of tryin' this stranger on what he says he is, oughta go to older heads than yours, Claudia."

"Send it to the law courts, then," she suggested with a certain bitterness. "They'll do a good job over it."

"Uncle Jed" raised his big hand. It was not over clean, but it gave me a feeling, I don't know why, that he was a supremely honest man.

"I don't intend to call in no law," he said. "This here thing was settled once outside of the law. Maybe it'll be settled again without ever gettin' inside the law. I dunno, but that's the way that it looks to me. I'd begin in the first place by sayin' what sort of a jury we had oughta have."

14

"All right," said the girl. "But I'm going to be in on this."

"Aye, Claudia," he answered rather abruptly. "You're most generally in on everything, so far as I can see, and I dunno how I can keep you out. What I suggest is that we get two people from each side, and one person that ain't on either side. That'll be a committee of five. If three out of the five can agree that this is Charles Dexter, then we'll say so, and I'll stand by the decision, for one."

"Does that sound right to you people?" said the girl, turning to the spectators.

Several voices spoke up quickly, and by acclaim the first four were quickly chosen. There was Claudia Laffitter, in the first place, the death of whose father seemed to give her a natural claim to consideration. She was a representative of the Dexter clan, one might say. The other for the same side was big Uncle Jed Raymond.

The two who were known to be opposed to the Dexter faction were a florid man of middle age whom they called "Dandy" Pete Bullen, perhaps because he was dressed in a gay Mexican style; and with him was nominated a man of some fifty years, I should have said—a small, lean fellow with very bright and steady eyes.

His name was Marvin Crowell.

When the four had been selected, the crowd looked about for a neutral, and Claudia, looking toward me, said suddenly: "Why everybody who lives around here has been on one side or the other, nearly all his life. But here's a stranger who hardly knows Dexter Valley from Monte Verde. This is Mr. Oliver Dean, and perhaps he'll help us make up our minds?"

Young Prince Charlie turned and gave me a single glance—I felt it flicker through me like the thrust of a ghostly rapier.

"A perfectly acceptable choice to me," he said slowly.

And that was how I was made a member of the committee and dragged into the grim affair that was to grow out of this day's work.

CHAPTER III.   QUESTIONS

WE all went into the hotel—that is to say, Dandy Pete Bullen, Marvin Crowell, Uncle Jed Raymond, the girl, I, and the man who claimed that he was Charles Dexter. He was to be tried, and we were to be judge, examining lawyers, and jury. It was an exciting business, of course, but I was not altogether sure that I was glad to be mixed up in it. If I could have looked forward clearly into the next three or four months, I certainly would have declined the post with thanks, packed my bags, and gone as far from Monte Verde as stage-coaches and fast horses and trains could carry me. But in I went with the rest, unconscious of what the future was to bring, except for a certain tingling along my nerves that might have passed for a prophetic foreboding.

We went into a little room at the corner of the hotel, so that its windows gave in two directions. From the eastern one, we looked straight down into Dexter Valley, which was in a way the theme of our argument. From the other window, we could look—at an angle—toward the mountains, seeing especially the outstanding king of the range, Thimble Peak. And a ridiculous name it is for that rough-shouldered, white-headed giant! The room in which we sat had a round table in the center of it. It was used, sometimes, to accommodate an overflow from the main dining room; and in the evening it was a place for a poker game of the friendly sort. On the floor was a matting which had been cut by spurs, here and there. The edge of the table had been nicked and whittled by absent-minded punchers and around the walls were photographs. One was a colored calendar showing a too-pretty girl with several wheat straws between her shining white teeth; there was a picture of Lincoln with an ancient wreath still

16

hanging beneath it, dust covered, half the leaves fallen off, but the remaining left religiously untouched. The haughty, weary face of Washington looked back from the other side of the room, and there was a sketch of Mad Anthony Wayne reining in a horse which seemed about to tumble backward. These insignificant details I mention merely because they are so firmly printed in my mind. I paid little heed to them at the time, or to anything else in the room except a thing to which our attention was called, with a little outburst of laughter. That was the distinctly outlined print of a foot exactly in the center of the ceiling, though how it could have been planted there, I never have heard or been able to guess.

We settled down around the table and Uncle Jed Raymond said:

"Well, friends, we might as well start right in. Dexter, would you mind sitting around on this side, where we'll get more light on your face?"

I almost smiled at this childish simplicity, and Dexter smiled outright.

"Certainly," said he. "You ought to have a chance to see me change face or color if I'm tripped in a lie."

With perfect good humor, he went around to the other side of the table where he faced both the windows. He was sitting, at that time, on my left, and Jed Raymond was on his left. Claudia Laffitter exactly faced him.

"You say, partner," said Uncle Jed, "that you're the real Charles Dexter, eh?"

"Yes, that's my claim," replied the young fellow, nodding a little. Or rather, I should say that he bowed a bit. This was his habitual gesture, his whole body inclining a trifle forward, from the waist. He usually kept his face very grave, though the lights went on and off in his eyes all the time.

"Why d'you want us to find out about you?" said Uncle Jed, very bluntly. "Why don't you give your proofs to the police, say? If they believe you, then we'd be more likely to."

"You mean that I should show my claims in the town,

there? Down in Dexter? There they have a Livingston for sheriff, and a Benson for judge, and what sort of a judgment do you think they would make on any claims I put forward when the admission of those claims would wipe out their estates?"

This point seemed pretty clearly established.

But he went on: "As for proving who I am to you people, you can imagine why I want to do that. If you give me your stamp of approval and declare that I'm really Charles Dexter, then at least half of the people in this part of the world will line up on my side. I take that for granted."

"And war will start again!" broke in old Marvin Crowell.

The young fellow looked across at him—he was just to the right of Claudia—and made his customary short bow.

At this, Crowell grew very excited and jumped a bit in his chair.

"By the old Harry," said he, "it sounds to me like you're here huntin' for an excuse to make trouble."

"As your brother, Manly, who was looking for trouble when he killed Jefferson Dexter, my own father," said the boy.

Though he said this without heat, one can imagine that it was like a blow in the face. Crowell stared for an instant, and almost forgot to retort, for a moment, but then he exploded: "It ain't true. Everybody knows that Manuel Scorpio done that killing."

"Manuel Scorpio killed several others of my family, as I'm aware," said Prince Charlie. "But he didn't kill my father."

"What makes you sure of that? It's your word against the world!" put in Dandy Pete, picking at one of the big silver buttons on the cuff of his jacket sleeve.

"It's my eyes against the world, too," replied the boy, "because I saw the killing!"

"Where were you when you seen?"

"I was in the door of the tank house ——"

"Hold on! Hold on!" said Uncle Jed, who from the

first took a very hostile attitude toward Prince Charlie. "What time of day was that?"

"It was a quarter past three in the morning."

"And what was you doin' in the door of the tank house at a quarter past three in the mornin'?"

"I had gone down to get ——"

"Wait a minute," put in Claudia, rather fiercely, as I thought. "We can break up this case in a simpler way than all that. If he's Charles Dexter, he owns that valley ——"

"Not even if he's Charles Dexter he don't," said Crowell firmly. "It ain't been proved that the Dexter land grant was ever ——"

"There's no use arguing about that," replied the girl. "Let it go, Mr. Crowell, please. You know that if he's Charles Dexter, he'll get so many people behind him that a part of his family's land will come back to him; and even a part of it would mean millions, now."

"We found it cattle range and we made it blossom like a garden!" declared Crowell. "But he'll never get back any part of it!"

"Mr. Crowell," I could not help putting in, "you're not the prosecuting attorney, here, but simply part judge and part jury."

My point was so obvious, considering Crowell's bitterness, that he could not make an answer. From the boy, I expected some glance, at least, of acknowledgment, but he merely looked me over with a blank eye of disinterest and then glanced away as if toward more important things.

This angered me. I said to myself that the cool young scoundrel was overacting his part; but this was the first proof I had of the steel-cold nerves of Dexter.

Claudia Laffitter went on:

"You're all interrupting all the time," she complained, rightly. "Let's try to get somewhere. I'll ask some questions, and when I'm through, I'll keep still and let somebody else try. There's no use arguing about the value to him of being acknowledged as Charlie Dexter. Of course that name has value. Millions of dollars of value. And something of higher value than dollars, too. The name for its own sake, is what I mean!"

She put her chin up, as she said this, and there was such a ring in her voice that I gathered, at once, that she attached some almost sacred significance to that family of the Dexters.

She went on, speaking straight to the boy: "How long ago did you leave Dexter Valley?"

"On the night we were betrayed by Manuel Scorpio."

"Where did you go?"

"Oh, I've been in half a dozen places, since that time."

"Well, recently, then?"

"In college, for the last four years."

"You knew that you were the heir to all of the Dexter claims?"

"Yes, I knew that, of course."

"And yet you let ten years go by without putting in a claim for what was yours?"

This question had so much point to it that I leaned forward a little to hear the answer, and to study Dexter's face. He seemed not at all confused and replied, readily: "Until I was a man, there was no use in coming back here to be swallowed alive by Scorpio, or some other of the family's enemies."

At this she cried out: "But Scorpio's dead. He was drowned in the river, that night, and everybody knows it."

"There never was any proof of his death," said the boy, "He's never been heard of since."

"Of course he hasn't. He's probably lying low, though, and keeping a new name. He would have been a madman to go about this part of the country, where so many of the people were ready and willing to make an end of him!"

"Aye!" broke in Uncle Jed Raymond. "More'n ready and willing, as a matter of fact."

He nodded, and his face was grim. I began to be anxious to learn more about this Manuel Scorpio.

"It looks a strange thing to me," said the girl. "That ten years' absence. I think it looks strange to the rest of us, here. Is there anybody who went off with you from Dexter Valley, or do you want us to believe that a twelve-year-old boy rode out of that place all by himself?"

"Phil Anson, the cow-puncher, was the fellow who rode with me."

"Aye, Phill disappeared!" broke in Uncle Jed, with a sudden light of belief in his eyes.

"Sure he disappeared," said Crowell. "And I think that the same thing that happened to Scorpio happened to him. The river got him and chopped him up on the rocks and made him food for the fishes. That's likely what happened to Phil Anson!"

"You can tell him what you think, in a few minutes," said the boy. "He's coming up here on the stage that's already overdue."

CHAPTER IV.   PROOF

THE proofs which I had heard of the youngster's identity, up to this point, seemed very slight and intangible, I must say, but the declaration that a man was arriving who had taken him from the valley ten years before and who presumably had been in touch with him, ever since, threw a bright and warm light over the affair. Claudia Laffitter cried out:

"Why didn't you tell us before?"

He answered her, rather dryly:

"Well, in twelve years Anson has changed in appearance almost as much as I have. You may want him to prove his identity also. Even if you accept him as the real Philip Anson, still you may say that if I'm an impostor, I simply have hired this man to help me in my intrigue. Philip Anson is hardly conclusive proof."

This quiet and logical speech, admitting instantly all the points that the opposition could bring forward, made an even greater impression on all of us than had the mention of Anson in the first place. Bullen and Marvin Crowell, who, of course, particularly did not wish the young fellow to establish the identity he claimed, began to scowl at the table.

Then Bullen said:

"We'll have to have a lot more proof. Lemme hear out of you what you was doing that night of the betrayal, as you call it."

"I'll tell you whatever you wish to know," said the boy.

"What time d'you go to bed that night?"

"I didn't go to bed at all," said Dexter.

"He says that he didn't go to bed that night," growled Crowell, looking around the table dismally.

"No, I stayed up all night."

"Why'd you do that?" bluntly demanded Bullen. "Kids of twelve ain't likely to stay up all night, are they?"

"I stayed up because I wasn't sleepy."

"Been drinkin' too much coffee, maybe?" asked Bullen, sneering.

"No, I was afraid."

"Hello! You was afraid? Afraid of what? You was there in that great big house of your father's, as you call him, and you had servants all around you. And still you was afraid?"

"Yes, I was afraid, because my cousin, Marshall Dexter, had been found dead the day before, with the mark on his forehead."

There was a stir at the table. For my part, I began to feel a cold puckering of gooseflesh up my back.

"What sort of a mark was it?" asked Claudia, cold and calm.

"I saw it," said the boy, nodding. "It was rather like a clumsy letter 'M,' with the last stroke, instead of curling up, prolonged straight downward. It was a queer-looking letter. It was drawn on the forehead of my dead cousin in charcoal—or something that looked like charcoal."

"Go on!" said Claudia.

"The morning after that killing, when we waked up, we found the same sign on the door of the house, and on every door where we were sleeping."

"You mean that sign was on every door in the house?" burst out Raymond, incredulous.

"No, but on the doors of the rooms where we were sleeping. My father's room, and mine. There was the same sign, exactly, on each of our doors. And that was why I was frightened. I felt, and my father felt, too, that whoever had murdered Marshall Dexter now intended to murder him and then murder me."

I shuddered as I listened.

"D'you find out anything what the sign meant?" asked Bullen.

"Well, we cast about in our minds for the name of some enemy of ours, or any one we knew, beginning with the letter 'M.' But we couldn't think of any one."

"Nobody you knew?"

"There was one puncher on the place called Maxwell. We talked about him, for a while, but my father decided that Maxwell was certainly an honest man, and I'm sure that he was right."

"You didn't guess what the thing meant, then?"

"Yes. Just at the end, my father guessed."

"Go on and tell me about it."

"We were having supper," Dexter said, "he and I alone, on the evening of the betrayal, and suddenly my father said that he had an idea, and he sent me after the big dictionary. He opened it up and looked in several places, and finally he came to the page where 'sign' was defined, and there were prints of the astronomical signs. He showed me one of them.

" 'That's what I've been looking for, Charlie,' he said."

Claudia Laffitter broke in with:

"They called you 'Buck,' in that house, most of the time."

"Only when my father was feeling jolly," replied Dexter. "When he was serious, he called me Charlie, or even Charles. He went on to show me that the sign for the

23

constellation called the Scorpion was almost exactly like the character which had been drawn on our doors and on the dead forehead of poor Marshall Dexter."

"Did that make him think of anything?" said Claudia Laffitter, leaning a bit forward on the table.

"Yes, it did, finally. Two or three times he said aloud: 'The Scorpion! The Scorpion! It is somebody who wants to tell us that he hates us as a scorpion hates, and that he'll kill us as a scorpion kills, in the dark, and as poor Marshall was killed! The Scorpion! The Scorpion!' he repeated. And then he exclaimed: 'The Latin for that word is Scorpio! By the Eternal!' "

"And then you thought of Manuel Scorpio?" asked the girl.

"Of course we thought of him then."

"Suppose that you describe Manuel Scorpio?" she asked.

"Yes. I can describe him to a T. He was a slenderly made Mexican—at least, I suppose from his name that he was a Mexican. But his skin was as white as any American's. He spoke perfect English, with very little slang in it. He was as quick as a cat and his football was as silent as feathers dropping. He was a good puncher and the boys in the bunk houses were fond of him because he played on an accordion and sang songs to them—some Mexican songs, and range songs, and all sorts of popular tunes."

"Had anything happened to make you think that Scorpio hated your family?"

"Nothing that had happened up to then," said Dexter, "but years before, when he was a youngster, my father suspected him of stealing a horse. He wouldn't have him arrested. That was not my father's way. But he had Manuel tied to a post and gave him a terrible flogging with a quirt."

"Did you see that happen?" asked the girl.

"Yes, and so did you," said he.

She started. He seemed to have touched her to the quick, with this remark.

He went on: "We were standing at the door of the

24

granary, and we were holding hands. We both trembled. We heard the sound of the quirt falling. We heard my father calling out in a rage, and we heard the boy screech. We saw his head fall. He had fainted."

At this, Claudia put both her hands over her face.

"Yes," she said. "I never shall forget."

"Very well," went on Prince Charlie, though this was a name which we gave him later on, "the flogging was finished, and your father told mine that he had better send Manuel Scorpio off the place. But my father wouldn't listen. He said that the boy had had enough punishment and now he should be allowed to start a new life, with his sins forgiven. And, after that, we discovered that Manuel had not stolen the horse after all."

"What was done?" snapped Claudia, her eyes bright.

"My father gave him fifty dollars—tossed it to him—and thought that everything would be all right. But on this night, when he had decided that the 'M'-shaped sign on the forehead of Marshall Dexter might stand as the sign for Scorpio, the constellation, then he remembered the flogging and decided that perhaps Manuel Scorpio had been nursing a grudge all this time."

"Then why didn't your father do something about it?" asked the girl.

"He did. He called Scorpio into the library. I listened at the door, because I liked Manuel and hoped that nothing would happen to him. I was sure that no one so young could have murdered Marshall Dexter."

"Well?" said the girl, impatiently. And we all were hanging on the next words.

"My father talked to him—not about the murder though. He told Manuel that he had been watching him, and was very pleased with his work, and intended to give him a piece of good land down by the river, so that he could set up by himself and be in a position to marry pretty little Rosita, when he chose. And Manuel thanked him, with tears in his voice. I was sure, listening in there, as I did, that Manuel was honest; and my father was sure, too. Though it turned out that he was wrong. Because it *was*

Scorpio's sign, after all, that had been put on the doors and on the forehead of the dead man."

"Aye," said Uncle Jed Raymond. "We all found that out, when it was too late."

"Will you go on," said Claudia, "and tell us what happened that night to you, afterward?"

"Well, I was telling you that after I went to bed I could not sleep, because I was frightened. Finally I made up my mind that I was a coward. I was young and foolish, but I decided that I would get up and walk out into the dark, just to test my own nerves. So I did go downstairs."

"Did you see anything on the way?"

"Well, no, except that I remember the face of the big clock in the hall. It gave a flash at me as I went down to the bottom of the stairs, and it was all I could do to keep from turning and bolting back to my room; but I made myself go on, and so I got out to the open yard. There was not much wind blowing, but the tops of the trees were bending slowly toward the north. A south wind was blowing. I decided that I would go into the tank house and get a drink of buttermilk. So I went in there and got it, and while I was drinking in the dark and the cool of that place, and listening to the sound of the water dripping over the coolers, I heard a door slam and a couple of voices raised.

"I was so startled that I dropped the glass of buttermilk and ran to the door, and there I saw my father standing on the side steps of the house, and below him was Manly Crowell, standing ——"

"It's a lie!" burst out Crowell, as he heard his brother's name mentioned.

Young Dexter looked at him for a considerable moment, and though he said nothing, I've never listened to a more eloquent silence. I could not see his full face, but Marvin Crowell could, and by the way Crowell lost color, I judged that the boy was not a pretty picture to watch.

"At length," said Dexter, still looking fixedly at the last interrupter, "Manly Crowell pulled out a revolver and fired. And my father, who was standing there in his night-gown, reached out at the empty air and fell down the steps and landed on the ground with a loud bump."

CHAPTER V.   THE MARK

AT this point in the narrative, I had lost all doubt, and something about the way in which Claudia Laffitter grasped her hands together told me that she could not help believing also. This was young Dexter. This was the right-ful heir to the rich valley lands; and infinite troubles were about to begin for many people! If I had only known how big and how many those troubles were, I should have left Monte Verde instantly.

"And then?" said Uncle Jed Raymond.

"Well," said the boy, "then I went into a sort of blind panic, because as soon as the revolver shot sounded, there was a cracking of firearms from the other side of the house, and then voices yelling, and above all a woman screaming and screaming as though a knife were being thrust into her. I started for the house, but before I got to it, there was a tall man running out of the night who saw me and caught me by the wrist. That was Phil Anson, the puncher. When he grabbed me, he said: 'This is no place for you, kid!'

"He took me on the run out to the barn and there we saddled a couple of horses and he made me ride off with him. I was rather confused. But he said something about a betrayal, and Manuel Scorpio, and he kept me riding all through that night. By the time morning came, we were at the head of the valley. And there we rested. By noon, a report came our way that Manuel Scorpio, helped out by a lot of people who had been renting land from my father, and who thought that they had as good a title to their ground as he had, had risen in the night and had

27

wiped out the entire Dexter family. They said that even I had been drowned in the river; that Scorpio had disappeared in the same way; and that Ben Laffitter had died, fighting for my family."

Here I saw him turn his big, dark eye, straight upon Claudia, and a shiver of excitement went through her. Well, I myself was shivering, for that matter.

I looked at the opposition camp, that is to say, at Crowell, and at Dandy Bullen, and they appeared thoughtful and out of sorts. No wonder. It would have taken a perfect skeptic to doubt the story that boy had told; but just then we heard the noise of horses and the groan of a heavy brake.

"There's the stage now," said Uncle Jed Raymond. "I'll go and get Phil Anson, if he's aboard of it."

"He's changed a good deal," said Dexter. "He's—I'd better meet him, I suppose."

"You'd better?" cried Raymond. "I'll tell a man that you had not better! I knew Phil Anson as well as I knew my own brother, in the old days. And I'd recognize him, I reckon, if he was a thousand years old!"

Dexter seemed a little disturbed, but he settled back in his chair and said nothing more, while big Raymond went out of the room. He came back almost at once with a tall fellow of middle age, a man dressed like a Westerner on a visit to the East. That is to say, he was dressed in ordinary "city" clothes, but on his head there was a towering, gray sombrero with a great brim on it.

He was not exactly a normal man in appearance. His left leg and his left arm seemed to be half helpless as though from the aftermath of paralysis. He had a professional invalid's way of smiling silently, bitterly to himself, as though his contempt for existence was a great deal too big to be put into words.

As they came up, we could hear Jed Raymond's heavy voice speaking to the other, and calling out his name. There was no doubt that he had recognized his man at the first glance. As they came through the doorway, side by side, big Raymond exclaimed: "Phil, d'you know this man?"

He pointed toward the boy, and Anson looked not at the boy but straight back at Raymond.

"I've been with him for ten years," he said. "I ought to know him."

"Then tell us his name," demanded Raymond.

"His name's Charles Dexter," said Philip Anson.

For my part, that ended the argument. The lean, saffron-colored face of Anson was that of a man who isn't long for this world. I took his speech as seriously as I would have taken a death-bed statement. And, in a sense, that is exactly what it was, though none of us could guess this at the time.

Raymond went up and shook Dexter cordially by the hand.

"I wouldn't believe till I had to," said he. "But you know that I knew your father, and that I fought for his family, and the reason that I left Dexter Valley was because the sneakin' murderers down there made things too hot for me. I been up here in Monte Verde like a hawk on a perch, waitin' for a time to get back, and now I reckon that the time has come!"

Dexter thanked him with a quiet word. He seemed to care very little, now, about the opinion of Raymond or the belief of any other person. He was more interested in that tall, lanky fellow, Anson. It was touching to see him bring out a chair for the cow-puncher and seat him in it, and leaning over with a hand resting lightly on his shoulder, ask him how he did. Anson replied with a mere grunt, and fell into a strong fit of coughing. It left him pale and his face shining with perspiration, and young Dexter stood by, biting his lip and frowning.

"Will you have a drink of something?" he asked.

"To heck with the drink!" said Anson. "It's that, more than anything else, that's broken me. I'm all right and ——"

But Claudia Laffitter got up and scurried from the room, leaving the door open, and she came back carrying a glass of water, and jerked the door to, behind her. Anson took the water and thanked her by lifting his eyes to her face silently. He had the dignity about him of a man who is finished with life. I've never seen it so clearly, before or since, though he rather spoiled things by his cynical, sneering ways.

Raymond suddenly said, in an unexpected way: "Now, gents, you've heard enough, I take it. I'd like to have the vote of you people on whether this here is Charles Dexter, or ain't."

"It's Charles Dexter!" cried Claudia. She had such a thrill in her voice as did a man good to hear. And she went to him and took his hands. "I had to fight against admitting that you were you, Charlie. There was so much depending on it! I had to fight against admitting."

"Why, Claudia," said he, gently, "of course, you had to fight against it. I understood perfectly, from the first!"

"Speakin' personal," roared Raymond, "I guessed ten minutes ago that the boy was straight. He's Dexter. He's got the Dexter eye. His skin seems a shade dark, but that's likely, too. His ma was sort of olive skinned, and I can remember that little Charlie was pretty dark, too. He's Dexter for me. I'd die for it."

"He ain't any Dexter for me," said Dandy Bullen sullenly.

"You've heard the proofs!" shouted Raymond. "What more'd you want?"

"I've heard a lot of slick talk that might be partly memorized, and partly made up. I ain't heard anything that's convinced me."

"Them that don't want to be convinced, they sure won't be," said Raymond. "But what about you, Crowell? You had oughta be able to see the nose on your face, even if Bullen won't!"

"If I can see the nose on my face," said Crowell, "I can see that he ain't a Dexter. He's too small, like I said before. And he's too dark—skin and eye. He ain't any more a Dexter than I am."

"You talk like a fool!" shouted Raymond.

"Steady, Uncle Jed," said the boy. "We don't want any fighting in here."

"It's two and two," said Uncle Jed Raymond. "Now there, you, stranger—Oliver Dean—what you say to us about this here job?"

I had hardly spoken a word during the entire interview and trial. And I hardly wanted to speak one now. I closed my eyes and looked into my own mind.

The testimony, so far as I had heard, and the arrival of tall Philip Anson seemed to show that the boy had claimed no more than the truth. All that was against it—or, at least, the principal thing—was the romantic nature of the event itself. One hardly felt it possible that such a strange story could be a true one. I tried to tell myself that it was not so extraordinary, after all, and that the boy had not been permitted by Anson to return simply because this business was sure to prove so extremely dangerous in every aspect. The life of Charles Dexter, if it were indeed he, was hardly worth a great deal, at this very moment. I don't think that a wise insurance company would have wanted to take a risk on him for three weeks, for that matter. It was only the romantic, fairytale atmosphere that told against the boy, so far as I was concerned. That and, perhaps, a little ingrained disbelief which I could not analyze.

But, as the matter stood, I could not have been honest and denied him. I was there, really, in a solemn capacity, and chance had made me the balancing power between two parties. If I voted against him, public opinion would deny him, because public opinion would declare that he had had his fair and equal trial before his peers and had been found wanting. If I voted for him, he would be established, in the eyes of the vast majority of those hardy mountain men, as the legitimate Dexter. And trouble would start in Dexter Valley, to be sure!

So, after weighing the matter back and forth for two or three long, anxious minutes, I opened my eyes and gave the boy a last look of inquisition. He met my glance with an unaffected steadiness, and finally I could not help nodding.

31

"You are Charles Dexter," said I.

Claudia Laffitter crowed with triumph and clapped her hands together. Uncle Jed Raymond cheered.

But the two of the Valley faction glowered solemnly upon me.

"Stranger," said Bullen, "you've stepped yourself into pretty tight shoes. Look out that you don't get some corns and chilblains from this here!"

Anson began to laugh unexpectedly.

"He's able to see the sun when it's shinin'. That's all. Bullen, you go and growl outside with the street dogs!"

And he laughed again.

"I'll remember this and you," said Bullen savagely.

"Remember and be darned," Anson advised him.

"Come on, Dandy," said that ferret-faced old sharpster, Crowell. "Come along with me, and get out of this."

He took Dandy Bullen by the arm and they started together toward the door, while young Dexter and the girl separated to let them pass. Not a single word of exultation had come from the lips of Dexter, during this test and the approval of him to be what he claimed. I admired his calm. I could put him down at once, I thought, as a lad at least ten years older than his age.

But, as they separated, I heard a loud, screeching cry from Crowell. It rang and bit against my eardrums. It rang and echoed through my head.

I saw the others turn, with a start, and in the meantime, Crowell was pointing out with a rigid arm at the thing that he had seen.

Well, it was big enough for us all to see, and when I noticed it, the hair fairly lifted on my head.

For there upon the central panel of the door, traced large and bold, was a character that looked like the letter "M" with the last stroke not curling up, as usual, but prolonged downward. It was done in black—charcoal, perhaps—and I knew it was what they had been talking about —the sign of Scorpio.

CHAPTER VI.   ONLY A HEIFER

THE effect of the sight on the people in the room was odd.
Nearly every one reacted in a different manner. I, for
instance, found speech and movement extremely difficult
for a moment. Dandy Bullen began to swear; Crowell
backed straight up until his shoulders were against the
opposite wall; Uncle Jed Raymond, gaping like a fish, took
out a little pearl-handled pocketknife and began to toss
it idly up and down in the air; Claudia Laffitter gave a
little screech and gripped the back of a chair; young
Dexter, with hardly a glance at the sign, amused himself
looking keenly about into the faces around him; and
Philip Anson, forgetting his sneer, keeled over in his chair
in a dead faint.

That gave us something to do, and I think every one
was glad of it. With what was left from his glass of water,
we sprinkled his face; I opened the window wider to the
west; and the rest employed themselves in one way or
another.

Dexter had dropped on his knee beside the chair of
Anson and, gripping the wrist of the puncher, appeared
to be feeling the pulse, while he looked at Anson in rather
a stern way, as one who was saying to himself that the
man did not dare to die from such a small cause.

It was not death, however, as I've said before. It was
merely a faint, out of which Anson roused himself with
a groan.

Dexter took him by the shoulders and said rapidly:
"It's all right, Phil. It's all right. I'm here. D'you see? I'm
here, and it's all right!"

As though what made Anson faint was not fear for
himself, but fear of what might happen to the boy.

Anson stretched out his long, cold, bony hands and

33

passed them over the face of Dexter. He drew a slow, groaning breath, and then pushed himself half erect in his chair. Then, turning his head with a jerk, he stared toward the door and the sign which sprawled upon it.

"It ain't a dream, Charlie!" he muttered. "It's there, as true as life, and Scorpio is still around!"

"We don't know," answered the boy. "It may be Scorpio —or a joker!"

As he said this, he flashed his glance around the room. It saw every one clearly. I know that when it rested on me it remained for only a tenth of a second, but in that instant, he looked right through and through me.

Then he took charge. Literally, he took that little, appalled group of humans in his hands.

Standing there with one elbow lightly drooped over the back of a chair, he said:

"Has any one any idea of who might have drawn that sign on the door?"

No one answered.

Then Bullen said: "When Claudia Laffitter went out of the room, she left the door open. It might have been done then."

"Maybe you mean," suggested Jed Raymond, with a growl, "that Claudia did it herself on her way back with the water?"

I looked at Claudia. She appeared too sick and white to hear what was being said. And no wonder, for her own father had died in that horrible fracas down in Dexter Valley, ten years before, and I suppose that the name of Scorpio had remained to her a blacker thing than the name of the devil.

"I ain't as big a fool as that," said Bullen. "But it must of been wrote on while she was away, and we didn't notice it after the door was closed until just now—or else somebody in this here room scrawled it on with his back turned!"

"Who was standing near the door?" asked Anson hoarsely.

"This here stranger was," said Crowell. "Who knows

34

anything about this man that was so sure that Dexter was Dexter anyway?"

He looked at me, and I remembered that I had, as a matter of fact, been standing close to the door all the time. I rolled my eyes to get an inspiration.

"I had nothing to write like that with," said I. "Or if you think so, I'm willing to be searched."

"You opened the window afterward," said Crowell, his eyes glinting with sparks.

"Yes, he could have dropped it outside, then," declared Anson.

And he began to glare at me in a horrible fashion.

I had wished before that I never had mixed up in this affair; now the wish was redoubled.

"Here!" said I, and held out my hands. "Is there any black on my fingers?"

They stared at my hands. Of course the point was not very convincing, but suddenly every pair of hands in the room was thrust out, to offer a mute proof of innocence.

"Let's not be fools," said Dexter, calm as could be. "The fingers that wrote that sign could have been cleaned afterward. There's no doubt about that. Personally I don't think that any person in this room had a chance to write the letter. It could not very well have been done behind the back. You see that the strokes are strong and regular. They would wobble, if a man wrote with his hands behind his back; and if any one of us had turned his face toward the door and leaned over to write the character, we would have noticed it. We're not blind men, you know."

"Then it was really Scorpio that done the thing?" asked Anson, mopping his wet forehead.

"It would of meant," said Uncle Raymond, "that he had the nerve to walk right into this here hotel in the middle of the day, and him a man that the law's been wantin' particular bad, since the night of the killings. Nobody would vouch for Scorpio, not even them that made the most out of the folks that he killed—not even men like the Dinmonts, the Crowells, and the Bensons, and the

35

rest of their crowd that swallowed up the estate of the Dexters!"

He looked hard and long at Crowell, as he said this, but the older man paid no heed to him at all.

Dexter, also, was still surveying faces. Then he said coldly: "I don't think that any one in this room wrote the letter on the door. It must have been some one from the outside, who had been standing out there and overheard part of our talk. It was Scorpio himself. He was standing yonder, outside of the door ———"

He turned, as he spoke, and snatched the door open, and I half expected—so taut were my nerves—to see a dark-faced, good-looking Mexican out there in the dullness of the hallway.

But the hall was empty.

We went out into it and thoroughly scanned the dust on the floor, and the window, and the ground outside the window.

"Is that a man climbing down the slope?" asked Bullen suddenly.

We all stared. This window opened toward the big, blue valley, and the wall of the valley dropped almost precipitously beneath it. In the slanting earth, some trees and shrubbery were growing, and some tufts of hardy grasses, but the slope was fairly open and bare, in most places. In a group of shrubs far down the hillside, I thought that I saw something move—yes, and then out stepped a brindled yearling heifer!

We looked at one another and suddenly laughed. If it had been a man, I think that one of those fellows was keyed highly enough to have sent a query after the stranger by means of a bullet. But it was only the brindled heifer, so we laughed.

"We've been acting like calves!" cried Bullen. "We oughta scatter around and tell the folks that the greaser has been here, and ask if they've seen anybody like him."

"A good chance I would have that you or any of your kind would spread the news or try to take Scorpio for me!" said Dexter bitterly.

36

"Young feller," said Bullen, scowling, "are you lookin' for trouble?"

Suddenly Dexter laughed. A rare thing to see one in his shoes able to laugh so outrightly.

"Why else do you think that I've come here, man?" he demanded. "Trouble? Of course I want trouble. I expect to have trouble with every meal, every day, until I've gotten back what's mine, and what belongs to my family!"

He looked Bullen straight in the eye.

"Them that wants trouble, they mostly get it," answered Bullen, sullen, and very angry, but not ready to fight.

"Go spread the news of *that*," said Dexter. "Go down to the valley and tell your family and tell your friends. I'm back here. You've set Scorpio on my trail. You've lost no time in doing that, so I know that down in your hearts you admit that I'm the real Dexter. Very well, tell them that I'm back, and tell them to stand on their guard because I intend to come and take what is my own!"

Crowell piped up in a voice as sharp and as sudden as the barking of a dog.

"You're witnesses, all of you," said he. "Here's this boy openly threatenin' the lives and the properties of the honest folks that are livin' down yonder in Dexter Valley! If ever they's any violence, the law has got a right to know what's been said this day!"

"Charlie," said Philip Anson, "I'm mighty tired. Send them away, will you?"

"Aye, I'll send them away," said the boy. "Of course I will. But I want them to take down a word that some of their friends ought to know, and that they ought to know themselves. I'm going to go peacefully to every house in that valley, and I'm going to leave a summons to get out of my way and turn over to me the things that they know are mine."

"Are you a fool?" broke in Jed Raymond. "You—one boy—agin' a hundred or so fightin' men?"

"I have my cause," said the boy, giving his talk an

37

odd turn that I had not expected. "And a good cause is a better thing than an army, I should say. At any rate, go back and tell them, there in the valley, just what I intend to do. I'll serve notices on them all. Then I'll begin to act."

Bullen started to make a rather hot answer, but Prince Charlie stopped him by holding up one hand, and Bullen cut off his words short. He and Crowell, side by side, walked away down the hall. At the foot of it, Crowell turned as though he wanted to throw back something in our teeth, to remember him by, but he, like Bullen, changed his mind when he saw the boy.

I didn't blame them. Danger was simply reeking in the attitude of that lad.

When the pair who represented the Dexter Valley people had disappeared, Dexter himself turned back to me and came up and shook hands with me.

"Mr. Dean," he said. "I think I understood what was passing in your mind when the decision was left to you. I think it took a good deal of courage for you to commit yourself, in this way, in a quarrel to which you're a stranger, and I want to thank you."

He gave my hand a good grip, but I was glad to get away from him, and outside the hotel, and let the clean open air blow on me, and the last of the sun's heat strike my face. I felt, in fact, as though I had been walking through a dream.

CHAPTER VII.   THE FIRST VICTIM

WALKING up the road to get my blood stirring again, I came up with an old chap in the most ragged clothes imaginable who was sauntering along behind a burro which he encouraged and guided by swearing at it. I gathered, from the hammer he swung in his hand, and from the misty look of his long-distance eyes, that he was one of the prospectors of whom I had heard——one of the men who spend their labor, who endure the fierce weather of the heights, who live close neighbors with disappointment every day, and who in the end are rewarded by making two or three discoveries which quickly slip out of their own hands and go to make the fortunes of others ——men they never have seen. This one apparently was setting out freshly on a trip of exploration. The load on the burro's back was fat and heavy, and the little gray beast went onward with tiny steps, now and then shaking its ears in mute protest.

"You're bound out, stranger?" said I.

He took me up in another sense, a little more literal than I had expected.

"Aye," said he, "I'm bound out. The seas that I'm bound for, they got frozen waves, partner, and there ain't any compass to go by. And every night you turn back for home, and every morning you figger out that you ain't got any home but the port at the end of the voyage. Yes, sir, I reckon that I'm bound out."

I was amused and not a little impressed by the whimsical gravity of the old prospector. His knees were bowed a little; he had a beard which was clipped off raggedly, like a pelt of a sheep; he looked half rusty, like an old gun, and half mossy, like a stone. But he had the shoulders of a youth, and a young man's swing to them.

I asked if he were an old inhabitant of this part of the world.

"Why," said he, keeping to his nautical phraseology to a degree, "I been cruisin' these waters quite a spell. Twenty-five, thirty year I been anchorin' and sailin', and sailin' and anchorin'. You know minin', any, stranger?"

"Not a thing about it," I confessed.

"You're a wise man to keep ignorant," said he. "Them that ever seen color, they're sure to dream of it, and them that dream of it, has gotta foller it farther than the sunset lies."

His mind and his eye left me, and lingered on some

39

distant peak, far ahead. I reverted to the thing which held my own mind.

"I've been hearing a good deal about the Dexters," said I.

"Well," said he, "they tell me that they's a young Dexter come back."

I ventured to correct him slightly.

"There's a lad who calls himself Dexter, at least," said I.

"Who that wasn't a Dexter would call himself one?" said the prospector.

"Why, they've been quite a family, haven't they?" I asked him.

"Family? They was kings, out here," he admitted. "But when kings is down, what's the good of worryin' about the throne that they've lost? And when kings that of been put off starts to climb back on, ag'in, they get a slip, and they get a fall. Look at that there George Third, now!"

This was a bit of history that needed correcting, but I saw that my proper rôle was that of listener, rather than teacher.

"Well, at one time they owned the whole valley, I've heard," said I.

"They've owned the whole valley, and more besides," he declared. "I've seen the time when the lowin' of their cows, you could hear it clean up to Monte Verde. They was kings, I tell you. They could go where they pleased, around here, and take what they wanted. In the end, they was always sure to pay double. Free and easy, that was their style. They was always walkin' the poop deck, it seemed like, whether they was on the back of a hoss, or the veranda of a hotel, or the shoulder of a mountain. They was kind, though, if they fancied you. Jefferson Dexter, he grubstaked me, off and on, for eight year."

"He took a fancy to you, then?" said I, willing to draw him out.

"He took a fancy to me," said the prospector. "It come of him shooting into bush with his shotgun for the sake of hitting what he thought might be a deer. But it was only a man. And that man happened to be me. And I got a buckshot into my shoulder."

He began to hum to himself, as though he were thinking back to the old days.

"So he paid you for the hurt by grubstaking you?"

"Paid me? He didn't have no idea of payin' for the bullets that he put into men," said the prospector. "If you didn't like his ways, you could fight 'em; and mostly you come out on the short end of the horn. All the Dexters, they ate gunpowder on their porridge, and the babies cut their teeth on cartridges, and they played on a single-action Colt like a fine performer on a piano. Oh, they was musical, the Dexters was!"

He laughed a little but I did not feel like laughter; only, the flight of big Jay Burgess was now explained. The Dexters obviously had such a name through the country that no ordinary man cared to stand before one of them.

At last I said: "Tell me, stranger. D'you think that the young fellow who is now claiming to be the last of the Dexters really could have lived through that night in the valley when they were attacked?"

"You mean, the night of the betrayal?" said the other. "Well, I dunno. Every Dexter has nine lives, they say, and if this here lad only lost eight of 'em, he's likely to be back here scratching off skin and gettin' his own back!"

He said this not lightly but with a great deal of conviction, and while I listened to him, I felt that my former doubts diminished perceptibly. After leaving the conference in the hotel, there had been more doubt than conviction in me, but now I said good-by to the prospector and turned back toward the town with my mind at rest.

I had begun to think that there was only one chance in three that the true Dexter had returned; I went back with the feeling that there was only one chance in three that he really was an impostor.

When I got back to the hotel, I found that my own position was indeed very sensibly changed. People, up to this moment during my short stay, had been inclined to act as though I were merely an uninteresting stranger and tenderfoot; but my accidental inclusion in the conference led them to look upon me at once as a person of importance. Several of them, that evening, took advantage of every chance to bring me into talk and get me to repeat the evidence which had been brought forward at the council of five. I did not think, however, that it was wise for me to talk too much out of school. Instead, I told them merely that three out of five had been convinced and that I was one of the three, but that as for the evidence, they had better wait until other men were ready to speak, because I was merely a stranger in the country.

In this way I put them off, and early after supper I went up to my room in the hotel.

Because of what was to happen, I must describe the position of this room somewhat more fully.

It stood in the second story of the building, directly over the small gaming and dining room in which we had held the conference that afternoon. Like it, it had a window to the east and one to the north; and when I went up to it this evening, I heard voices through the thin partitions to my right and eventually I thought that I distinguished the soft, smooth, and calm tones of young Dexter. I could not make out his words, for he was apparently speaking very gently, as he had done that afternoon, in fact, and as I guessed to be his habit. The man with whom he talked, however, sometimes cried out aloud, so that I distinctly heard a few disconnected words.

These were, shortly after I arrived, the repeated exclamation of: "Time! Time! Time!" disjointedly, and not put together, as though the man were exclaiming about some matter in which time was an important element, or as if he were bitterly complaining that there were not, perhaps, enough time left to him, or to them, in some project.

Later on in the evening, as I sat before the northern window, looking at the dimly-etched outline of the mountains, against the stippling of the starry sky, I heard another word of a different nature which was brought out with an equal loudness, and which thoroughly chilled me, hearing it. For it was clearly the word "death," as though the speaker were using several sentences, each of which ended on that dismal word.

I told myself that it must be some invalid, like myself, in that room, complaining, as I was myself in the habit of complaining, against his time in life cut short, and against a too early death. This feeling of sympathy, and the loneliness of the night, oppressed me like a weight, and I went to bed, eventually, to listen to the irregular tremors and racing of my heart, and to wonder if I were out here fighting a lost cause, or whether the pure, icy air which I was breathing would really make me a sound and healthy man again.

At last, after lying for a long time staring into the darkness, I fell asleep, and naturally my dream turned back to the horrors which I had heard during the conference that day; for I began to envision that terrible young Mexican, Manuel Scorpio, he whose footfall was as light as a feather, and swift as a cat's.

Out of this sleep I wakened with a sense that something was fumbling at the door of my room.

In another instant, there was a faint rushing sound, though no louder than a whisper, and a freshening in the gust of air which blew across my bed, exactly as may happen when the door of a room is opened, and a new draft comes into play.

Fear turned me to ice.

I remembered that my vote had been the one which turned opinion in the favor of young Dexter's honesty. Perhaps I would be made a victim next!

I could not move. There was a dizzy sickness in my brain, and my body trembled violently.

Next, I heard the most hideous voice that it is possible to imagine. It is impossible to describe it properly, except to say that it was half speaking, and half whispering: "Charlie! Charlie!"

I could endure no more.

I cried out: "Who's there?"

There was no answer. Then I heard a heavy, slumping sound, as of a body falling heavily.

At this, I instantly scratched a match, and holding it in the cup of my shaking hand, I directed the light toward the last noise I had heard.

There I saw a crowning horror.

For there the tall man, Philip Anson, had sunk to his knees; his hands were both clasped against his throat, from the base of which blood was running fast, his face contorted to a stony mask of grinning terror and horror, and upon his forehead, boldly worked in black, was the sign of Scorpio.

CHAPTER VIII.   PHILIP'S WORDS

I LIFTED the chimney of the lamp which stood on the little table at the head of my bed; I touched the flame to the wick, and jamming the chimney back in place, I leaped from the bed.

I ran to the wounded man. Just then he fell over on his side and began to kick and struggle, in what I was convinced was his last convulsion.

I had to have help, and now I remembered the voices which I had heard in the room to my right, and I was convinced that Anson, wounded by the murderer, Scorpio, in his agony had mistaken my door for that of young Dexter, who must be adjoining.

I ran, therefore, through my open door to that of the next room. My hand had barely rapped against it when the door was jerked open.

"What is it?" said Dexter. "What is it, Mr. Dean?"

No matter how excited I was at that moment, I remember that I was amazed by his manner of speech. That is to say, at such a time one expects stammering breathlessness, stumbling speed, exclamations. But the words of Dexter came out with no inflection whatever. They were merely swiftly uttered, and as distinct as though he were talking over a long-distance telephone.

I managed to point toward my room and exclaim something about poor Anson, when Dexter left me like a flash, bounding across the hall. He had himself described the tread of Scorpio as being like that of the fall of feathers. I thought of the comparison as I watched him spring across the passage and into my room.

I followed, and closing the door behind me, I stared at that odd scene which never will leave my mind until I die.

There was Dexter on the floor beside the dying man.

Dying he was, for I came just in time to see the boy strongly draw away the hands with which Anson seemed trying to stifle himself. For one long fraction of a second, the boy looked at the wound, and then released his grip on the wrists of Anson.

I knew that he had decided, in that glance, that Anson was a dying man.

It was not Anson, in his death agony, who fascinated and overwhelmed me most. It was the expression of Dexter's face, for he was kneeling there with his profile turned to me, and with the lamplight falling clearly upon him. I looked to see him turn greasy gray, as men do under the stress of such terrible emotion. I looked to see the sweat running on his skin; to see his mouth compressed, and the muscles bulging at the base of his jaw.

Instead, I give you my word that he was as composed as though he were idly looking down at a printed page, and not a very interesting page, at that.

This amazed me, I think, more than anything I ever had seen before, and more than anything that I saw in all of the strange narrative which I have to tell, more than anything that Dexter himself ever did and said.

It is true that he often appeared in a more tremendous light, but the first impression of such a man, once vividly revealed, is greater than all second thoughts, whatever they may be.

And I saw, then, surely and clearly, that this was not a

45

man like other men, but a prodigy, a freak of nature, a soul and a mind such as I never met before.

I could look at last from his terrible calm to the struggle of the dying man.

Anson, now that he seemed to know that death was coming rapidly upon him, was spending the last effort of his strength, the last stream of his life in speaking, or trying to speak. In the vastness of his desire, the veins swelled upon his forehead. His face turned a hideous livid hue. His eyes leaped from his head, while the blood, started by these exertions, welled up faster and faster, and choked him, flowing liberally over the breast of his pajamas. I remember that the poor man was making wide and powerful gestures, such as one makes when using the strongest sort of speech.

His moving hands were clearly asking something of the boy, asking with palms turned up, and with fingers stiffened and clutching with enormous earnestness. So did the eyes speak, already growing glassy with death, but yet attempting to give a clear message.

The conduct of young Dexter, at this time, was most remarkable. He spoke to his friend as though nothing of importance were taking place.

"You will have to relax, Phil," he said. "Every strong effort that you make forces the blood more strongly into your throat and helps to choke you. There, now. Relax. Let me wipe your lips. Don't try to speak, but whisper. That will cause less effort and the sound has a better chance of coming through. Or, better still, write what you have to say on the floor. Here—I'll support you so that you can write. Write it on the floor, Phil, old fellow!"

I suppose that these words seem calm enough, but nothing can express the perfect indifference with which the boy was speaking, so far as inflection could make any ear judge. The velvet, soothing, confidential note never for an instant was absent from his throat!

In the meantime, he supported the dying man around the shoulders, and Anson, thus supported and raised, seemed incapable of understanding what was suggested to him. I suppose that he already was too far gone with the loss of blood and with strangulation. As a matter of fact, he was in the very midst of the death agony, and therefore, instead of writing on the floor with his own blood, which he might have done so easily, he continued to strain and struggle to speak, prolonging that most exquisitely hideous spectacle. I could hardly endure it. I felt once more as though I should faint, but with a sick man's calm and an invalid's coolness, I removed my mind a little from the picture and controlled myself.

Perhaps it was the more raised position that cleared the throat of Anson for an instant as suddenly, against my expectation, I heard a ghastly voice break out.

I have spoken of the horror of that half whisper and half-vocal sound which I had heard before in the darkness of my room, and this was the same sound, but raised to a frightful sort of smothered screech—a sound at once unutterably piercing, and chokingly thick:

"Scorpio—revenge ——" were the words he gasped and screamed aloud. He made a further effort, but could only soundlessly gibber, though the frenzy was blackening his face.

The boy seemed to realize that he had heard the last words which poor Philip Anson would ever utter. With one arm beneath the man, he stood up, raising the body as he did so, firmly embraced in that single arm. He rose, I say, with the large weight of that grown man, as easily as I should rise with a new-born infant in my arms.

So standing erect, with the lamplight gleaming on him, with the blood of Anson running over his own breast, he lifted his free hand to the sky and to God.

It made a solemn picture. But in the face and in the voice of the lad there was no more emotion, even now, than there is in the droning voice of a child reading a passage he does not understand. Not that I would convey any sense of stupidity in the intonation of Dexter, but rather depict the mere soft, lifeless method of his speech.

"Phil," he said, "you see me and you hear me. I shall never rest. I shall never breathe easily. I shall never sleep in peace. Food shall never have a taste for me. Nothing shall exist for me, and all of the affairs which have brought me here will be nothing, until I have found Scorpio, and killed him, exactly as he killed you! Do you hear me? Does that make you feel quieter, and happier?"

A fresh and last convulsion seized unlucky Philip Anson. His head moved violently from side to side, as though he were denying or refusing the last words, or else merely biting at and gasping for the breath which he could not take.

Then, as if stabbed by a fresh stroke, and this one through the heart, his body became limp and he hung loosely over the arm of the boy.

By this time the slamming of my door, and the shriek of the wounded man, had roused the hotel, and steps came running up the hall.

"Close the door and keep them out," said the boy to me, over his shoulder.

So I closed the door and locked it.

I was twenty years older than he, but the simplest private in Napoleon's army never looked more explicitly for commands to the Little Corporal than I looked for my directions to young Dexter.

He was placing the body on the floor and straightening it into a position of composure when the first of the inquirers came to my door. They had seen it open, and the light of the lamp shining through it down the passage. Suddenly, I heard the excited cry of Claudia Laffitter.

"What's happened? Mr. Dean! Are you there? Are you all right?"

I blessed her, for some reason, because she should think of me. Who was I in a house containing an Anson, a Dexter—and a Scorpio, unknown!

"I'm here and perfectly safe," said I.

I glanced back toward Dexter.

"You may talk," said he, looking over his shoulder at that instant as though, uncannily, he had felt the weight of my questioning eyes.

48

"Then what was the horrible screech? Was it only a bad dream?" asked Claudia Laffitter.

"Look here!" said a man's voice in the hall. "There's blood on the floor."

"Yes," said Claudia. "There's blood—there's blood! And it leads to this door—Mr. Dean, you must open. Something has happened. You haven't a right to conceal it, on this night, and in this place!"

I wondered what, exactly, she meant by that.

But I answered:

"Philip Anson has been stabbed; he came to my room, mistaking it for Dexter's. He is dead, now, on the floor of my room, and Dexter is with him. If there's an officer of the law in the town, he had better be sent for before any one is admitted or anything disturbed!"

Then she said a very odd thing, which slid through my brain like a cold gleam of steel.

"He's dead—so quickly!" said the girl.

As if she expected his death as a matter of course, and only the suddenness of it made any difference to her, or surprised or horrified her.

Then she turned back upon the others who were coming, and I heard her stop them with a perfectly calm voice, and tell them in a few words what had happened, and urge them to go to Sheriff Whalely, because he had arrived in the hotel that same night.

CHAPTER IX.   A BLACK BAG

THERE was still a good deal of uproar in the hotel, but for the moment it ebbed away from the immediate vicinity of our door.

And then young Dexter stood up.

He was looking down at the body of the dead man; and the whole front of his pajamas was covered, patterned

49

and streaked with the crimson of Anson's blood. Yet, though it was blood, it only seemed to heighten the youthfulness and the slender boyishness of Dexter.

In his gentle, matter-of-fact voice he said to me, though without shifting his eyes: "You were mastering yourself, toward the end of it, Mr. Dean. You saw clearly what happened?"

How did he have time to notice that I had been mastering myself, toward the end of the death struggle?

I merely answered: "Yes, I saw everything that happened toward the end, I think."

"Then," said he, "what you have to say will be valuable to me—more valuable than anything in the world, as a matter of fact. Do you think, in the final struggle, that he was simply fighting for breath, or that he was saying 'no' to the last words I spoke to him?"

I paused. It was a hard question to answer, but as I looked down at the face of poor Anson, I saw it resigned in what appeared a perfect peace, and the relaxed smile of death was on his lips. There was no token of his horrible death upon him except for the great purple and crimson pool at the hollow of his throat.

I pointed toward him.

"It must have been merely the death struggle," said I. Dexter shook his head.

"Because he seems peaceful, now? Death seems to be a wit; it turns all sorts of tricks. No, I wouldn't trust to that alone."

"Otherwise, it's hard to tell," said I.

"Yes, it's hard to tell, otherwise I wouldn't be asking you, because I was using my own eyes for all they were worth," said Dexter. "But now I beg you to think back to that picture. Close your eyes to this one and try to remember exactly how he appeared in the final struggle."

I set my teeth and did as he requested.

It was not a pretty picture to summon up, and my nerves were already jumping, but the wonderful example of the boy steadied me a good deal.

Finally I was able to say: "Well, Dexter. I may be

wrong, but it appeared to me that he was not saying 'no' to your last words, but that he was really merely fighting for breath. How else could he have been reacting, when you had given him the promise that he had just asked?"

"It might have been the reverse of the question which we heard," said the boy. "One word, of course, would have changed it completely. He might have been trying to say: 'Scorpio—no revenge.' Or perhaps: 'It was not Scorpio. Revenge me on—somebody else.' In a moment of frenzy like that, he may have thought he was saying, and actually have been trying to speak, a great deal more than you and I have heard him say."

"Yes," said I. "He may."

"And if we are wrong," said the boy, "it may mean than I am throwing away a ——"

He stopped himself from the full current of what he was about to say, but nothing could be clearer than that he was in the grip of a great difficulty. Finally he said, more to himself than to me: "Yes, I think that you're right. It was only Scorpio that he had in mind. Scorpio, who put the mark on him. Scorpio—Scorpio, of course!"

This decision to which he came seemed, for some reason, to be a great drain upon him, a great regret. Just why, I could not say. No matter what was in the mind of poor Philip Anson, it was clear that Scorpio was the murderer. Yet something else was in the mind of the boy. He went, now, to the window, and from it he looked over the western valley where the people, whose name he claimed, had once been kings. I stood a little behind him and had the same view, and I must say that few things in my life have impressed me more.

For the night had come to its end and the day was beginning. It came as a pale fringe of fire behind the mountains, making them great black outlines with rosy flushings along the snow of the heights, and now the dawn light sank into the valley like dust of gold filtering through the profound waters of a well. It made the river sparkle, and the windows in the town of Dexter began to gleam brokenly, and then the green fields and the shadowy

51

trees were visible and finally, even at this distance, we could see the sheen of the dew upon the meadows.

All these changes required only a few moments, and during them the boy hung over the picture as though he wished to drink it down deeply into his heart, to have for a clear image, always. I thought, once or twice, that I could see a tremor in him, but this may have been only the effect of the chilly morning wind, which was blowing straight in upon him.

A moment later, the sheriff arrived.

Of course, the door had to be opened to him at once. Several other men came with him, including the editor of the little Monte Verde newspaper, and as the world poured into the room, I had the feeling that the open light of day must now shine upon the mystery.

This man of the law was named Thomas Winchell, and he had a good reputation among the mountain men because he kept peace among all the rough canyons and the ravines of his district. Yet I don't suppose that a less formidable man ever appeared. He seemed simply innocuous. He was not only very little, but he was very faded. As a small boy he must have been one of those golden-haired, blue-eyed children with eyes wide open, half in stupidity and half in innocence. He still had them wide open, and the very blue of them had faded; I don't like to say that they looked like the eyes of a dead fish, because that has a disgusting sound, but there was the same weary film over them. His hair was faded to rust and gray also. He had a thin streak of mustache on each side of his upper lip but I cannot say that this made him appear more manly, as hair on the face often does, because his mouth was usually a little open, and increased his general appearance of vacant wondering. To make everything perfect, his head thrust forward at the end of a rather long and scraggy neck, and was so weakly supported that it nodded a bit with every step that he made and gave him an absurd appearance of greeting his own shadow on the ground.

I hardly noticed the sheriff, at first, I was so busy looking at the big, rough-looking fellows who accompanied him. I kept to a corner, except when I was asked questions. Young Dexter remained by the window, with his arms folded, and his expression as indifferent as ever.

The first time I noticed the sheriff was when I saw the little man lean over and pick up a corner of the rug, very much like a housewife feeling the texture of some material.

"Tut-tut!" says the sheriff. "Pretty well spoiled! Pretty well spoiled, I'm afraid!"

And he shook his head at the dark, wet stains which were on the surface of the rug. Then he turned his attention to young Dexter, shook his head again, blinked his eyes and opened his mouth, and looked, in fact, so much like the village half-wit, that I began to wish they could turn the foolish little man out of the room at once.

"And you're little Charlie Dexter?" said the sheriff.

"Yes, Sheriff Winchell," said he.

The sheriff went up and held out his almost tiny paw. Dexter shook it, as Winchell still nodded and bobbed his head from side to side in his idiotic fashion.

"I'm glad to see you, but I ain't glad to see you in this here room, Charlie," said he. "But to think of you comin' back here, and to think of there bein' a Prince Charlie ag'in for the boys to look up to and the girls to admire! Why, it'll put a lot of life into things around here, lemme tell you. They'll be a good many fires will burn brighter, and a good many guns will be flashin' for Prince Charlie, to my way of thinkin'. But welcome home, Charlie. A good, hearty welcome to you."

This rambling speech appeared to me a little more out of place than any words I ever have heard, though after learning that this was the sheriff, I was a trifle more willing to respect him. Prince Charlie gave the sheriff one of his bows which were no more, really, than nods; and Winchell went on with his investigation.

He took his time, I must say. He went across the hall, and he entered the room where Anson had been sleeping when he was stabbed. There he moved about, and looked, and examined with a pocket glass, certain smudges of the blood.

"I always have to admire folks that could work with gloves on," said the sheriff, finally. "From a hayfork to a knife, I ain't never at home if I gotta have something between my fingers and what they've laid their hold onto."

He looked at the window sill and bobbed his head up and down as usual.

"There's where he come in at, and he must 'a' been like a cat walkin' up a wall!" said the sheriff.

The rest of us went to see what we could see, but I could make nothing of it and neither could the others, until the sheriff pointed out a flake of paint gone at one spot, and a projecting nail from which the rust had been newly ground off at another.

"You got an eye in your head, sheriff!" said one of the men, admiringly.

"Oh, I got a mighty bad eye," said the sheriff. "But there's such a thing as findin' what you wanta see, and there's such a thing as good strong glasses to help out them that has weak eyes." Then he asked that Claudia Laffitter be sent for, and she came, looking pale and hard-set, as though she were bracing her nerves, and I have no doubt that she was.

"Claudia, dear," said he, "will you tell me what kind of luggage this poor Anson fellow was carryin' with him when he came to the hotel?"

"Just a suitcase, and a small black bag."

"I see a suitcase, but I don't see a little black bag," said the sheriff.

He turned to Dexter.

"You tell me, Prince Charlie," said he. "You tell me what might be in that little black bag that people would want to steal it for?"

Prince Charlie answered in his unemotional voice: "Well, I suppose that I ought to tell you, though it's important only to me. In that little black bag were all the proofs of my birth and enough to convince any court in the land that I am Charles Dexter."

"Ah-ah-ah!" said the sheriff. "But we all take that for granted already. And who would be murderin' a man for that?"

"Oh, that was only part of the reason," said Dexter. "The main cause was that Scorpio always hated Phil Anson, and now he has the thing put to rights, so far as he is concerned."

CHAPTER X.   EARTHLY END

"ABOUT the proofs of your birth," said the sheriff, "if you was to give me a list of 'em, we'd have a better chance of gettin' them back."

"If you can make things whole out of ashes," said the boy, "it would be a useful thing, and I'd be glad to give you the list, as you suggest. But if you can't do that little miracle, there's no use in troubling about the thing."

"And how would you expect to go about the gettin' back of your birthright, me lad?" said the sheriff.

"I can hope, only, and pray a little, now and then," said Dexter, and he smiled sardonically. One could guess that not many prayers would come between those fine, white teeth of his.

When the sheriff had finished inside the house, he went outside of it to try to follow the back trail of the murderer, and young Dexter went with him. Before he left, I touched his arm.

"If I can be of any use to you ——" said I. "About arrangements, I mean?"

He turned and looked at me as though he never had seen me before. In ways, he had the most unsympathetic eye in the world. But now he said: "You're very kind, Mr. Dean. You can make the arrangements at the cemetery and get a coffin made, if there is none here—I don't suppose there's an undertaker. I have something to do besides burying dead men."

Words like the last part of this speech were enough to alienate most men forever, of course, and they struck me like a blow in the face, but I put up with them. I had seen this lad pass through too many things. I knew that he was made of steel, but being an invalid myself, I had perhaps an exaggerated respect for the strongest of metals. It can be relied on where the shame and the follies break down. Kindness and perfect manners never built a kingdom—or a man, for that matter.

So I went off to execute my mission as soon as I had nervously swallowed a small breakfast and made the usual wry faces over the bitter black lye which was called coffee in that hotel. There were half a dozen other people in the room while I was sitting there, and I saw them nodding toward me and even pointing, but I paid little attention. Suddenly I could have laughed, but not exactly with an outburst of mirth. I was simply remembering that for something like three years I never had been able to take my mind from my own physical infirmities, and now I had been up half the night, had passed through two great nervous strains within less than twenty-four hours, and yet I had no headache, my pulse temperately kept time, as the poet says, and my face was neither hot nor cold. For the first time in years, I was filling my mind with purely objective interests, and this seemed to be better for me than anything the doctors had prescribed.

After breakfast, I made inquiries and found out where I should go. This was to the drug store.

Drug stores are not what one expects to find in a little village like Monte Verde. The drugs usually are sold, I suppose, over a special counter in the general merchandise store, but Monte Verde had its own drug store. Over the front of it was a big sign: "Keenan's Pharmacy." I went in through a front door that set a bell ja gling and found myself in a small room, the walls of which were glittering with glass jars of many sizes, and containing liquids, powders and crystals of all imaginable colors.

Under a glass counter there was a display of tooth-brushes, combs, pocket-knives, and a host of odds and ends. And through the back door of the room came a man in overalls and a blue flannel shirt out of which stuck a leathery brown neck that supported a head covered with shaggy gray hair. He was brushing the breakfast crumbs from his lips, but left at each corner of his mouth a glistening streak of bacon grease. He came forward with an amiable air and smiled on me.

"Why," said he, "you're the gent that was in on the murder, ain't ye?"

He spoke with the gentleness of one asking about the weather. I could not help smiling. And, determined to say nothing about what I had seen during that night of horror, I told him, frankly, that I had been directed to see him about getting a coffin, although I supposed that I had been misdirected.

"No, sir, you ain't been misdirected," said the pharma-cist. "Them that I don't get goin', I get 'em comin'."

"Going? Coming?" I repeated, not understanding.

"Them that are born, they're comin', ain't they?" said he.

"Why, I suppose they are."

"And for a new-born baby, they's gotta be supplies from the drug store, ain't there? They's gotta be powders and lotions and cough medicines, and something to warm their stomachs for 'em when they got colic, and something to get the wind out of 'em when they're windy, and all sorts of things that'll sooth a baby in this here rough kind of a world, partner."

"Yes," said I. "That's true."

"But if I miss 'em when they come into the world, I get 'em when they go out. Partly it's the medicines that they need and got to have as they lie sick, countin' the cracks in the ceiling, and partly it's the layin' out of the corpse—which it's more of a trick than you'd think, maybe!—and partly it's the coffin that they gotta be buried in! Step right this way and take your pick."

I followed him into a shed beside his store and there I

57

found sawdust and shavings on the floor, a vise, and various tools of the carpenter's trade. Sitting on hurdles at the end of the room there were a number of rectangular troughs. They looked very much like watering troughs with both the ends knocked out.

"There you are," said he. "Soft pine and fir, most of them is, but there's a coupla cedar that take a higher price. Women, they're mostly likely to cotton to the cedar, because they have a better smell, but men, they don't care much, usually. Worms'll get through a thicker fence than any man can make."

I wanted to get out of this place as soon as possible, and yet the callous talk of this fellow Keenan amused me, too.

"Do you mean to say that those are coffins?" I asked him.

"Yes, sir," said he. "And what else would they be? I got 'em in about all sizes from two year up to six foot three. They got some big-shouldered men, around here, and you can see the size of them at the pottom of the pile. One thing I give you, here, is a good fit, and I don't charge no more for it neither. It's one of the advantages of havin' a good, big stock on hand. It don't cost me nothin' more but foresight, and if I got a few odd sizes, I'm willin' to keep 'em on hand for an emergency. You never can tell when people are gonna up and die and need a coffin real quick—particular in the summer weather."

He was proud as Punch of his layout.

"But there are no ends to these things," said I.

"How could I have ready-made ends onto 'em?" said he. "Wideness I've took care of, but nobody can tell how long a corpse is gonna be after it stretches. So I keep the ends off. Along comes a dead man, and I get his measure. Gimme his length, that's all I ask you to do, and inside of an hour, I'll have him suited, I tell you. Gimme his length and maybe one of his old coats to get the bulk of him, and I'll dress him up like it was tailor-made. All I have to do is to pick out the right width from my pile, and then I mark off the man's length, and I saw off the boards all around, and I nail on the headboard, and the footboard. A good, tight fit like that, it keeps a corpse from jouncin' around, and slidin' and slitherin' a lot, which ain't a pleasant thing. The most unlikeliest and most unpleasantest thing in the world is to hear a corpse a-jouncin' inside of his coffin when they're fetchin' him out to the cemetery. It ain't right, and it ain't necessary. It upsets the womenfolks. It makes a bad impression. And it gives a kind of general sloppy and careless touch to everything. It don't hardly make no difference how much green and how much flowers is piled onto the top of a coffin, if the dead man ain't restin' and fitted snug inside of it, as I always says to my wife, and she agrees with me, too."

I managed to cut short this digressive talker at last. We agreed on a coffin; I paid him for it; and then I went out to the cemetery. It was hardly more than a quarter of a mile from the edge of the village, and it lay on a fine, open southern hillside. There were half a dozen cows enjoying the good grazing outside the fence, and one long-legged heifer had jumped the barrier and was getting fat on the long grass that grew inside.

The burial ground was not in very good repair. Brush had grown thickly, here and there, to replace the forest that had been cleared away in the first place. Young slips were hastily turning themselves into young saplings, and one could almost feel the yearn of the soil to cover itself with the familiar green gloom of the woods. Since there was no question about price for a burial lot, the ground being freely contributed by the community, I went in to pick out a proper place, and spent a little time wandering about through the long grass and the shrubbery while the heifer, as wild as an antelope, ran bawling up and down the farther fence, asking for help, but without wits to make her exit as she had made her entrance. Cemeteries are never very cheery places, I suppose, but this one was the least depressing I ever have found. The first time I parted the grass and peered at a headboard, I made out in dull letters:

Here lies the body of Lobo Jack.
He was a brave man. Why couldn't he be true?

I smiled a little at this wistful query. The very name of the dead man seemed the sufficient answer. Another board said that "Christian Petersen lies here. We hope he fits his grave better than he fitted his town." Another read: "Under your feet sleeps Will McKay, the straightest shot, the straightest tongue, and the straightest friend that ever was in Monte Verde."

Most of the inscriptions were much shorter. One said simply: "Good-by, Joe Cruthers." But only a few began with the formal: "Here lies ———" or proceeded to useless dates. There was generally a touch of personal feeling that I liked, and yet I was glad that the forest was taking this ground again for its own. I felt, also, that the men who had died and were buried here were probably like those I had seen in Monte Verde, rough, strong fellows who were perfectly willing to return their bodies to the soil from which they had sprung without foolish monuments or well-kept graves to shelter their remains. In an open, grassy place in a corner I selected the site of Anson's grave, and hired a strong lad at the nearest house to dig the hole for me. Then I went back to town.

There was excitement ahead of me, I saw at once. For several men and boys were in view running at full speed toward the hotel, and when I came in sight of it, I saw a crowd of forty or fifty people in front of the veranda. I knew, without being told, that this interest must have something to do with young Charles Dexter and his affairs.

CHAPTER XI.   CALLERS

WELL, I was right. As I came closer to the crowd, I noticed that four or five men sat in the center of the group on horses, and that these men were all facing toward the front door of the hotel. Now I mixed with the bystanders and saw that the riders were the center of all attention. They were worth it. I never saw a more splendid set of fellows. One was of middle age, with the face of a statesman of the grim ancient school; the rest were young fellows in the very flower of life; and every one of them, young or old, had the look of a king, or the look which kings, at least, ought to have. The arch of their chests and the straightness of their backs made me feel smaller and weaker than ever.

"Who are they?" I asked a neighbor among the spectators.

The fellow looked at me as if I had asked the name of the sun in heaven. Then he realized that I was the tenderfoot.

"That's Judge Benson, and those are Clay Livingston's boys," came the answer.

One man to have four such sons!

But then, they plainly came of a mold. I could admire them without envy, such physical perfection being at a stellar distance from me.

"Will he come out?" some one asked.

"Sure he'll come out—if he's a fool!" said another.

"He'd come out in spite of all the men in Dexter Valley," said a third.

And I knew, instantly, that they were speaking of Charlie Dexter. Had the five riders, then, come to see him? Suddenly I was aware that lightning was in the air—the sort of lightning that causes men to be struck dead in a quick explosion of battle.

Then a fellow bawled out—the sort of a fool who loves to make more trouble than he is willing to share: "There's the man who's Dexter's friend! That's him—the little feller."

I saw Judge Benson turn toward me on his horse. The crowd melted away to either side and he rode straight up to me, and behind him came that wedge of heroic young riders. Those five pairs of eyes fastened upon me, and loaded me with a weight. I never have felt more uncomfortable, but being in the first place called a "little feller," I naturally straightened to my full height and forced myself to look back at them as straightly as they were looking at me.

"You're a friend to the young impostor who calls himself Charles Dexter, are you?" began Benson.

This was a little too much for me. When a man asks a question that can't be answered, he ought to feel some shame, but the judge seemed bent on putting me in a foolish light. I heard some one snicker, and then I answered: "I'm a friend of Charles Dexter."

The rage which I felt at the attitude of the crowd stung me so that I went on: "And so are the rest of these people. They're all friends of Charles Dexter! Ask them— let me see which one of them denies it!"

The judge was a match for that question.

He said: "So am I the friend of Charles Dexter—the poor dead boy who lost his life ten years ago. But I ask you, pointblank, how you dare to encourage the pretensions of an impostor—and you a stranger to the community!"

I found it hard to say anything in answer to this, and I'm afraid that my eyes began to grow big with the pressure he was putting upon me.

He went on: "How long have you known the young reprobate who gives himself a name like that of Charles Dexter?"

"Less than one day," says I.

The judge smiled in his contempt.

"I thought so," said he.

"Some truths are self-evident," I managed to say.

"What?" he exclaimed. "Self-evident?"

He reined his horse back at me, furiously, almost as though he were about to ride me down, and the people around me shrank away. But a man as physically helpless as I was, grows used to embarrassment, I may say.

"Self-evident," said I. "You can define the word yourself, when you see Prince Charlie."

62

I don't know why that expression came to my tongue, but it turned the face of the judge black.

"By Heaven!" he cried out in his deep voice. "Credulous fools cause half of the misery in the world. And if this young criminal and pretender dares to show himself to me ——"

Suddenly, turning my eyes toward the veranda, I saw what I wanted, and it came in so pat that I could not help pointing.

"People who are willfully blind never can see, Judge Benson," said I.

He jerked his head around, and then he saw Dexter at last. The crowd disappeared from between them. I saw the judge straighten in his saddle. The four young knights with him stiffened likewise, and I saw a contemptuous smile appear on the lips of one of them.

"Ah, my lad," I thought, "you may soon learn a different sort of a smile, if you have much to do with that young man!"

I must say, however, that Dexter did not present a heroic appearance, contrasted with the five giants on horseback. He looked slender, sallow, almost like an invalid. And he was lounging lightly against one of the wooden pillars which held up the veranda's roof. In his left hand a cigarette was burning. His black hair was brushed sleekly down over his head, so that one could see the big bumps behind his forehead. Phrenologists probably would have admired those enlargements, but at times they gave his head an almost deformed appearance. He was dressed as dapperly as usual, but he had chosen to put on a blue suit, with gray spats of box cloth, and he wore a wing collar with a bow tie which was spotted with tiny white polka dots. It wasn't exactly the sort of an outfit that one expects to meet with in a wilderness such as the mountains of Monte Verde. Suddenly I myself felt my face growing hot, and it seemed patent that the lad must be a charlatan, after all.

There was a moment of silence, during which the judge stared at the boy.

Then he broke out in a scornful voice: "So you're the true Charles Dexter, are you? You?"

"My name is Charles Dexter," said he.

"So I hear you say. But any man with half an eye in his head can see that what you say is ——"

"That will do," said the boy.

He did not raise his voice, and yet he cut into and stopped the speech of the big judge as easily as a father checks a child.

"We won't call names until they're asked for," said Dexter, and gave the judge the benefit of his faint smile.

"Young man," said the judge, "do you know what the law says must be done to those who steal names?"

"My dear Judge Benson," said Dexter, "perhaps you need to be on a horse to ask that question, but I don't need to be on a horse to answer it."

"We've stood enough!" exclaimed one of the Livingston boys. "We don't have to stand here and listen to that crook back-chat, Uncle Benson."

They started forward, pouring around the judge.

Dexter did not move, except to straighten and put his weight on both feet. There was a gasp from the crowd. I thought that bullets would begin to fly at once, but that calm, precise voice of Dexter's cut in:

"You'd better keep your young men in hand, Judge Benson."

The judge did not wait, If he had, for another half of a second, I think that Monte Verde would have seen some amazing things. But it happened that Charles Dexter was to reveal himself gradually to the town, and to the valley, and to all of the people of the district.

Benson shouted: "Slade, Harry, Joe, Ben! Get back here and don't start trouble. Keep behind me and out of the way!"

They reined in their horses. They were flushed with anger. They were fairly growling their rage.

"All four, and on horseback!" said Dexter, with his shadowy smile that could make the flesh of men creep. "Four to one! Four to one! But what big, strapping boys

64

they've grown to be. Big fellows! Worth something, I dare say, if they could be sold by the pound!"

There was a ghastly second of silence, and then some one snickered irrepressibly in the crowd, and there was a sudden roar of laughter—half hysterical, I have no doubt.

This wave of mirth maddened the young fellows, and they looked to their older companion for guidance. He himself had a brow that was black with fury, but he kept the four young giants in leash with a lifted hand.

"You're Slade, of course," said Dexter, to one of the youngsters. "And you'll be remembering the day when I blacked your eye for you at the swimming pool, Slade? Remember it, old fellow. Always remember it. And when you come again, don't come with four, but with fourteen!"

Perhaps there was something childish in this taunt, but the light and casual manner in which it was spoken had a peculiar effect, and the reference to such a particular instance out of the past also had its decided point in the minds of all who heard. I think it was this moment that decided Monte Verde to believe in Charles Dexter.

The judge was naturally in a fury. He had come up here to make a show of the "pretender" and instead, he himself was being made to look like a foolish schoolboy.

"My lad," he said, with a heavy attempt at kindness, "I advise you to leave this community and betake yourself to smaller crimes. You'll find this a dangerous atmosphere."

"My dear judge," said Dexter, "I don't aspire toward the crimes by which you've distinguished yourself. I, for one, never expect to murder my landlord in order to keep the rent that belongs to him."

The judge shouted something, I don't know what. His anger simply exploded in his throat. And the four young Livingstons stared at him, waiting impatiently for a signal.

"You infernal young puppy!" cried the judge. "There never was a Dexter who wouldn't make two of you!"

Dexter deliberately walked down the steps of the veranda.

He sauntered slowly out until he was standing right

before that row of horses' heads. He folded his hands behind his back, and looked from one rider's face to the next.

"You see, however," said he, "that I keep the old Dexter characteristics. I never hunt in couples, and I never run from packs of village dogs, judge!"

CHAPTER XII.   CLEWS

HERE the judge called out loudly to the Livingston boys to keep their hands from their guns and to bear back. And he was in the nick of time, because those lads had been badgered by Prince Charlie to such a point that they were beginning to reach for weapons. Even if they had been able to shoot down Charlie—which I'm not at all sure that they could have done—they would then have had rough handling from the crowd which had gathered, and which was thickening every instant. The bearing of Dexter and his inimitable cool manner were telling very heavily in his favor, and I could hear, all around me, deep-throated mutterings and murmurings which threatened the men from the valley with immediate destruction if they attempted any foul play. The judge must have seen what was in the air.

I suppose that he had come up there hoping to brush the boy before him by weight of numbers, by weight of authority. The tables were turned.

"Whatever nonsense may be in your mind," said he, "there are equitable courts of law in which you can present your claims."

"For instance," said the boy, "in the court where you preside?"

He smiled, and there was a quick little murmuring that ran through the crowd—a sort of hasty agreement, the point was so manifestly and aptly taken.

"And, as you know," said Dexter, "the man who could have given the best testimony on my behalf has been murdered and the documents have been stolen from him."

"Come, come, come!" said the judge. "What documents could there have been?"

"What I had in my pockets, only, when I left home."

"And what documents," said the judge, looking around upon the crowd with a smile, "would you have been carrying in your pockets—after being roused out in the middle of the night, suddenly, during the unlucky battle in Dexter Valley ten years ago?"

Prince Charlie was not moved in the least by the superior attitude of Benson.

He said: "I was carrying what any lad is apt to have in the pockets of his coat. I had a new wallet, and of course I always had the wallet with me, and in that wallet were some things of importance—now. They were not important then. There was a picture, for instance, of my mother and myself, and a few words written by myself under the face of the picture."

"A very simple matter," said the judge, "for any one to get at a picture of poor Mrs. Dexter and her dead boy. What would it prove?"

"In the first place," said Dexter, "it would prove that my handwriting was simply the boyish forerunner of the handwriting which I use now. Any handwriting expert could see the truth at a glance. In the second place, it isn't true that it would have been easy to get a copy of that picture. My mother never had snapshots taken. Neither did I. That picture was taken almost by accident. But in my pockets there were other things, such, for instance, as a key to the cellar door, and another key for the wire run where I kept my rabbits."

"A snapshot—a key to a rabbit run," said the judge, smiling contemptuously again. "A great deal must hang from that sort of thing! But, whatever it might have been, you only *claim* to have had the trifles. No one in this part of the country has seen any of them."

"No," said the boy, "because your thief and murderer

took care of that, when he killed Philip Anson and stole the black satchel."

"*My* thief and murderer?" fairly shouted the judge. "Do you dare to accuse me of ——"

He stifled with rage and real excitement.

Then he roared out: "Wasn't the sign of Scorpio on his forehead, as they say? Isn't that a proof that the Mexican did the work?"

"Very likely," answered Prince Charlie. "And very likely Scorpio would have done the thing just for fun, eh? After hiding for ten years, he would come out of his hiding place and do a murder, and steal a thing in which *he* had no interest. Not a bit! There was nothing for Scorpio to gain in keeping me from my rightful inheritance. Not a penny in pocket for him. But it meant millions to the men who have been living on my father's land, rent free, for ten years! It meant keeping the houses they stole, and the houses they built. It meant keeping the barns they had put up on the stolen ground. It meant no payment of the back rent in sums which would have bankrupted every Dinmont, Crowell, Benson, Livingston in the lot. It meant keeping you all from the disgrace of a shameful exposure. It meant saving you from becoming contemptible in the eyes of all the honest men in the region around you. All of these objects were to be gained for your party by the murder of poor Phil Anson and the theft of the little black bag. Then, Judge Benson, I want you to consider that if you had much to gain by the death of Anson, Manuel Scorpio had almost as much to lose by making himself known. Wherever he had been sheltering himself, his whereabouts were entirely unknown to the law officers; He was out of the danger of the hangman's noose.

"Then what sort of madness made him kill Anson, steal the bag which was useless to him, and finally confess the murder by putting his own well-known sign on the forehead of the dead man?"

This arraignment made that crowd tense with interest and anger. The Livingston boys began to lose color. Certainly their case looked black and the damning finger pointed straight at the men of the Dexter Valley as the probable criminals, or inspirers of the crime.

The judge said: "What made him so mad, ten years ago, that he should have put the sign on the foreheads of his victims then?"

"Partly because he hated people of the Dexter name, and he had some reason for his hatred. Furthermore, when he put the sign on his dead men, he did not dream that any one would be able to recognize it as the sign for the constellation which carries the same name as his. No, no! If Scorpio came here of his own volition, he would come to murder another Dexter. If he came here to kill Anson and steal the satchel, then he came because he was hired, and hired at such an enormous price that he was willing to sign the deed he committed!"

This was about as clear a statement of the case against the men of Dexter Valley as could have been made, and I saw the people in the listening crowd look sharply at one another. For that matter the Livingston boys were doing some staring also—and the direction they looked was toward Benson. No matter what had been contrived, it was pretty apparent that those clean-eyed lads had had nothing to do with any plotting.

The judge was plainly hard hit by the talk of Dexter. If the boy had shouted or raged, or grown either red or white, or if his voice had trembled, it might have been another matter, but the deliberate and easy speech of Prince Charlie gave a double weight to everything he had said.

"Malignant traducing of character!" bust out the judge. "This sort of talk is cheap. You will learn, young man, that one has to have proof—and good proofs—before charging even a considerable number of men with such a crime."

"I have the proof," said the boy.

My heart jumped into my throat.

"You *have* proof?" shouted the judge.

And he turned gray. Yes, under my eyes, his face grew ashen and puckered with emotion. The thing was so startling that I heard one of the men standing near me point out the judge's expression to another watcher.

"I have proof," repeated Prince Charlie. "I followed the back trail of the man who killed Anson and left the sign of Scorpio upon him. I went with the sheriff, and we followed down into Dexter Valley."

At this, there was a general gasp.

"Dexter Valley is a big place!" cried the judge.

"Yes," said the boy instantly. "It's a place big enough to hold all the enemies of my family."

"You followed down into the valley, and there you lost the trail?" suggested the judge.

"Yes, we lost the trail, after a time."

"Poppycock and nonsense!" said Benson. "This is not even interesting. You follow a trail into the depth and the width of Dexter Valley, and you say that trail has any definite meaning?"

"I do," said the boy.

"Let me hear your reason, then?" said the judge.

"You wish to have me lay all of my cards on the table, I see," said Prince Charlie. "Well, I suppose that is hardly a reasonable request, but I'll show you everything that I know, judge. It may be," he added, and that velvet voice of his suddenly warmed a little, "it may be that every man in the valley is not a scoundrel. I'd hate to think that these four fellows are sneakin' murderers, or connivers at murder, for instance. I find it hard to think that *you* would countenance such things, Judge Benson ——"

A very strong effect was there. The judge turned from pale to crimson. His big chest began to labor. Certainly he had been touched in an unexpected place.

"But," said the boy, continuing, "I can't say the same thing of every one, and the first person I accuse is Steven Dinmont."

"Infernal rot!" shouted the judge, who could not keep his voice down under any circumstances. "I know and respect Steve Dinmont as though he were my own brother."

"Why, no doubt you do," said the boy, "but the trail of the man who used Scorpio's sign went out from under the eyes of the sheriff and me when we came to the tangle of corral fencing around the place of Steven Dinmont."

"It ain't me that accuses him," said a quiet, drawling voice.

And there was Sheriff Tom Winchell, looking a great deal more like a half-wit than ever before. But you can believe that when I looked at him now, I looked with respect. I began to see that if he were half freak, he was also half genius.

"Ah, Winchell," cried the judge. "You're not on the side of this young pretender here? Why, Tom Winchell, of course you're not!"

"No," said the sheriff, "I ain't on his side."

"Good!" cried the judge, and one could hear in the vibration of his voice that his heart had been warmed by that answer.

Winchell went on in his drawl:

"I ain't on anybody's side. I'm on the side of the law. I'm just on the side opposite to stealin' and murder and ——"

"But all that nonsense about the black bag and the wallet, and the keys, and such rot?" exclaimed the judge. "And a trail that vanishes at Steven Dinmont's place ——"

"That's where the trail went out," said the sheriff, "and here's a coupla things I found in the ashes of a little dead fire down that same trail."

And he pulled from his pocket and showed us in his hand the blackened and half-melted remains of two keys!

CHAPTER XIII.   DUST TO DUST

THE thing came in unbelievably pat. The boy had claimed to have left two keys in his companion's keeping. Here was the blackened metal of two such keys. Then what was the conclusion to be drawn?

It was perfectly simple.

The men of Dexter Valley had gained information of the proof with which young Dexter was about to reinforce his claims to the land which they had usurped, and therefore they had sent as an emissary of robbery and murder, either Scorpio himself, or a man ready to use the sign of Scorpio to cover his true identity.

At that moment, there was a deep, angry voice from the entire crowd.

Even the judge was moved. He shifted his glance from side to side, as though to measure the strength of the sentiment which surrounded him, and then he said:

"My dear lad, if you have any real claims to present to the men of Dexter Valley, why don't you present them fairly before us?"

"Do you suggest," said Dexter, "that I should go down there among you and talk to representatives?"

"That's what I suggest," said the judge, "because then ——"

He paused. His strong face hardened.

"I'll give you my personal guarantee that you'll go and come safely," said he.

"Don't do it, Prince Charlie!" burst out some one. "Don't you go and be a fool! You'll get your throat cut!"

"It's a lie!" said the judge, with great force. "Come down there and you'd be as safe as if you were in the heart of your own family. Come down there, and I'll make sure of your safety. Make up your mind what claims you wish to prefer. Come to Dexter House to-morrow night. You know that I live there now. I'll receive you. You'll be my guest, and hospitality has sacred claims in this part of the world, my young friend. There we'll talk over the thing amicably. We are not robbers, but people who wish to do what is right and what is just."

This was a very good speech, expressed in the judge's deep and manly voice, and all at once I had my first hope that the matter might be smoothed over in a friendly fashion.

Prince Charlie, for a moment, looked quietly at Benson, and then at the four young riders with him.

"I think I might trust you, all five," said he.

And that had a great effect, too. I mean to say, there had been such imminent danger of a brawl a moment before, that it was a great pleasure to hear this quiet little acknowledgment from the lips of Dexter.

The judge did not wait, once he had received his favorable answer.

"Good-by," said he, "and good luck to you until we meet again. Whatever the truth may be, let the truth be known about this matter."

That was a very considerable admission on his part—that there might be even a ghost of truth behind what Prince Charlie claimed. But though he had made what he thought was a handsome concession, the judge got no applause from the crowd as he rode away with his escort of fighting men.

In fact, as they rode away, some one in the group broke into loud, jeering laughter. At this, young Ben Livingston whipped his horse around and came riding straight back at us. He looked ready to jump into a cage filled with wildcats.

"Who laughed?" he asked, his handsome face all in a snarl. "What cur laughed?"

No one answered, and Ben Livingston allowed himself the privilege of a contemptuous smile, while his eyes ran over us, man by man. I, for one, found it quite impossible to meet his blazing young eye, and it amazed me to find that the others were silent. One didn't expect to see half a hundred burly mountaineers overmastered with such ease!

Well, Ben Livingston, after enjoying his triumph for a few seconds, pulled his horse around and rode after his companions, slowly, as though inviting some one to take up his challenge, but no voice stirred in pursuit of him.

After the party was out of sight, tipping over the edge of the road where it bent down into the valley, the crowd broke up as well, and formed into groups which busily discussed what had been heard on this day, and there was no doubt as to where the sympathy of the talkers lay.

Whatever Dexter Valley might think of the new claimant, there was no question in the mind of Monte Verde. It accepted Prince Charlie exactly as it found him.

For my own part, I suppose that I was professionally more of a skeptic than the townsmen. Invalids are apt to be great doubters. I was an invalid. Moreover, the fairy-story part of the thing was still a good deal too much for me.

I went into the hotel and took a sponge bath and changed my clothes. I lay down for a half hour, and at the end of that time, just as I was dropping off into a doze, there was a tap at my door. I called out, and the door was opened by Prince Charlie.

I had left word at the hotel office as to the arrangements which I had made for the burial of the body of Anson, and the boy now asked me if I would attend the funeral. I agreed to go, and getting up, with an uncontrollable yawn, I brushed my disarranged hair and put on a hat.

I found that Charlie Dexter was watching me with his grave, dark eyes.

"You're not very strong, Mr. Dean?" said he.

"I'm not a Hercules," I admitted.

"A year out here will make you into a new man," he told me.

We went down the stairs together, and now and then I felt that his glance was fixed upon me again, searching, inquiring.

"That sheriff is a mighty intelligent fellow," I suggested.

"He's intelligent," admitted the boy, but would say no more on the subject, where I had expected him to break out into praise.

We went down to the street and there I found that the hearse was already there. It was simply a buckboard, with the trap at the rear of it open.

In the front room of the hotel was the coffin, closed,

and with some flowers placed carefully over it. They were wild flowers and were already wilting.

It was not a very cheerful thing to look at. The rude, blind look of the box which covered the human remains of poor Philip Anson made me shake my head. For three years the picture of a coffin had never been very far from my mind.

Well, young Charlie Dexter surprised me again by asking me to act as a pall-bearer. There already had been an inquest. The verdict had been given: "Murder, by hands unknown." And I was amazed to think of any jury arriving at a verdict without first hearing the testimony of the star witness—myself! However, that was the way that things were done in Monte Verde. Other men had heard what I had to say, and therefore I was not called.

When I was asked to be a pall-bearer, I said to Dexter: "But I never knew this man."

"Neither did he know you," said the boy, "except at the end. But he had no other friends in Monte Verde. Neither have I. No better friend than you, Mr. Dean, to call upon."

The flattery of this little remark made me quite willing to serve.

I found that the sheriff was another pall-bearer, and besides Dexter, there were two others, men I never had seen before. They helped me to carry the box out to the wagon, and then we walked through the town behind the dust of the hearse until we came to the cemetery. And there the coffin was taken from the buckboard, and carried into the little graveyard.

The grave, by this time, had been dug. The boy who had done the work was leaning on his shovel at one side, waiting to be paid, or given a bit extra for filling in the grave again. Behind us poured the whole of Monte Verde. They came in a thick crowd, including even the women and the little children. There was not a soul left in the village, as I understood afterward, except one bedridden old fellow who could not move—he was just recovering from pneumonia.

This throng went trampling around through the shrubbery, making a good deal of noise, but all anxious to get in proper places to see the ceremony. They seemed to feel that something extraordinary was about to happen. I felt that way myself. The very feel of the wind was telling me of something exciting ahead. The clouds in the sky had an unusual look.

Well, everything went straight forward. We lowered the coffin into the grave and then the minister read the service.

I mean to say that he first delivered a little speech, short and to the point. He was a good man, that minister, with a sad, sincere sort of a face. His clothes looked ten years old, and they were polished to the shining point at the knees and at the elbows. You could see that he literally starved himself in order to feed the needy.

As near as I can remember, he said: "I am sorry that I don't know more about this man, who is a stranger to us. He lived in Dexter Valley, ten years ago, and all we know is that when his friends were attacked, he saved the lone survivor of the Dexter family, rode away with him, and raised him to manhood.

"I have no doubt that Charles Dexter, who stands here, will eventually get all that is justly owing to him. In that case, poor Philip Anson is robbed of certain great rewards. He would have been made rich. He would have been given a chance to enjoy the reward of his faith and his long service. But this reward has been stolen away from him, like a cup knocked from the lips of a thirsty man.

"There are other rewards, however. No one serves without being rewarded. The God who watches over us sees such acts, and remembers them. We, too, who never knew the man, never will forget him. We may be inspired to similar acts, or lesser ones of charity, and of faithful kindliness. Philip Anson, yesterday, was not even a name to me. Now he is a shining light and a leader. So may he be to all of you. Only let us remember that no good thing is done or even strongly attempted in vain!"

Here he paused. The coffin was now in the ground,

and he read the regular service, after which young Charles Dexter stepped forward and picked up a handful of the loose soil at the edge of the hole where Anson lay at rest.

He lifted his hand with a sober face toward the sky, and he said in his velvet, soft, regular voice, that held no emotion: "If I give my life to anything but the finding of your murderer, Philip Anson, may I be damned forever!"

Well, there was enough in that to give us the thrill which we had sensed in the air, but it was nothing to what came. For a wild voice suddenly shrilled out: "No, no! Charlie Dexter, don't say it——"

I turned about, amazed, and saw the white face of pretty Claudia Laffitter, with her lips still parted on the last word.

CHAPTER XIV.   AN INVITATION

WOMEN, it is reputed, will cry out more quickly than men. They are more easily brought to a semi-hysterical state, but Claudia Laffitter was not like other girls. She had the steady eye and the calm manner of a man. She walked like a man, with a free, easy step. She talked like a man, too—that is to say, she didn't chatter and gossip but spoke straight to her point, whatever it might be. She could ride a horse, shoot with a rifle, swing an ax, throw a ball like a boy, and in general she could share with the men whatever the men were interested in, all the while remaining distinctly and delightfully feminine. But for Claudia Laffitter to screech out in this manner at the burial of Philip Anson was so extraordinary that every one turned and gaped at her, without speaking a word, until her mother—a fine-looking, buxom woman, took Claudia by the arm and hurried her away from the grave.

She seemed to go unwillingly, and at the entrance to the cemetery she turned and looked back at the group, and I never have forgotten her appearance—her face had grown so pale and her eyes so large.

Young Dexter generally took everything in one free-and-easy swing, and never was upset, no matter what was happening around him, but on this occasion he differed from his usual mode of action. When the girl first cried out, he took two or three rapid steps in her direction, and then, recalling himself, he stopped short.

He turned, and encountering my eye, looked at me with a curiously wondering stare, as though he hoped that I or some other man could give him an explanation. But of course I was as bewildered as he.

Why had she cried out? Why had that solemn vow of vengeance upon Scorpio struck her so suddenly to the heart?

Well, it was a problem and a serious one, and I hardly was surprised that young Dexter should take the thing so gravely.

Yet I *was* surprised that he should remain impressed for a long period afterward. Most of the crowd remained only until the grave was nearly filled by two shovelers, and then they began to wander back toward the town, but I stayed there in the wild greenery of the cemetery, puzzled and doubting, and when I turned to start back to the center of Monte Verde, I was overtaken by Dexter. He went on beside me, never speaking a word, though several times he glanced at me in such a manner that I guessed that he had something in his mind to speak out.

I was not surprised, then, when on reaching the hotel he asked if he could have a few words with me. I told him that I should be delighted. I was flattered, in fact, and that, of course, was not strange.

He was, of course, younger, and in many ways, I suppose I may say that he had done far less than I in the world. I could at least point back to certain business accomplishments, and though I never had set the world on fire, yet it is true that I had made my small mark in my own way. Yet the attention which Dexter gave to me, accidentally as I had been thrown in his way, pleased

78

me more than almost anything that had gone before in my life. The lad had a power which had gripped all of Monte Verde, for that matter. Perhaps I valued him very largely because of the way in which all of the other inhabitants of the village were now looking up to him.

We went up to my room, and sat there in the warmth and the golden color of the afternoon, sunning ourselves, relaxing, and speaking very little together until we each had smoked a cigarette.

Then he said to me in that curiously soft voice, which I cannot help mentioning so often, simply because it was such a pronounced and unusual characteristic of his: "Mr. Dean, I'm about to say a strange thing to you."

I nodded at him. Perhaps I blinked a little. Something was coming, and I was as prepared to catch a shock as any baseball player is prepared to catch a line drive in the infield.

"Very well," said I, smiling. "I'm here to listen."

"You've seen me through several odd moments," he said. "From the start you've been the greatest sort of help to me."

"If you mean that matter of the decision," said I, willing to make light of what I had said or done, "that was spoken merely because it seemed justice to me."

"I don't refer so much to that," said he. "I never really can thank a man for doing and saying what seems right to him. But I must thank you for another thing. Out here on the rim of the world—I suppose I may call it that?"

He halted, here, in the middle of his idea, and as he waved out the window toward great Thimble Peak, I saw at once that it *did* look like the rim of the world, and the great "falling off" place must be just at the back of the mountain.

"Yes, you might call it that, I suppose," said I.

"Very well. Out here in the wilderness, a man reverts to nature to a strange degree. And I've felt myself reverting."

His grave eyes were here fixed upon me, as much as

though he were asking if I could understand and agree with him. In my place, I stared soberly back at him, for I was recalling several pictures of moments in which I had watched him.

Then I said, suddenly: "I think I know what you mean. I could even name an instant when the primitive urge almost mastered you."

He leaned forward at this, though his expression did not change and he allowed no curiosity to enter into the tone of his voice.

"What moment was that, Mr. Dean?"

"When you left the steps of the veranda and walked toward the riders, to-day," said I, "it was not merely that which you first had in mind."

"Then what did I have in mind?" said he.

I hesitated. It seemed that I was about to say a foolish thing, and yet it was so on the tip of my tongue that I could not keep it back.

"You were thinking, in the first place, that you would like to draw a gun, and to leap out at them, firing as you ran."

Now that the thing was out, I felt doubly the fool. He rose and walked to the window, without answering me. He gave me his back to stare at, for a moment, and then he suddenly faced toward me again.

"What makes you think that I carry a gun?" he asked me.

"Well," said I, "the other day you invited that hulking brute and bully to a gun fight. And besides—a man can't fight with his teeth, like a tiger."

I laughed, to cover the last sentence, but he was not laughing. He moved with his shadowy, soft step back to the center of the room and there he stood quietly, looking down on me.

"Why do you use that word—tiger?" he asked.

I hunted through my mind, quickly, to find another expression that might serve as an alternative, but finally I saw that I had better rely upon the honesty of my impression, just as it first had come to me.

"Because from the first moment you seemed to me

dangerous," said I. "And because that's the way the other people look on you."

He shook his head.

"You've heard them talk about Dexters, before," he suggested.

"No. I never had heard of the Dexters, I'm sure, when I first laid eyes on you. It's not the past reputation of your family that made Jay Burgess run for his life!"

He nodded, after a moment of thoughtful pause.

"Perhaps not," said he. "No, perhaps not!"

He continued, when I said nothing: "However that may be, I *was* rather tempted to leap out at those Livingstons, and at Judge Benson, in spite of their numbers. But as I was turning the thing in my mind, my eye happened to fall upon your face, among the crowd, and the peace of it, the pallor, and the calmness of your eyes, Mr. Dean, did me a great deal of good, because it reminded me that man is, or ought to be, a civilized animal. It helped me a great deal, just then, to have you to look at."

"Thank you," said I. "That's a thorough compliment."

He waved aside the notion of such politeness as this.

"You've helped me so much in the past," he went on, "and you've come so close to the heart of my mystery, if I may call it that, and you've had the blood of Phil Anson on your hands—you've done so much for me, in short, that I'm inspired to ask a greater favor than this from you."

"I'd like to do what I can for you," said I, truthfully.

"I want you to go in my place to the old Dexter house and make them my terms in a formal proposal."

This, as one may imagine, was enough to flabbergast me.

"That I should go in your place?" I exclaimed.

The mere idea made me sweat.

"If I went for myself," said he, "I would almost certainly be walking into a trap."

"No, no!" said I. "I think that Judge Benson intends to act like an honorable man, and so do the young Livingston boys."

"They may intend to do so," said he. "I've no doubt

of that. But there are others in their families whom they couldn't control. No, I wouldn't trust my life in their hands for ten seconds. Rifles may be fired by unknown hands through windows, and such things, you know."

I could not help nodding. The danger seemed far more than imagination to me.

"But there are these other men, these hardy fellows of Monte Verde who admire you, Dexter! Why not send one of them along on this errand?"

"Shall I tell you why not? For a very simple and a very full reason. None of them would go. They might accompany *me*, but they wouldn't go alone. And if I go, accompanied, then it means a bloody battle to begin with. Blood in the very start of things!"

A new note crept into his voice. It was like the ringing of a bell at a distance. A big, brazen, ominous bell. The tremor of the tone went straight through me, and danced along all of my nerves.

Blood he said that he wished to avoid, but as he spoke the word there was no horror in his voice, I thought. There was rather a hungry yearning after it.

"Dexter," I said frankly, "I'm not a hero. I don't pretend to be one. The mere thought of going down there as your representative ———"

"You'd be in no danger. They wouldn't dare. They couldn't blame your death upon some old feud, some mysterious agency. You've been here too short a time to have entered into any of the blood feuds that exist around here. You'd be as safe as you are sitting in this room."

Then he waited, murmuring as a sort of afterthought: "Besides, you've handled men before this, and you could read their minds for me, in part."

"What terms do you want me to put to them?" I asked him.

"You think over the matter of going," said he. "I'll see you again to-morrow morning, and then, if you want to do this great thing for me, I'll tell you the terms."

CHAPTER XV.

IMMEDIATELY after supper I went to bed. I was exhausted after the events of the past twenty-four hours, but nevertheless I was unable to turn in without certain precautions. To be frank, I locked my door and slid home the bolt which secured it. I drew down and turned the latch of the northern window, and in front of the western window I laid two chairs on the floor, so as to hamper as much as possible any one who tried to enter in that manner.

When I had done these things, I went to bed, but before I turned out the light, I fell to wondering whether or not it wouldn't be a better thing to have doors and windows all unlocked, so as to facilitate flight in case an enemy should try to get at me. However, after I had turned the matter back and forth through my mind, several times, I summoned courage, told myself that not the slightest danger was pointed at me and finally was able to lie down and close my eyes. Sleep came slowly. No matter what reason might tell me, instinct was giving me a profound warning that I had embarked on a perilous sea.

When I wakened in the morning, I was surprised to find that the sun was already high; a bracing wind cut in through the open western window, and I jumped out of bed and began to whistle. Over to the window I sauntered and leaning on the sill, I looked down into the ample green arms of the valley below. And suddenly I remembered that it was the first time in six months that I had slept solidly through a night; that there was no heaviness in my head, and no jumping along my nerves, and that my blood ran strong and hot in my body. I was hungry as a wolf and eager as a horse for this day's course.

When I looked at myself in the dusty mirror, the fixed

and hopeless look was gone from my eyes. I looked close enough to fifty, but not ten years older, as usual.

"Prince Charlie," said I to myself, "you are the tonic I have needed—you and your affairs!"

That instant I made up my mind that I would actually accept his commission and go down into the valley to old Dexter House to interview the usurpers and try to make terms with them.

By the time I had shaved and taken a quick bath, my hunger had to be held hard on the rein; and at breakfast I distinguished myself. Young Dexter already had breakfasted, at dawn, and Claudia Laffitter kindly came and sat down at my table and chatted with me. She said that Dexter had gone off to buy a pair of horses from a fellow on the edge of the town.

She, watching me with her fine, direct eyes, said suddenly to me: "Tell me, Mr. Dean. What did you think yesterday, when I squealed out like that, at the cemetery?"

"I thought nothing," said I. "I didn't know what to think. I was stumped by it!"

"Other people were, too," said she.

She flushed.

"I suppose I made a fool of myself," she said.

"I don't see that," I told her. "Not in my eyes. Not in the eyes of others. After all, you're a woman, Miss Laffitter, and your nerves had a right to jump a bit, when you heard Dexter swearing that he would have his pound of flesh for the death of poor Anson."

She nodded.

"You see how it is?" she put the thing to me, gravely. "He's the last Dexter; and he won't be long on earth, anyway."

"Why do you say that?"

"Don't you think that it's in his face?" she said. "I mean, that when you notice the set expression he has, and the way every emotion is held on the curb, it makes one feel that he is bound to go down soon. Besides, see what he's attempting."

She waved toward the western window of the dining room.

"All those people!" she said. "He'll surely try to go down there among them, and if he does, how long will he last? Oh, he'll be swept away by them!"

"I don't understand it," I said, irritably. "If the Dexters had a real claim on the ground, how can it be taken away from them? If they disappeared, I should imagine that the State would get it, or some such thing."

She nodded.

"You're thinking of eastern ways and the settled law. Ten years ago law hadn't much more face than a scared rabbit, out here. And it still appears only about once a week, for half an hour. And when you have people like the Crowells and Bensons and Livingstons and the rest, why, they're strong enough to hold on to what they have a ghost of a claim to. The Dexters have disappeared. For ten years those people have gone on improving the land they call their own. They used to rent it, you see? And now comes one poor fellow, without many real proofs, to claim the Dexter inheritance—well, what do you think will happen to him? He's in enough danger, but when he swears, as he did yesterday, that he's going to follow one man's trail, and when we know that that trail dips straight down into the valley—well, don't you see that he's tying a stone around his neck and then vowing that he'll jump into the water?"

When she had finished explaining, she sat back with a puckered brow, to wait for my assent. And there was nothing I could do but give it.

"Yes," I had to say, "almost from the first moment I laid eyes on him, I felt, somehow, that he was tied to a lost cause."

"That's it!" said she. "A lost cause. He has the look of it. Hullo, Jerry. How's things on the ranch?"

She broke off to call to a big, burly lad who had just come into the room, and presently she left me and went over to him. There was no restraint about Claudia. She talked to men as though she were a man herself. That was her charm, or a large part of it. She could be as free and easy as any rough mountaineer, and yet keep all her woman's dignity and essential aloofness.

A moment after this, the dining room was in a turmoil.

For out in the street we heard a crackling of revolver shots, people shouting, and then a prolonged and screeching cry.

Of course, we got outside on the double-quick.

People were flocking on the dead run toward a little house down the street, and I ran after them. The agonized yelling came out of that house, and when we got into the place, we found a man writhing and twisting and gasping on the floor, and occasionally a fresh scream came from him.

Young Dexter kneeled beside him, holding him by the shoulders, and saying: "Who sent you? That's all I want to know. Who hired you? Tell me that and I'll leave you alone—and we'll take care of you!"

The man on the floor was one of those big fellows whose heads are in proportion to the rest of them, but whose faces pinch out and draw to a point, till they look like ferrets. This one had the jaw of a bull and the little thin mouth of a cat. His eyes were small, and animal bright.

He still kicked and groaned, for he was badly hit, but when Dexter asked questions, he refused to make an answer, and finally yelled out at him: "I ain't gonna tell. To heck with you! I ain't gonna tell. Are the rest of you gonna stand by and see me bleed to death? Are you gonna let him torture me here, to death?"

Dexter got up and stepped back, dusting his hands, and still watching the face of the other, while my friend Keenan stepped in and took charge of the wounded man.

I mixed around with the crowd and at last found an eye-witness telling the story to a group of open-mouthed listeners.

What had happened was that when Dexter rode back down the street on his newly purchased horse, leading a second one behind him, out of this house, which belonged to the wounded man, Marsin by name, came a sudden chattering of guns, and Dexter's horse fell with him, shot dead.

He landed clear of the body, however, and using the bulk of the horse as a bulwark, he opened a return fire on the house. Almost his first shot struck Stew Marsin, and as the latter began to yell and the shooting from the house ended, Dexter charged straight across the street and into the house.

The others were already clattering out of the place by the back way, and they scooted off on horses which they had tethered in the brush before any of them could be identified. The tracks, later on, showed that three confederates had been with Marsin in the house. Or that three men, at least, had fled.

What impressed me, and what fairly froze my blood, was the amazing courage and ferocity of young Dexter in running across an open roadway toward a house filled with gunmen who could shoot at him from that cover.

They must have thought he was a ghost, also, for they had not waited for the charge to be driven home. They fled, whooping with terror, and left behind them only Stew Marsin, writhing in the apparent agony of death.

He was not to die of that bullet, however.

It was a grisly wound. It had torn through the ribs of his right side, crushing and splintering the bones, but driving none of the splinters actually into the lungs. He lay in frightful misery, but even the inexpert Keenan was able to say, after a brief examination, that the man would probably live.

They put him on a bed in his own house, and two neighbors volunteered to nurse him until he could ride a horse.

I heard one of these volunteers say: "I'll take care of Stew till he can ride out of town. And if he stays here a day after that, I reckon that he won't be needin' any more nursin'. He'll just need a hole in the cemetery."

"We don't bury hounds like him in that cemetery,"

said another. "And what're we gonna do about this? Are we gonna let the other three get off scot-free?"

It appeared that a dozen riders were already in pursuit of the fugitives, and then the group went on to another matter. Mr. Keenan, having finished with his doctoring, came out and proposed that every living thing in Monte Verde should believe that Charles Dexter was the true Prince Charlie—every living thing, from man to dog. This proposal was met with a howling cheer that still tingles in my ears.

Keenan went on to suggest that they fight for him, follow him, trust in him, and let the people of Dexter Valley know that the next time an attack was made on Prince Charlie, retribution would be exacted for the crime.

I went back to the hotel very thoughtful in spirit, and remembering what the garrulous old sheriff had said: that guns would soon be flashing because of Prince Charlie.

Well, the flashing of the guns had already started.

CHAPTER XVI.   INTO THE VALLEY

MUCH already had happened in the feud between Dexter and the people of Dexter Valley, but this wanton attack upon him, and the murderous cowardice with which the attempt was made was like the firing on Fort Sumter. From that moment public opinion all through the mountain was convinced that Prince Charlie was no false claimant but the real heir to the throne. However, though opinion outside the valley might be one thing, that inside of the valley was sure to be another, and it was really what the men of the valley were willing to think and do that counted. How this war would turn out, no man could say, but a veritable blue shadow of murder seemed to be sloping athwart Dexter Valley. It had climbed to the

88

height of Monte Verde, and no man who looked at Prince Charlie could doubt that there would be ample reprisals.

It was nearly noon before I saw young Dexter again. He had gone calmly back to the horse dealer at the verge of the town and bought another animal to take the place of that which had been killed. With this he returned, and he looked me up at once. I was in my room, resting, turning over the affair in my mind, when he dropped in.

He went right to the point.

He said: "I've tried to get six men from Monte Verde to go down to Dexter House for me. They won't budge. This business of to-day has finished them. They won't trust themselves in Dexter Valley. I don't blame them much, either. But still I have hope that you may take the chance."

I was almost amused. To expect more courage from poor hollow-chested me than the big men of Monte Verde were willing to show was ridiculous, on the face of it—except that I afforded a more meager target.

"My boy," said I, "I never have fired a gun in my life."

"And they know it," answered he, quickly. "That makes a great difference. If they tackled any one of these mountain men and dropped him, it might be called the result of a natural brawl. But no one would accuse you of drawing a gun or making a motion to do so. It would be murder, Mr. Dean, and even the people in Dexter Valley shrink from that idea—unless they should have a chance at Charles Dexter!"

He added the last with a glint in his eyes. It was not an expression of anger or of hate; it really was simply a gleam of amusement, and suddenly I saw that the frightful affair of that morning had not upset him at all. It had been merely a stirring touch that made a good day for him.

"I think that I'll ride down there for you," said I. "I'll ride down, unless I lose my nerve, this afternoon. Suppose that you tell me what I'm to say to them."

I expected a little immediate gratitude for this offer, and perhaps a little praise. Instead, he drove straight into the matter. As he talked, he took out a sheet of paper and sketched in the lay of the land, and noted down the houses, and gave me the names. I won't reproduce, here, what he told me, because it will appear in due course, in another place. Of course I listened carefully to what he told me. I made copious notes and afterward rehearsed the thing to make sure that I had it straight. We had lunch together and talked some more, and afterward Dexter said:

"Now for your share in the deal, Mr. Dean."

"My share?" said I.

"Yes. I suggest that you and I work on a percentage basis."

"I really don't understand that," said I.

"If you're my diplomat," said he, "and go places and do things that I can't do myself, and which no one else around here can do, then I think you ought to get—say twenty-five per cent, of everything that I salvage out of Dexter Valley."

He waited, his eyes keenly upon me. I could not help frowning, because in spite of his shrewdness he had misunderstood me.

"No," said I. "I'm out here in the West for my health, and not for business. I have enough to live on. It's life itself that I want out of this country, and not a fortune."

He looked straight at me, for a moment. He showed neither surprise nor anger, but appeared to be weighing something.

"It's true that you're taking a long chance," said he. "Perhaps you'd find the country more healthful if I offered you—say a third of the whole proceeds?"

At this, the frown left me, and I smiled.

"I wouldn't take a penny, or a blade of grass, or an acre of ground, Dexter," said I. "I believe that you're in the right. If I can help you to win what is yours, I'm contented."

His expression did not change in the least.

"Are you willing to shake hands on that?" said he.

"With all my heart," said I, and he stretched out his hand to me.

I grasped it. It was a cold hand, and it closed slowly

90

but hard on mine. At the same time the astonishment which I had half hoped to see in him before now appeared.

"You *mean* it!" said he. "You actually *mean* it!"

"Every word," said I.

"But to go down among those hungry wolves—Dean, what are you made of? Are you above money?"

"I'm beyond it," I told him, frankly. "I've lived so many years without much hope of life itself that money doesn't concern me, Dexter."

He passed a hand suddenly over his face.

"You haven't been through ten years of ——"

Then he checked himself, and merely added: "It isn't the first time that I've accepted charity, during these last ten years. And I'll accept yours, if you're still minded to go down there for me."

In ten minutes I was mounted on one of his horses, and he strapped on behind the saddle a small pack containing what necessaries I might use if I had to remain in the valley overnight, as seemed likely.

He stood for just a moment at the shoulder of the horse, looking up at me.

"This is a mighty brave thing, sir," said he.

"Stuff," said I, very pleased.

"I was going to give you some advice about the proper way of dealing with them," he went on. "But I won't. You'll see the proper thing to do, when the time comes, and I think that I'd rather trust your judgment than to my own."

He shook hands with me, and I started. I think there were twenty people out to see me off. Half of their attention was given to my bumpy seat in the saddle; but they were mainly rather bewildered as I started on the road into the valley. I suppose they realized that I was the emissary of Prince Charlie, and they didn't expect to see me come back up that same road again.

For my part, as I look back, I see that I had the courage of the helpless. The same courage, I suppose, that inspires a woman among men. It shames me to say so, but I'm afraid that that was the case.

Only when I came to the brink of the downward slope, I hesitated, and was about to draw in upon the reins. Shame kept me from doing so, for I knew that many eyes were still fixed upon me; but it seemed to me that beautiful Dexter Valley, at that moment, was a land of death for me.

It was now well on into the afternoon, a time when the grass-green colors of the fields were softened a little by the slant of the sunlight from the west, and the big groves of trees which swallowed up the farmhouses were islands of deep shadow here and there. The river, too, no longer burned as bright as the sun, but with the wind upon it it looked like hammered silver. But all of this beauty left me cold—made me cold, I might almost say—for I realized that, the lovelier Dexter Valley was, the harder men would fight to possess it, and the lower they would stoop to crimes on its account.

With the steeper slope gone, I entered into the pleasantly rolling lands of the lower valley, and saw the sleek-sided cattle grazing everywhere. There were amazing numbers of them, for the valley was so situated among the mountains that it was rarely long between rains, and the grass grew here as it grows in England—only it was a darker green. These cows had not the look of range animals. They lacked the hunched backs and the fiery, wild eyes. They were rather like dairy stock, munching away contentedly, or lying down to chew their cuds in the shade of some wide-armed tree. All seemed pastoral peace in Dexter Valley.

At least, so I felt as I rode through the land, and above all when I came to the river bottom, where the plowed fields began. Gold grew out of that soil, gold in abundance in its kinder forms of corn, and hay taller than my head, and maize as tall as horse and man. Yes, they would fight to keep this ground. They would fight inside the law, and outside of it!

I came to a good stone bridge that went across the

river on big piers. It echoed hollowly under me. There were several boys fishing from the down-stream side of it, and they turned to stare as I went by.

I was well beyond them when I heard a shrill voice saying: "That's one of Dexter's men, right now!"

What a chill I felt when I heard it!

But I went on, still comforted by the strength of weakness, I suppose, and somehow unable to do the sensible thing, which was simply to turn the head of my horse the other way and go back to Monte Verde as fast as I could.

I looked back only once, and saw the big hills rising, and the little town of Monte Verde blinking its windows at me like a sleepy Argus; after that I dared not look again, for fear that cowardly temptation would be too much for me.

A man driving a rattling hayrick encountered me on the far side of the bridge. At my question he shouted to his trotting team, and when they had halted, he looked me over leisurely. He was a middle-aged fellow with the chest of a Hercules, and the bluest eyes I ever saw.

"You dunno where the judge lives?" he queried.

I admitted my ignorance, and after he had surveyed me once more, he finally extended a massive arm and pointed.

"Second farmhouse on the right. It's got a windin' sort of a driveway. I reckon you'll know it by that."

I went on, and forced my horse into a gallop, even when the way began to slope upwards. It seemed to me that if I went more slowly, I would lose the necessary impetus for carrying through the work that lay ahead.

So I came to the designated driveway, and whirled my horse through the gate, and presently was scattering the gravel, as the horse came to a stop, before Dexter House itself.

There I dismounted, and stood in the presence of as wild an adventure as ever comes to the lives of men.

CHAPTER XVII. A MISSING PICTURE

IT was not a very big or imposing place. It was built rather long, to be sure, but only in the central section was there a second story with an attic over it. The walls were made of logs of varying sizes. I have seen a hundred better built log cabins. This was simply a big one and it looked as though the trees nearest at hand had been felled, helter-skelter, and squared on the ground to fit into the first place that could be found for them. In this way, quite a space had been cleared around the house, but no effort had been made to make a garden. The only things that bloomed before the house were a couple of long hitching racks, with holes pawed out along them. Three or four horses were tethered there at this moment, and I thought that their wild eyes and shaggy manes were telling what sort of people I might expect to find inside.

I tied up my horse, and patted his honest nose for him, and went to the door, at which I knocked.

"Hey!" called a voice from inside. "Come in, can't you?"

I went in, at that singular invitation, and saw a big young man seated in a large, half-furnished room, pulling at some straps which I gathered formed part of a bridle.

He paused in his work to look up at me in annoyance, though I gathered that he was more annoyed by his repair job than by my presence. His sleeves were rolled up to the elbows over arms fit for a blacksmith, and a tangle of hair poured over his forehead and almost across his eyes. He wore faded and patched blue overalls, and altogether looked like a common laborer.

"Hello, stranger," said he. "Lost your way?"

"Not if this is Judge Benson's house," said I.

"This is his house," said the boy. "Set down and rest your feet. Pa's out. You wanta see him?"

I said that I did, and that I was in no hurry. I sat down.

"Hey, Mike, Mike!" bawled my host.

There was a shuffling of feet, and a Chinaman appeared in the doorway.

"Fetch in a snack of something to eat," said the boy, "and a mug of coffee. Or would you rather have some corn whisky, stranger?"

I said that I was not hungry, and I meant it. There was a naked power and simplicity of fact about this room and the man in it that had taken all the edge from the arguments I had been preparing while I rode down into the valley; with them, my appetite had gone.

"He don't want nothin'," said the boy.

The Chinaman disappeared.

"I'm Pete Benson," said the youngster. "What's your name?"

"My name is Oliver Dean," said I.

"Oliver Dean—Oliver Dean?" said he.

He raised his head, and his fleshy brow puckered in thought.

"Why, ain't there an Oliver Dean mixed up with that lyin' sneak of a pretender that calls himself Charles Dexter, up there in Monte Verde?"

Forthright frankness? Yes, it might be called that. I assured myself that I had been a consummate ass for coming on this diplomatic mission to a place where such a thing as diplomacy was not known. But I saw that frankness must be met with frankness.

"I'm the Oliver Dean you refer to," said I, "and I believe the young fellow is really Charles Dexter."

I expected an explosion, after this. Pete Benson dropped the bridle with a rattle upon the floor, but he did not leap up to his feet to berate me. Instead, he muttered: "The deuce you do!"

And then he looked down from my face—not far down, or lower than my hip. And suddenly I saw that he was searching me with his glance to see whether or not I wore a gun!

What a country of the strong hand that was!

"You believe in him!" he went on, and nodding heavily at me, as though bewildered by such idiocy as mine, he shouted: "Hey, ma!"

"Hello, Pete!" called a woman's voice.

She came into the room immediately afterward. She was dressed in calico. Her hair was twisted into a tidy knot. Her arms, bare to the elbows like her sons, were as big and almost as powerful as his. And her step was like a man's, long and swinging.

"Them pigs have gone and busted through the fence and got into that corn in the thirty-acre field," she said. "You better go get 'em out. That worthless Banner, he ain't nowhere in calling range."

"Here's a stranger, ma," said Pete, nodding at me, and without rising. "He's Oliver Dean, the gent that's backing up the one that calls himself Charlie Dexter."

"You don't say!" said ma.

But she came straight up to me and shook my hand, and stood there towering above me, massive and at ease.

"You think he's the real thing, do you?" said she.

"Yes," said I, politely but firmly. "I do, indeed."

"He ain't growed to the Dexter size," she told me. "All the Dexters was what you might call eighteen-hand men. But set down and make yourself at home. I guess you wanta see the judge?"

I said that I did, and on the heels of this meeting, the judge himself came into the house. He seemed amazed to see me.

"You're from the boy, I suppose?" said he.

"Yes," said I.

"Got a proposition for us?"

"Yes."

"I'll get some men together inside of a coupla hours," he remarked. "Pete, get up and stir your bones. Ride over to the Crowell place and get Marvin Crowell; and stop in on the way and tell Clay Livingston that I want him; and

96

send somebody over to Steve Dinmont's, because I want Steve right pronto."

The boy went out of the room, carrying his broken bridle, and saying something about his bay mare having pulled back.

"You ought not to be such a fool as to tie her by the reins," said the judge. I've told you that before. You ought to get some of your growth into your brain, Pete!"

This over-frank criticism brought no answer from Pete, who disappeared through the front door, and the judge sat down to talk to me.

He said not a word about Charlie Dexter, however. His talk was about crops and prices, and road building, and such matters, and what the fall price of beef might be. This conversation I relished simply because it gave me a chance to size up my host a little more carefully and to take my bearings in the new position in which I found myself.

By the time it ended, however, the dusk was commencing, and the judge told me that I must stay there for the night. So he gave directions for putting up my horse, and then he himself carried my pack up to a room which he said was to be mine that night.

He left me there, with the remark that supper would soon be ready, and the other members of the conference would be on hand for it.

It was now time to light lamps, but I preferred, after washing with chilly water at the washstand, to sit for a time quietly in front of the window, looking eastward across the shadowy valley toward Monte Verde, where there was still a hint of the light of the day on the heights.

I saw this light vanish, and the dim lamps of the mountain town were beginning to glisten more and more brightly when I was called for supper.

I went down and found that we five were eating alone. Mrs. Benson and her children had a table in another room —and a riotous lot of noise they made. But the five of us had the old dining room to ourselves.

I took note of the guests, first of all. Marvin Crowell I had seen before, and he appeared even more withered and leathery hard than at our first meeting. Clay Livingston, quite unlike his stalwart and handsome sons, was a lean, sour, melancholy man; and Steven Dinmont was different from all the rest. He was not more than my own unimpressive height, but he must have weighed almost twice as much. He was both broad and deep, with a round face that was all brown and red, forever smiling.

In true Western style, there was not much conversation, once the food had been brought to the table. We had a typical ranch meal, of cornbread—very good, at that—and steak cut thin and fried till the inside of it was gray, and heaps of greasy fried potatoes, and canned tomatoes sweetened with sugar and filled out with little squares of bread. The dessert was a vast apple pie, served cold; and all through the meal they drank enormous cups of coffee strong enough to have made a mule wince.

Hardly a word was spoken, as I have said, until the eating was finished, but as the judge was stirring the third or the fourth spoonful of sugar into his coffee, he pointed to some pictures on the wall.

"There's some *real* Dexters," said he. "Does your friend look at all like them?"

I looked carefully at them—four or five or six of them, in all. They were the enlargements of photographs which once were so popular, particularly in the West, and I remember that the men were, without exception, big fellows, darkly handsome, and the women seemed a tall and haughty lot.

"They seem to have swarthy skins," said I. "And this Charles Dexter has exactly such a skin. They're dark, and he has dark hair and eyes, too. As to features ——"

I had to pause, here, and the judge cut in:

"Hair and eyes—rot!" said he. "Look at the size and the cut of 'em, compared to that hunting cat up yonder in Monte Verde!"

I could not help saying: "He seems enough of a man to hold up his end of a fight. He did this morning, as a matter of fact, when four hired thugs tried to murder him."

"Hired thugs? Who hired them?" asked the judge promptly.

"Ah," said I, "about that there's a good deal of argument. People, doubtless, who have good reason to wish that Charles Dexter were out of the way."

Before he could answer, I noticed an odd thing and pointed it out.

"Between those two pictures, Judge Benson, it looks as though the wall paper were darker—as though another picture had been hanging there, until recently. Is any of the collection missing?"

CHAPTER XVIII.   TERMS

THE judge, at this, gave me a quick side flash of his eyes, but he answered at once.

"Used to be a picture of an elk that Tom Dexter killed a whale of a time ago," said the judge. "I got tired of looking at the thing, and the fool smile that Tom wears, standing beside it. But now that supper's over, if you fellows all have had enough to eat, let's get down to business. There's no better place to talk than right around a table, I suppose?"

I agreed that there was no better place. And the conversation began at once, but on a very disagreeable note.

It was Clay Livingston, who said in his harsh, nasal voice: "Well, I dunno why you got us over here, judge. You like talk. But I don't. It never leads nowhere. We're gonna sit around here and confab, and nothin' will come of it but a big waste of time."

"We'll find that out later on," said the judge. "The thing to learn, now, is what the young lad up there in Monte Verde has to say for himself, and to us!"

"That's good sense," remarked cheerful Steve Dinmont. "Let's have it!"

He had lighted a cigar on which he was puffing rapidly, and now looked at me through a ragged cloud of smoke.

In the meantime, my opinions had been not exactly changing but altering in emphasis. After my acquaintance with Prince Charlie, I somehow had expected to find the Dexter house a big, comfortable mansion with an air of old grace and dignity about it. I had found, instead, a great rough barn of a place. And the two pictures did not fit in together, at all. One could hardly imagine young Dexter in such a house as this.

"Let's have it," said the judge. "What does this lad want to say to us?"

"He says that he wants to put the thing fairly before you, in the beginning. He feels that you murdered his family ——"

I ran in this in the most casual manner, but I expected a roar and I got one.

"There ain't a shade of proof about that!" boomed the judge.

I raised one finger.

"With his own eyes," said I, "Dexter saw Manly Crowell shoot down his father."

"It's a lie!" cried little Crowell, his face turning purple and crimson with anger.

I turned a little toward him. They were such a rough lot that I saw the only thing I could do would be to talk as roughly as they.

"Then why," I challenged him, "didn't you bring Manly Crowell here to refute the statement? You must have known that it would be made."

"Manly's had a hard day," said his brother. "He wouldn't be bothered to come over here and gab for nothin'; and besides, the judge didn't ask him to come."

I did not press the point, but I felt that I had scored on him, distinctly, and I knew by the expression of the others that they agreed.

I went back to listing the points in Dexter's position.

"He feels that a frightful wrong has been done to his family. There are two people whom he excludes from any

100

treaty of peace which he may make with you. One is Manly Crowell. The other is Scorpio."

"Hold on, my friend," broke in the judge. "We'll take those things one at a time.

"Any treaty of peace that he may make with us? Who asked him to make any treaty? Who wants one with him? Why should we bother about one impostor?

"As for Manly Crowell, supposing that we *should* wish to make an agreement with this fellow who calls himself a Dexter, Manly is one of us, and would have to be protected.

"As for Scorpio, we have nothing to do with him. We never *did* have anything to do with him. Why should you bring up his name to us?

The judge, with his legal mind—though he actually knew very little law—was making a hedge of difficulties bristle before me.

"You want to make peace because you yourself asked him to make his proposition," said I. "Manly Crowell is a murderer, according to Dexter, and cannot come in with the rest. Scorpio was a tool in your hands—or in the hands of some of you. I think this answers your three points."

"Answer be jiggered!" snarled Livingston in the most ugly fashion. "What do we care for Dexter or his answers? And what's the good of any more talk? You see where it leads, judge?"

"It leads nowhere," cried Crowell. "I always said that it wouldn't lead nowhere!"

"Wait just a minute, boys," suggested Steve Dinmont. "It ain't ended, yet. They's still a chance it might be worth while. No matter what we *think* about the thing, maybe this *is* Dexter. And if it's Dexter, maybe he's got a right on the ground. And maybe Scorpio *was* hired by some of the valley people. And certainly this here boy has gotta kind of a right to be suspicious when four thugs try to murder him as he walks down a street in Monte Verde!"

I was amazed to hear my side of the case so clearly

101

presented, or suggested; it gave me my first faint hope that perhaps this affair could be peaceably untangled.

Said the judge, to whom the others were always turning, and who was obviously the controlling spirit in Dexter Valley: "Steve, you got a kind heart, but you talk rather simply, now and then. As for the four who tried to murder Dexter, what do we know of his past life, or how many enemies he may have? And even if he's a Dexter, which he isn't, we don't know what real right he has to any of the land in the valley. As a matter of fact, the old Dexter grant was such thin tissue and so full of legal holes that it wouldn't hold water in any court."

I could not help smiling a little at his surety.

"We've had murder and crookedness talked down to us," put in Livingston. "I'm tired of it. I'm gonna go home now."

He actually pushed back his chair and stood up, and the judge rose, also.

"There's not much use in arguing any longer," he observed. "I wanted to find what was in the poor boy's mind —even if he's a criminal. I see that it's simply encouraged his effrontery."

All four of them were on their feet, breaking up the meeting, and I looked from one to the other, without budging. It was a good bluff; but the instant they made it, I felt thrillingly convinced of two things: that they feared young Dexter, and that they actually—or some of them—were guilty of the things which he charged against them. It was a good bluff, as I said before, but though they acted their parts well, they did not act them well enough to deceive me. I had sat in at too many board meetings when the keenest business minds were trying to push across their arguments, resorting to all devices of trickery, sham, and pretense. Now I simply remained in my chair and looked quietly about at the four of them. Livingston was already headed for the door.

"Sorry you had the ride for nothing," said the judge. "But you see that we can't be talked to in this way,"

At this, I laughed outright. Laughter was what I wanted,

102

and I let it go, and made it even heartier than the mirth I felt.

They turned about, all four of them, and glowered at me.

"My dear judge," said I, "I like a good bluff as well as a good joke. But if you're through with the play acting, suppose you sit down and pick up the argument where we left off."

"Play acting? Play acting?" exclaimed the judge, who really would have done very well on the stage. "Do you think we don't mean what we say?"

"I *know* you don't," said I. "So sit down again, all of you, and let's talk turkey."

"I never intended any discourtesy to you," said the judge, in a new tone, "and if you really have something important to say, of course we'll sit down and listen to you."

But Livingston was rubbed the wrong way by my cocksureness.

"I'm through with it!" he exclaimed, and jerked the door open.

"Clay!" said the judge, sharply.

It was as though he reproved a child. Clay Livingston, with a sullen muttering, slammed the door shut again and turned back to us, scowling, his hands in his pockets, his head thrust forward. Plainly he was in a dangerous mood.

"Well?" he demanded.

"Remember that we're entertaining a stranger," said the judge.

"Oh, stranger be hanged!" muttered Livingston.

Nevertheless, he raked out a chair and slumped down into it, staring gloomily, straight before him. The others hesitated. They waited for the judge to give the clew.

"If you can give us an idea," said he, "of what actually is in your mind, besides naked accusations that have no foundation, of course we'll listen to what you have to say. You're a man of education, Dean, and I hope that you haven't come here to amuse us with nonsense."

The others seemed pleased by the dignity of his language.

"Sit down, Judge Benson," I said. "I can tell you, briefly, how we stand."

Suddenly the judge sat down, and I knew that I had gained my first important victory. The others followed his example as a matter of course.

Then I went on: "If you people are innocent, then you have nothing to fear, and you will, of course, disregard everything that I have to say. When I use the phrase 'you people,' I mean by that not necessarily you four, but some of the inhabitants of the valley. And even if your own hands are clean, you can hardly be in complete ignorance as to who they may be. If you are clean of any guilt in this affair of the murder of the Dexters, and the recent attempt on the life of Charles Dexter, then of course I'll make no headway. But if you refuse to come to terms with me to-night, perhaps Dexter will decide to take matters into his own hands."

"Suppose you tell us," said the judge, "how he could take things into his own hands?"

"Suppose you imagine," I echoed him, "that Dexter should happen to ride down into Dexter Valley just to look over the scenery, and suppose that while he is down here he finds one of the Crowells, or the Livingstons, or the Bensons, or the Dinmonts, and decides to ask the man, or the boy, a few questions—questions with a point, and asked in a pointed way which I rather believe young Dexter would understand the trick of. Now, if that should happen, as I've pointed out, and one of the men he questions should find that he hardly could keep from telling everything he knew ——"

"You mean," snapped Livingston, "that this fellow might come down here and try to torture a lie out of some one?"

"A lie?" said I, gently as possible. "Of course, I don't mean a lie. I mean the truth—the sacred truth—the whole truth, such as a man blurts out when he can't hold his

104

tongue any longer. Just suppose that some one in the valley *has* something to tell, you can see the results?"

"I don't see nothin' except the crookedness anywhere around!" exclaimed Livingston.

"Wait a minute," urged the judge. "Let's hear what he has to say!"

"I've heard enough!" shouted Livingston, suddenly enraged more than ever.

"It would make an interesting case for the law courts," I suggested, looking straight at the judge. "And if there were a confession which described how the men of the valley planned to attack the Dexter family, and how Scorpio was hired, and how the murders took place, and how, afterward, four men were sent to murder the sole survivor in Monte Verde—mind you, I don't say that any of these things actually happened—but if such a confession should be made, it would be enough to tear you from your places, throw you into prison, and keep you there for the remainder of your lives!"

I brought this out with all the passion I could command, and I was greeted, at the close, with a dead silence, out of which the voice of the judge finally made me an answer.

"No one knows," he said, "the mystery of the attack on Dexter House, ten years ago. It was Scorpio who committed the murders, we're sure. If other people in the valley took up arms at that time, it was because they had heard shooting, or rumors of the alarms, and whispers about something that was perhaps to happen ———"

I looked him in the face and smiled broadly.

He went on, after a little hesitation: "You've told us a great deal about what your friend says, but you really haven't given us any definite proposals from him."

"You have kept his land, rent free," said I, "for ten years. You have, to be sure, made a good many improvements here and there, and you have added more stock, the cattle are more numerous, there are more horses, implements of all kinds, bigger barns, and in general the valley has been improved. This his family might have done and probably would have done on its own account.

At any rate, the fact remains that for ten years he has not received a cent from his estate. Now he does not ask for the back rent, which would probably ruin most of the farmers, if they had to pay it in a lump sum."

As I strung out my talk, I watched them, and saw them growing tense, and showing interest which no doubt they would have been glad to conceal.

I went on, more hopeful, now, that they would come to terms: "As a matter of fact, Dexter doesn't ask for a penny of the back rent, and he doesn't ask any man in the valley to remove from the. ground he is occupying. But he wants half the value of every farm turned over to him in the form of a secure deed."

Livingston shouted. It was like the yelp of a dog which has been kicked, as he cried out, smashing his fist against the top of the table: "Blackmail! I knew that's all it was. Either we turn over half of everything that belongs to us, or else he hounds us like a mad dog, and tries to cut off our boys!"

"I haven't suggested that," said I.

"Half?" said Judge Benson, actually sweating with emotion. "Half of everything? We'd rather die, first!"

I stood up, at last.

"I suppose you'll want to talk the thing over," said I. "You have Dexter's offer. If I'm out of the room, no doubt you can talk more frankly."

And I went up to my room.

CHAPTER XIX.   CHARLIE APPEARS

As I walked into the blackness of my bedroom, fumbling for a match, I heard a soft voice saying: "Steady, old fellow. Don't be alarmed."

Immediately afterward, a match scratched, and the

flame was touched to the round burner of the lamp, which showed to me Charlie Dexter himself, glowing with the light.

He stepped back into a corner where there was a small table, and half sitting against this, he folded his arms and smiled at me.

Yes, smiled at me, the first true smile that I had seen on his mouth, the first sign of actual cheerfulness and mirth!

But the whole man was changed. He had discarded the dapper gray flannels which he usually wore, and instead he was dressed as a true son of the range. He even went a little further than the range dandies, in his shirt of blue silk, with a big yellow flower worked across the shoulders of it, his sombrero banded with golden Mexican wheelwork, and the crimson pattern at the top of his boots. This flashy costume, but his gay face even more, bewildered me; and the very fact that he was here in the house of his enemies made me weak. My legs shook under me and I sank into a chair.

"Dexter," I whispered hoarsely, "do you know what you've done? Do you know that they'd murder you without a second's thought? They're downstairs now, and they've had a bomb exploded among them."

He tilted back his head and laughed. Yes, he actually laughed in a silent ecstasy that swayed him back and forth. The sound he suppressed, but the joy was rippling out of him.

"Of course they'd murder me," he said, "but did you think that I'd wait up there in Monte Verde and give them a chance to murder *you*, Dean?"

I pulled out my handkerchief and dabbed my forehead dry with it. I was beginning to shake.

"You don't know your frightful danger!" said I.

At this, he sobered a little. But still his eyes danced. He was as if at his first party, radiant and careless.

"Stuff, Mr. Dean," said he. "I've just begun to live. This is the first day I've lived, after ten years. For now I'm among them, and they can look to themselves. As for me, I know every rafter, every rat hole of this house, and I'm safe in it. Don't fear for me!"

I stared at him. Certainly he appeared to be a remade man, a new soul in his body.

"When you looked around that dining room," said he, "did you notice that one of the pictures had been removed recently?"

"Yes," said I.

"Good for you!" exclaimed he, as though he were surprised by this closeness of attention on my part. "Did you say anything about it?"

"Yes. I asked them what had become of it. The judge answered that it was a picture of one of the Dexters hunting—I don't remember who. Picture of a man beside a dead elk. He was tired of it and had taken it down."

"I don't blame him for being tired of it," said Dexter. "He was so tired that he put it up in the attic of the house, and there I've found it."

With that, he pulled out a roll of paper and spread it out before my eyes. What I saw was the enlarged photograph of a man in his late thirties or early forties, a man with a short, pointed beard, and a closely cropped mustache darkening his upper lip. It was not a handsome face. There were wide and high cheek bones, for instance, and, on the whole, the same type of features that appeared in young Dexter.

"Why," I exclaimed suddenly, "that's a good deal like you!"

"Of course it is," said the boy, "and that's why it wouldn't do to let it remain hanging on the wall of the dining room, after the judge had a look at me in Monte Verde. A Dexter standing by a dead elk, eh? Well, the dead elk is there, too, if you look hard enough—and that dead elk is coming to life, now. It's standing in the Dexter House, once more, ready to fight. It's I, Mr. Dean!"

He went on, rapidly, gayly: "Bungling work for an old hand like the judge, who ought to have known better than to take the picture down and put it in the attic. Rats get into the best kept attics, you know!"

He could not help the laughter bubbling as he talked.

"You can see how the judge was troubled, Mr. Dean. If that picture were to appear in a courtroom, it would be a pretty good proof, I take it, that I'm really the last of the Dexters, come back to life. No doubt the judge wanted to burn it, but where was he to do it? Where was he to break the glass and take out the picture without exciting some sort of comment? Somebody might notice and remember. He felt like a murderer that has a dead body to dispose of. Well, he remembered that, and he decided that for the time being, he simply would put the incriminating thing out of sight. Out of sight, out of mind, for the time, and after a while, he would slip up to the attic some day and get rid of this. Do you know who it is?"

"No," said I.

"It's the picture of Delaware Dexter. He was my grandfather, and they called him 'Delaware,' because for a long time he was on the plains working with a number of the Delaware Indians, who were the best hunters and guides between the two seas. Look at it, Mr. Dean, and tell me if it's not a dead ringer for me?"

I looked at it, willingly enough.

"It's like you—very like," said I. "I noticed the resemblance at once. It's a big link in your chain of evidence— but you'll have to have more links than this one to convince a judge. There are too many chance resemblances, of course. Far too many. No judge that I've heard of would be much influenced by such a thing, I'm sure, unless you could present other things to go with it."

"I can, I can!" said he. "Not only this, but the known attack on me in Monte Verde, and that little mystery of the stolen bag, and the two keys which the sheriff found in the ashes—it doesn't take many such things to make up a case."

I shook my head in doubt.

"If not before a judge, at least before a jury," he went on. "Juries would be pretty apt to side with me, I should say. What do you think?"

Well, no matter how doubtful I might be about the

value of that old photograph, certainly the fact that it had been taken down from the dining room wall and lodged in the attic made a damning fact against the whole Benson-Livingston-Crowell-Dinmont tribe.

I was in the midst of assenting that this would be a powerful argument before most juries, when there was a sharp knock at the door.

"Dean?" called the voice of the judge.

I turned cold and gaped at the boy, and he, after a first swift glance toward the window, slithered out of sight most unromantically on his stomach, and disappeared beneath the bed.

Then I went to the door.

CHAPTER XX.   A SNEEZE

THE judge came in with so much on his mind, apparently, that I hoped he would not notice my perturbation.

He said: "Dean, we've talked the thing over. As far as we can see, this boy hasn't much to stand on. But we all have decided that we don't want to run into a long lawsuit with some wretched shyster lawyer fighting us for the sake of a split in the profits, if he ever can induce us to settle out of court. Otherwise, we'll have to spend a good deal inside the law, I suppose. Besides that, we see that on the face of things the boy must feel that the attempt on him in Monte Verde was probably made through the instigation of the valley people. Now, then, we're willing to do something handsome for him. As for the fifty per cent which he asks, of course that's foolish. But we'll put him on his feet for life. We'll guarantee him an annuity of five thousand a year."

I looked him in the face. But if he were dishonest, I could not see it in his eyes.

Finally I said: "Judge Benson, either my friend is an unprincipled young rogue who deserves nothing but a cell in a penitentiary for an attempt to defraud on a gigantic scale, or else he has a right to every acre in Dexter Valley, and, in return for ten years of rents that have been missing, to every building and animal and implement that exist here. He's chosen to take a step toward a compromise. He's offered to accept fifty per cent of all that belongs to him. Do you think that I can advise him to take less?"

The judge bit his lip and then looked at me from under his bent brows. I must say that he filled out the picture of an honest man, thoroughly angered, and for a good cause.

At length he said: "Mr. Dean, I don't know what share you will get from any settlement ———"

At this, I lifted my hand and shook my head.

"I'm here for the sake of helping a friend, not to line my pockets. I'm an engineer, Judge Benson, with a record you can easily look up and no tar on my hands from shady deals of any kind. I'm here to represent young Dexter because I'm his friend, not because I'm hoping to fill my wallet."

This put him back, as the saying is, upon his heels, so that he blinked at me before going on:

"Whatever may be your arrangement with him, I want you to assure him that the very top limit to which we'll go is ten thousand a year!"

"Ten thousand as an annuity which may be ended by a bullet at any time?" said I. And I let myself smile at the judge again.

He grew angry once more, then controlled himself and said: "Dean, I hope you'll see that you have a moral obligation in this matter. Your client is a young lad and probably hot-headed, even if not criminal. If he throws himself across the path of the number of determined men in Dexter Valley, he's liable to run into no end of trouble!"

"Judge Benson," said I, roused in my turn, "it seems to me that you have a moral obligation of your own. If you try to put off my client with pin money instead of

111

what is right, you and the other determined men of Dexter Valley are likely to find a tiger in your path!"

"It comes to open threats, I see," said he.

"Not open threats, but open truth."

"What is open truth, Mr. Dean? Everything that this boy claims to be, and perhaps is not? Is that your attitude?"

"What is this whole valley worth—cattle, land, houses and all?" I asked him.

"I suppose that you know," said he.

"There are nearly seventy thousand acres of woodland, grazing land, and farmland," said I.

He lifted his brows, surprised.

"Well, it wouldn't be hard to find that out," said he.

"The land alone ought to be worth fifty dollars an acre, and that makes a total of three millions and a half."

"Maybe that's right."

"You know that the figure is low, rather than high. The timber, houses, cattle, implements, improvement, should stand for another sum half as large as the first, and lumping the two together, no matter what deductions are made, there's something like five million in the whole deal. As a matter of fact, both you and I know that a cash offer of five million would never tempt the landholders of Dexter Valley!"

He flushed a little, and then shrugged.

"Go on, Dean, and tell us some more about our business," said he, ironically.

"I shall not," said I. "I've given you the round figures. I'm equipped with details, though, if you want to hear them ——"

And I reached for my notes, but he held up his hand, surrendering on the point at once.

"What's your conclusion?" he asked.

"That in reply to his request for fifty per cent, you are countering with an offer of the interest on four per cent of the total, and that in the form of an annuity!"

The judge could not but feel the force of this reply. He began to walk up and down the room with his heavy

112

step. He said, pausing in the end of a turn: "The boy ought to be reasonable. Ten thousand a year is a fine, handsome income for a lad who never did a stroke of work in his life, apparently ——"

"What makes you think that?" said I.

"Why, the inside of his hand, they tell me, is as soft as a girl's."

"You've been watching this youngster pretty closely, judge."

"Naturally one watches a pretender and a cheat, Dean, when he's pretending to your own pocketbook."

"In this case," said I, "I've no doubt that young Mr. Dexter will decide to go to law."

The judge smashed his fist into his open palm.

"In that case, he'll be licked!" he shouted at me. "He'll be made a fool of and shut out without a cent!"

I listened to him in such a manner that he saw I would not attempt to interrupt or match passion with passion. This silenced him and I put in: "No one can tell how the courts of law will decide such a matter. One thing is sure, that for such a great reward, some very able lawyers will be willing to undertake the prosecution of the affairs of Dexter in the courts, no matter through how many appeals. And before they were through with the business, every detailed circumstance of life and action here in Dexter Valley would be before the eyes of the world."

He walked straight up to me. The man was a giant and made me feel like a child, but I screwed up my courage and met his eye.

"Investigation we don't shrink from. We welcome it," said he.

"That I doubt," said I.

Actually he swung back his ponderous arm, and I was afraid that he would knock me flat. He held his hand, however, with his face twitching, and his eyes devilish with anger.

"This is the end of any possible agreement, then?" he blurted out, at last.

"I hope not, but I'm afraid that it is," I answered. "I'm

almost ashamed to offer your suggestion to Dexter. He'll think that I've played more the part of a fool than of a representative."

The judge resumed his pacing of the room, growling out, from time to time: "A darned, awkward, unpleasant business in every aspect. I don't like it. I hate it. I never did like it. If the boy by any chance has any Dexter blood in him, he ought to have some rights to the valley ———"

He paused before me once again.

"I've offered you the limit that I'm authorized to offer. But I'll tell you what I'll do. I'll go back and argue with those fellows. You saw them. They're a stubborn lot, They're stubborn as the devil. They don't care for arguments or for reason, and they simply won't give up what they feel is their own. You can hardly blame them. They've offered ten thousand a year. Mind you, not a sum for any young man to throw out the window. But, my friend, you have to remember this: that if it comes to a law fight or any other kind of a fight, we have odds of position and money in our favor. Nevertheless, I'll tell you what I'll do, I'll go back and try to screw five hundred thousand dollars out of those people. A whole half million, Mr. Dean, is what I'll try to get for your client!"

It was as though a door suddenly had opened before me. I felt no further doubt about the rights of Dexter, for men may pay an annuity as blackmail, but they will not pay half a million except because of a guilty conscience.

I said to him, quietly: "Judge, you may go back and talk to them as you will. But if you wish to say what will satisfy my client, you will have to ask them for five times half a million."

"Two millions and a half!" he shouted at me, furiously.

"And even that is not really a half. It's hardly more than a third, by a fair survey," said I.

"You're talking rot—you're talking nonsense," said he. "By the eternal heavens, I never heard such rot. Two and a half millions, indeed! Well, sir, good-night!"

And he made for the door.

"Good-night," said I.

114

I was sure that he would not leave the room, and I was right. I swallowed a smile when he turned back toward me.

"Blackmail and highway robbery combined," roared the judge, "are something that I've never seen attempted before."

"Yes," said I, "I agree with you. I've never seen them attempted. And I've never heard of innocent people offering half a million as hush money."

This was going too far, of course, and I regretted it as soon as I had spoken. As for the judge, he fairly turned purple, and his big hand jumped inside his coat.

I knew that the fingers must be locked around the handle of a revolver. I half expected that I had come to my last second of life, as I saw his eyes reduce to veritable sparks of brilliance.

Then he jerked out his hand, and folded his arms, manacling his own violence of humor.

"Insults, too!" exploded the judge.

"No—facts," said I. "Though I'm sorry that I used harsh language, judge."

He gripped at this small apology.

"I think you are, Mr. Dean," said he. "I think that you regret ——"

But here the course of the most promising of negotiations was cut short by an explosive sneeze from beneath the bed!

CHAPTER XXI.   PURSUIT

WHAT might have happened to our discussion I can't tell. The explosive rage of the judge led me to feel that he was arguing with much noise because he had decided that he would have to give way. He had come to my room, however, prepared for more than mere argument, as he now showed.

For, when the sneeze exploded like a bomb in that room, he gave one startled look at the bed and then shouted an order, and into the room charged three armed men, weapons in hand, led by big young Benson, and behind him, Dandy Bullen, my old acquaintance at the town of Monte Verde.

They came with a businesslike air, and made straight at me, until the judge shouted: "The bed! The bed! There's somebody there under the bed!"

At the same time, from the shadow beneath the narrow cot, out slithered young Dexter, and leaped from hands and feet straight toward the window.

The judge already had a revolver in his hand, poised, and he brought it down with an oath that ground out between his teeth.

I reached for the gun, and as it exploded, my hand knocked it up. The bullet crashed through the frame of the window a few inches over the head of Dexter, and then I saw him dive out of the window into the dark of the night.

It was a good long fall to the ground, and I expected him to get a broken neck on the way down. But the rays from the lamp fell upon the green branch of a tree that spread before the window, and into this greenery Dexter dived, as into water. He disappeared, and I heard the sweep of the bough dragging down, crackling, and then as the judge's men leaned from the window, shooting wildly into the night, the bough flung up again into view without its human freight.

Was he safe?

A revolver rang in answer to the shooting from the window. And the third of the three men who had entered the room staggered backward, gripping his face with both hands. The judge, at the same time, turned with a sort of howl of rage and disappointment, and knocked me flat against the wall.

The force of the blow dropped me to my knees, on the

116

rebound; but I was not too stunned to hear and to see what followed.

"It's Dexter! It's Dexter!" yelled the judge. "After him, every man jack of you! Call out the boys! Get the horses. Ride like thunder on a vacation. Get that man! Get that man! We'll make you all rich if you shoot him down. Dead or alive, we want him!"

He spurred them with this shouting, hurrying them forth to the man trail, but the judge himself remained behind to deal with me.

I did not attempt to resist. In the first place, I had no weapon. In the second place, his bulk and his strength were so overmastering that he could have crushed me with his empty hands.

His furious face, as the younger men stampeded from the room I shall never forget. He paid not the slightest heed to the fellow whom Dexter had wounded with that snap shot from the ground level. The man I could not see or recognize clearly, because his face was one red blur, though I learned afterward that the bullet had not seriously wounded him—simply plowed a furrow through the flesh and in the wake of that furrow left the features forever distorted.

He staggered out of the room at the heels of the others, and the judge let him go without a word, to get what comfort and help he could elsewhere. For his own part, the judge was fully occupied with me, and the way he handled his revolver gave me the impression that he wished he had used the gun on me instead of the mere weight of his hand.

I was badly frightened, of course. But when a man sees that there is no hope, it is easier for him to submit with a certain amount of dignity and of grace.

I got up to my feet and dabbed my handkerchief against the broken skin of my cheek, where his fist had gone home.

"March along with me!" said the judge.

He took me by the coat, gathering a good gripful of it between my shoulder blades, and so thrust me ahead of him out of the room and down the hall.

I did not speak. His own words were inarticulate curses and snarlings. And so he brought me to the same dining room where we had eaten that evening. I could see ashes and cigarette stubs scattered around the floor, where the four of them had been carrying on their discussion after I left the room. The talk must have been sufficiently hot. One cigar had been hurled clear across the room. It left a black spot, and lay itself crumpled and broken on the floor beneath.

The judge fairly hurled me into a chair, and I fell into it so hard that it skidded almost a yard under the impact.

Still I said nothing.

I spent my time rearranging my necktie, and straightening my vest. Two buttons had been lost from my coat, and I employed myself pulling out the projecting, broken threads.

As I did so, I watched the judge, of course, from time to time.

The man was not recovering from his outburst.

The blow which felled me had been the distant flicker of lightning upon the horizon. Now the storm was gathering and blackening right over my head.

In order to heat the room in the winter, there was a good big stove at the side of the room and the force of winter habit now made the judge stand with his back to the stove, spreading his hands out behind him, and shifting a little from foot to foot, while he stared at me.

The foolishness of this behavior might have made me laugh at any other time. Now I assure you that it did not so much as make me smile. For, as I looked back into his gleaming eyes, almost lost under the hanging shrubbery of his brows, I saw that death was in the mind of the judge.

Well, not many days before death would not have been exactly a horrible thing to me. It had been in my mind for so many years that it had an old familiar acquaintance, and sometimes I had felt that it would prove my only friend. Now, however, matters had changed with me. I had breathed a new air, tasted a new life. Weak and broken as my nerves were, I wondered that I had not

118

fainted under the strain of these experiences. But I had not. I was frightened. The cold of fear was running in my veins, but still it *ran,* and my brain was not numbed.

Very distinctly I called up that picture—the big room, the old photographs vainly striving to decorate the walls, the faded place that had been left behind the picture of Delaware Dexter when it was removed, the noise of shouting and stamping echoing through the house and passing outside, finally fading away in distant hoofbeats.

Gradually a quiet came over the house, except that from a far room a baby began to cry, and its wailing continued endlessly, turning from a sound actually heard to something felt, pulsing like a heartbeat through the body, keeping up a ghostly rhythm in the brain.

The judge, all this time, did not speak, but every time fury swelled his throat, he locked his jaws and pursed his mouth upon it, and shut it back. And still he blackened.

"When he comes back," he said at last, "then the pair of you ——"

He stopped himself, not that he wished to hold back any words, but because his passion stifled him.

"I would have had him," went on Benson. "I had a dead bead on him, between his shoulders. I would have broken his back if ——"

Fury throttled him again.

He opened his mouth and dragged down a huge breath.

"The whole business would have been ended!" he shouted. "You sneaking, hypocritical, murdering cur! You got him into the house under your wing, a snake to turn loose in the middle of the night, did you?"

I shook my head.

I was about to speak, when he bellowed: "Don't say a word. Don't whisper a word. Don't think a word, even, or I'll bash in your face and your skull like a rotten orange."

I watched him with almost more curiosity than fear. His passion was so huge that he became a natural phenomenon somewhat like the eruption of a distant volcano rather than a mere passionate man.

"The whole thing would have been rubbed out—forever! But you—you—treacherous, lying, crooked ——"

He bit at the air again, like a dog at raw meat.

"When they bring him back," he said through his teeth, after that, "we'll decide what to do with him—and you. The same thing for the two of you. You're the impartial friend, the disinterested representative! Faugh! I almost was taken in by you. Almost! Almost! But now I see the truth. You'll be an easy man for the world to forget! A danged easy man, and the world is going to have its chance to forget, I'll promise you!"

"No doubt it will," said I.

They were the first words I had spoken, and they almost were the last.

In his insane, blind rage, when he heard me, and listened to the singular calm which appeared in my voice at that moment, he snatched up a chair. His strength was so prodigious that he swung up the heavy, rudely made chair easily with one hand, and stood there above me with the thing poised loftily, towering toward the ceiling.

I watched it as a small chicken might watch a stooping hawk. But the blow did not fall. Instead, he hurled the chair away from him, and when it struck the wall, so great was its weight and so vast his strength that it crumpled into a shapeless heap and dropped with a crash to the floor.

After this, he began pacing the room, still stopping to warm himself, now and again, before the imaginary heat of the stove, and to teeter ridiculously back and forth on his heels and toes. Still his eyes like a basilisk's fabled glance, were turning me to stone.

And the seconds turned into minutes, and the minutes into an hour.

Then he said aloud: "They know every road. They've got fast horses. Every man jack of 'em is a dead shot. They'll overtake him. They'll mob him. They'll beat him down. They'll trample him into the ground, and bring him back like dead game thrown over the pommel of the saddle!"

120

And, as if in comment upon what he had said, at that moment I heard the distant trampling of horses along the road!

CHAPTER XXII.   A HOSTAGE

ONE cannot hear the sound of approaching travelers without having the heart leap up, at least for a moment. And in that first moment I told myself that it was help coming toward me—the sheriff from Monte Verde, and a posse of trusty men—the little sheriff, coming through yonder door! How beautiful his half-witted look would be, in my estimation, now!

Then I saw the downward look of listening, and the savage, poisonous smile of satisfaction upon the face of Judge Benson. He was foretasting a frightful triumph. An Indian might wait thus for the return of the war party and the disposal of the prisoner.

His expression, after a moment, changed. He threw up his head. His eyes rolled.

"By the great ——" he began. Then he stopped, and added, "What if ——"

I knew what he meant. My own heart suddenly raged with joyous hope in my breast. What if young Dexter had escaped from their hands? What if he were gone from them? Then, what would they do with me? It might alter matters. If he were a prisoner beside me, I was a mere cipher. If he were still free, then I was dignified into the position of his friend.

The moment that I saw this thing, strength returned to me, and my shoulders squared themselves instinctively.

What gave him pause, and what gave me hope was the slow pace of those searchers. The victorious in the West are apt to come like wild Indians, with a yell and a rush, guns exploding. But there was no rushing and yelling here.

121

The hoofbeats pattered like heavy, distant rain, but approached only very slowly.

He looked down at me, did the judge; and suddenly a devil made me smile at him. The thing was totally irresistible. I could not help the twitching at the corners of my mouth.

I thought he would go mad. The eyes literally started from his head, and striding up to me, he bent and shook a fist in my face. His great balled hand was almost as large as my whole head.

"Whatever happens to him, we've got you," said the judge with infinite relish.

Now, with that fist in my face, the same devil that had taken hold of me before made me answer: "I don't think that you'll ever be a complete fool, judge. Only a partial one, from time to time!"

And I deliberately patted my cut and swelling cheek with my handkerchief and I looked up into his infuriated eyes and searched them, deliberately.

If ever a man came close to death by a single blow, or by throttling, it was I.

Or was I really so close? Did I not realize, instinctively, that if young Dexter were free, all close danger was removed from me?

At any rate, there was no tremor in me as the riders came pouring slowly up around the house.

Half a dozen of them trooped into the room, and the first face I saw was that of Dandy Bullen. The expression on it was to me like the most delicious music. It was salve on my wound, and balm for my soul. For he was as dark as the night outside, and he gave only a glowering glance to the leader of the clans, Judge Benson himself.

They did not report, at first. They asked for a drink, and got a ration of corn whisky from the Chinaman, who appeared mysteriously when needed, and disappeared again through the kitchen door with his pigtail wagging behind him.

Then Clay Livingston sat down and rested his face between his hands, but all of the others remained standing.

"Well? Well?" said the judge at last. "You've come back like a pretty pack, with your tails between your legs. Dogs? I wouldn't compare you with dogs! You've let one fox get away from you!"

Clay Livingston looked up, steadily, toward the judge, and his face was not a pretty study.

"He has my boy, Slade!" said he.

"He has—what?" shouted the judge.

"Tell him, somebody," said Livingston, and buried his face in his hands once more.

I felt a pang of pity for him, and yet wonder overcame me. I had seen the rush of those hunters. They had failed. Fleetness of foot and cunning might have saved Dexter, but actually to have caught Slade Livingston, big, formidable lad that he was, seemed utterly impossible; not only to save himself, but to take a prisoner in flight!

"You mean he shot down Slade? We'll have the law for it!" cried the judge, almost triumphantly. "We'll hang him for this. It's the end of him. The sheriff will have to take his trail, now. We'll make an end of him. Clay, my heart bleeds for you!"

"Blast you and your heart both!" said Livingston. "If you'd had a brain in your head, we'd 'a' settled the matter before it come to this."

Seeing that Livingston had been the chief malcontent when it came to peaceful discussion, this remark was illogical enough, but the judge appeared unwilling to argue the point.

"Are you all dumb?" he shouted. "Will you tell me how it happened?"

"Slade ain't dead," said Bullen, "but Dexter has him!"

"Durned if I ever seen such a thing," said another.

"Not dead—but Dexter has him?" groaned the judge. "Then everything is spoiled! Slade—Livingston, can that boy hold his tongue? Will he talk?"

"How do I know? And why should I care how much he talks?" demanded Livingston.

And he glared toward me.

The judge, taking the hint, whirled around on me and

snarled out some threat. But Livingston's voice rang out like the report of a gun.

"You treat this feller with gloves, Benson. You hear me? You treat this feller Dean like he was your own brother—or better—or you'll hear from me about it."

There was no doubt, of course, as to his meaning. Whatever they performed upon me, would be performed upon fine young Slade Livingston in requital.

I could afford to sit there and actually indulge in another smile, with which I favored the judge, and his blackened face burst into a glistening sweat.

"Say something!" he roared, turning on the others. "What happened? Were you fools all paralyzed? Couldn't you ride? Couldn't you shoot?"

"We ride as well as the next," said Bullen sullenly. "But him—he can fade out like a ghost. I never seen anything like it. We rode. We seen him, too. We seen him go into the woods down on the Dinmont ranch, and when we seen that, we headed for him."

"Did you all rush blind into the trees?" exclaimed the judge.

"No, we done the right thing," said Bullen. "Livingston, there, was giving orders. He ain't no fool. He sent part of us down the Dinmont lane, and another chunk of the boys riding like blazes across the fields to the west of the woods, and him and Slade and two more went straight into the woods behind Dexter."

He stopped, and shook his head. I was half stifled with excitement, and my head spun in bewilderment. I could not understand how such a man could effect anything against such enemies—not even such a man as Dexter.

"I was going to the left, between the woods and the water," said Bullen, while most of the others stared disconsolately at the floor, or helped themselves to another round of the corn whisky. "And I heard the hosses of the two Livingstons and the rest go crash into the wood. Then I didn't hear nothing more worth while, for a time, till suddenly I saw Chip Hooker, riding at my right, turn his hoss around with a terrible yell, pointing back.

"I turned around in the saddle, then, and what I seen was enough. I seen a pair of riders away off in the distance, and one of the hosses was poor Slade's pinto. I could tell that paint hoss by the slab of color along his side, looking white even at night. And right alongside of him, sort of hitched to him, there was another gent, and they were heading out of the tail of the Dinmont woods, and straight over to the ford. They were almost at the edge of the water, when we seen 'em, Hooker and me!

"I couldn't believe it, hardly. How could anybody?

"He must've turned straight back, when he got inside of the woods, and instead of running any longer, he waited and he snagged Slade as Slade went piling by him in the dark of the trees. And then he started back toward the river, while Clay Livingston and the other two, they saw nothing because of the trees and they heard nothing because of the noise that their own hosses was making. Anyway, there was Slade being taken away, though how anybody the size of Dexter could've done ——"

"Shut up your comments, and go on with what happened!" cried the judge. "What did you do then? Twiddle your thumbs and go home? You didn't follow across the ford?"

"We piled right down to the edge of the river," said Bullen, "and then out of the brush on the far bank comes a rifle bullet that tips my hat mighty polite for me!"

He took off his hat and showed us the neatly drilled hole through the crown of it.

"Would you've stayed there for Prince Charlie to shoot at you, judge?" he asked pointedly.

"You could have crossed at the lower ford!" shouted the judge. "You simply came back here and left in his hands a hostage who will mean ——"

"Suppose that some of us watched the upper ford," broke in Bullen, "and the rest of the pack of us went down to the lower ford, he would simply have faded away through the brush and been miles away. How could we tell when he was gone? Only by going down to the water's edge, every few minutes, and getting ourselves shot down.

He tipped my hat for me, shooting right across the river, and there wasn't much moon for him to see by, either. He's out to kill, is Prince Charlie, and he's shootin' for the head!"

"You talk like a fool, calling him Prince Charlie!" said the angry judge.

"If he ain't the Prince, how can he shoot so straight?" said Bullen, with naïve simplicity.

And the others, it appeared, seemed to feel very much the same way.

Clay Livingston stood up.

"Benson," said he, "it's Dean, here, and maybe something to boot, to get back my oldest son. I'm going to trust you to arrange it, or you can trust me to raise more trouble than you ever seen in all of your born days."

And he turned and stalked with a long stride from the room.

CHAPTER XXIII.   ESCAPE

No lullaby was ever so soothing to a child's ear as was to me the knowledge that Dexter now had a pawn which he could play for my release. After the departure of Livingston, the judge and several of the others continued to talk about the situation and possible means of meeting it. The chief worry of the judge was that young Livingston, while he was in the power of Dexter, might be induced to talk too much, but, after his first explosion on the subject, he was careful to conceal his idea from me as much as possible.

Sometimes I was brought into the conversation, but I had very little interest in it now. Besides, I was so soundly tired that since I could afford to forget my own dangers, I sank back in my chair and was quickly asleep.

I wakened, after a time, rather chilled and stiff, and my head had been nodding so hard that the back of my neck was aching. A stiff wind was rising, and the shutters of the old house were being banged back and forth, here and there. No doubt it was the mournful complaining and whistle of the wind, together with the clapping of the shutters, that wakened me.

I yawned two or three times, rubbed my neck, and looked about me. Every one had left the room except Bullen and one other, whose name I did not know. They were watching me with a sullen persistence, Bullen having a shotgun across his knees, and the other, a rifle against his chair. Plainly this pair had been set to guard me, a thing that would have been ridiculous—either one of them being more than enough to guard me—if it had not been that there was the danger of Dexter reaching for me from the outside of the house.

"You fellows have a dull job," I suggested to them.

Bullen shrugged his shoulders.

"You take it easy," he said. "But don't you forget—you ain't out of hot water yet, stranger. And you're likely to leave your scalp behind you when you leave!"

He was in a very ugly humor, either because of the guard duty which had fallen to him, or because of an early dislike which he had taken to me. I could afford to overlook the display of temper.

I composed myself for another nap, and gradually sank off to sleep. I wakened, a good deal later on, with a veritable thunderclap in my ears. One of the shutters of the dining room had blown wide and slammed with a huge report against the side of the house.

I heard Bullen swear.

"Go latch it again, Billy," said he.

Billy got up and stretched.

"The wind must be changing," said he. "It ain't been blowing in a direction to bother these windows, up to now."

He sauntered across the room with his hands in his pockets. He walked like a rooster, his head going back and forth on his long neck. No one could have called Billy a graceful lad, but he had a good-natured eye that pleased me a great deal more than the make-up of a man like Bullen.

127

"It's blowing up pretty wild," said Billy, at the window, leaning out a bit into the dark.

"Aw, close the window, and shut up, will you?" ordered Bullen.

I looked across at the youth, expecting to hear an angry retort. Instead, he started back half a step and jerked up his hands shoulder-high. The hands remained there for a moment; his whole attitude, even viewed from behind, suggested horror and astonishment. I looked past him into the black of the night which he was facing and made out, very faintly, the glimmering of a gun pointed at his heart!

That sight raised me out of my chair. I glanced at Bullen, and saw him covering a yawn, so I took it for granted that he had seen nothing.

For my part, I started for that window, sauntering, wondering how soon Bullen would become suspicious, for I knew, instantly, that behind that gun in the outer dark was Prince Charlie. I measured the difficulties at a glance. The window was low and wide, Such a wildcat as Charlie Dexter would have leaped through it like a circus dog through a ring. But for me, I would have to climb over the sill—and Dandy Bullen was back there in the corner, watching me, with a shotgun across his knee.

Billy, perhaps in response to a whispered order from outside, had lowered his hands at once and thrust them deeply into his pockets. There was nothing highly suspicious about the situation except that he so long delayed in securing the window.

"Where are *you* aiming to go, Dean?" asked Dandy. "He's aiming to take a little walk out through the window, Billy," he added to his companion guard.

And Dandy laughed.

There was no answering laughter from Billy. I saw a quiver in his shoulders; otherwise, he was turned to stone as I came up beside him.

And then I saw, in the dark, the outline of Prince Charlie, and the clear, cold gleam of his steady gun as it pointed at the heart of the youth within.

"Billy!" snapped Dandy. "Mind Dean. He's right be-

128

hind you. Say, what the heck is the matter with you, you blockhead?"

He was enough irritated by the continued silence and frozen stillness of Billy to jump up from his chair. That moment I selected for getting through the window.

I don't know exactly how I managed it. I only remember that it seemed to me, during that second of time, that all of my muscles had turned numb, and that I was swimming toward the outer darkness as toward a haven of safety. I was half in and half out when Dexter caught me with an amazing strength and jerked me the rest of the way into the kind dark. At the same time, Billy risked his life by leaping sidewise and shouting: "Dexter! It's Prince Charlie!"

There was a yowl from Bullen, like that of a lion dropped into a roaring fire. And the next moment a charge of buckshot crashed into the window and hissed over my head as I landed on hands and knees upon the ground.

There was a spur of infinite keenness that got me to my feet on the bound. I sprinted right down the side of the house before the man who was leading the way, then turned behind him and angled off among the trees. There I saw the loom of horses. The tethering rope I jerked free, together with the little twig to which it was secured, and then like any Wild West rider I bounded into the saddle. I think I could have jumped over the horse, for that matter —fear had made me so light and so strong.

For all my speed, I was behind Dexter, as he headed away from the house.

And behind us, I heard Dexter House wake up with a roar that boomed heavily along the strong current of the wind. Guns exploded, too, though none of the bullets came near us, and I suppose that Billy and the infuriated Dandy Bullen were firing at the swaying of the shrubs and the dark saplings in the woods, taking them for men.

Dexter pulled back beside me.

"Can you sit a jumping horse?" he shouted.

Well, I had ridden a little over the jumps, but only in an amateurish way, of course.

I answered that I would stick to the saddle, and the next minute he was firing instructions.

"Give him his head as he rises. Don't fight him, and he'll see you through all right!"

And then a fence rose before us and looked to me as lofty as the wall of a house. The bars shot downward as the horse rose. I hung dizzily in midair, at the top of the rise, and then the ground rushed darkly up toward me. We landed. I lost a stirrup. The jolt took half my breath and all my wits, and for the next few minutes all I remember was a succession of dizzy ups and downs as we flew half a dozen fences. And then, at last, with my feet out of the stirrups, which were flying wildly, and with my body slewed far to one side, we struck the heavenly smoothness of the Monte Verde road.

My horse was nearly out of control, by this time, and Dexter helped straighten him out with a sharp order and an extra tug on the reins.

At last we sat still in the saddle in the middle of the road. The moon came out from behind a cloud and looked at us, just then, for the wind was blowing the sky as clean and cold as steel.

"Let's get on, Dexter," I called to him. "They'll be pouring after us, in no time, and I'm no expert rider!"

I stared behind me. Every moment I expected that from the midst of some copse that was trembling and shining under the moon, a volley of terrible riders would burst out on us.

Dexter merely laughed.

"They'll wait a while to curse," said he. "And I don't think that they'll take to the saddle at all. They've had one useless chase, to-night, already. Ah, man," he went on, exultation and joy in his voice beyond my describing, "ah, Dean, now would be the time to go straight back to the house and get in among them—if I wanted to do them a mischief! But a little later, for that. Break their morale, first and then drive 'em, some day, like sheep—like sheep!"

And he laughed once more, the mirth choking off his words.

I almost forgot my sense of peril, as I stared at that

130

strange youth. I looked again over my shoulder, and pulled impatiently at the reins of my horse.

"Here's the road to Monte Verde, straight as a string," said he. "Ride straight down it. If you feel a little jumpy in the nerves, ride hard all the way. That gelding will take you all right. He has the legs and he has the barrel, too!"

I stared up that winding road and yearned after it so greatly that it seemed to me like the road to heaven. I could not see Monte Verde itself, but I could see the shoulder of the mountain on which the town stood.

But then, something stopped me for a moment.

I glanced aside at the youth.

"Dexter," said I, "if I leave you, it's war to the knife between you and all the men in the valley."

"Aye, it's war to the knife, anyway," he replied carelessly. "They would have it that way. They asked for it, and now they have it!"

"Well," I told him, "you may amuse yourself for a while, like a cat catching rats, but it's a diet that would soon be the end of you. If you'll let me stay with you, Dexter, I'll try to be your emissary once more, and carry terms of a new peace to them!"

He brought his horse closer to me and looked at me with his bright, steady eyes.

"Why, man," said he, "that's the offer of a true friend."

"I hope to be one to you," said I.

He put out his hand, silently, and gripped mine, and my heart leaped very oddly. Then he turned his horse off the road, and my gelding followed him, without control from my hands.

CHAPTER XXIV. TORTURE

I WAS still more than a little upset and anxious about our enemies, but Dexter was at ease. He pointed out that no one had been on hand to see our actual course of flight and that the others would hardly suspect us of having flown the many fences between that part of the house and the Monte Verde road. And so he led the way without any haste along a winding cow trail across the meadows of a pasture land, darkly blooming with groves and thickets here and there.

On the way, I asked him what actually had happened in the capture of Slade Livingston.

Dexter made light of that. He declared that there was nothing to it except a lucky idea that came to him when, on the verge of the wood into which he had ridden, he had looked back and seen that his pursuers were scattered, and that the four immediately behind were aiming to enter the trees behind him at various points. Then, he said, the plan came to him.

"Tell me, Dexter," said I. "When you started for that forest, you hadn't planned on turning back and trying to trap one of them?"

"Only vaguely, only vaguely," said he. "It was what I wanted to do, but, later on, the opportunity was held right under my nose. I couldn't fail to take it."

"But Slade—he's a big fellow and looks like a fighter!"

"A rope is a great subduer of energy," said Prince Charlie, chuckling. "A horse soon learns not to run against it, and what a horse learns at one lesson, you'd think that a man could learn at least as fast. But Slade Livingston had needed two. And he's getting the second one now!"

Something more than merriment came into his voice as he said this, and I asked him where Slade was. He said that he would show me presently, and then called my attention to the river below us, and the way the water darkened at the margins of the stream, and brightened in the middle.

"I'd like to be a painter," said Prince Charlie. "Night pictures would be my style, though."

He laughed again. He was bubbling with delight.

"You're happy, Dexter," said I.

"As if I had wings! As if I had wings!" said he. "After ten years, this is heaven, Dean. Smell the fresh of the grass in that wind, will you? Why, one night like this is worth

132

an ordinary year. Tell me, Dean, how they felt in the house when they learned that Slade was with me. And what did the judge say? There's the villain, I think. The judge is the man, I'd say. What do you think, Dean?"

"The judge," I said, as judicially as I could, "is no ordinary person. There's bad in him. There may be a lot of good in him, too. I can't say, as yet, except that I'm glad that you got me out of his hands."

"I never could have done it," he said, "if you hadn't budged his gun, just as he was drawing his bead on me, this evening. He had the look of a fellow who doesn't miss a pointblank target, no matter how fast it's moving."

"How in the world could you see what I did?" I asked. "Your back was turned, and you were diving through the window, as nearly as I can remember."

"I have an eye in the back of my head," said he. "That's my great advantage, in a pinch." He began to chuckle. "It takes practice, and that's about all, Dean."

"And where's Livingston now?" I asked him.

"You want to change the subject, do you?" he remarked. "Well, you're modest, but I know what it must have cost you to interfere with the judge, at that moment!"

"No," I told him frankly. "As a matter of fact, I reached out on a sudden impulse that I wouldn't have had the courage to follow, on second thought. But where's Livingston?"

"Stretching," said this remarkable youth. "Just having a good stretch to take all the lies out of him and leave him nothing but the truth. I hate a liar, Dean."

"I don't know what you're driving at," I said.

"You'll see, in a minute," he assured me.

And I did!

He led the way into a small copse to our left. Inside of it, the moonlight shot down pale streams of silver, and the shadows of the tree trunks were painted black against the ground. Inside of this covert, the wind was not felt, though it roared and groaned overhead, and I was feeling much more comfortable in spirit and in body, when it seemed to me that I saw a man leaping at me, with his hands stretched above his head.

I jerked back my horse so hard that the gelding reared, and then, as my mount settled forward once more, I made out what it was.

It is a thing which I still hate to think of. The picture of it sickens me now, on reflection, just as it sickened me at the time.

For there was Slade Livingston tied up by the wrists to the bough of a tree with his feet just touching the ground. That was the ingenious and terrible part of the thing. The inhuman craft of Dexter had arranged the matter so exactly, and hoisted his victim to such a nice height, that by standing on tiptoes, Slade could support all of his weight on his feet.

But have you ever tried to stand on tiptoe for any length of time? A man's weight is intended to come down through the bones of the leg, and the major part of it rests on the heel. There's nothing falser than a tiptoe position, except for a dancer.

Poor Livingston was strung up there in such a way that he could put part of the burden on his legs, and part of it on his arms.

But who can hang by the arms for long? Not even those who have a good deal of ape in the make-up can do it very long, and Slade Livingston had had to endure this torment for a long time. His weight sagged straight down from the shoulders; his numb legs vainly strove to take off some of the pressure from the straining, stretching ligaments of the shoulders, but they were simply bending uselessly at the knees. He was limp from head to foot, except for his head and neck. And the neck of the youth was swollen and rigid with agony.

His mouth was open, and his expression was that of a frozen screech of protest. I wondered why the sound did not come out until, looking closer through the shadows, I saw that the jaws were distended, not by his will, but by a gag.

I have tried to describe this picture in detail, but nothing can convey the horror of its effect upon me, nor the terrible bulging eyes of the tortured man. It left me speechless.

Dexter dismounted. I think I slid down to the ground because I was unable to keep the saddle any longer.

And Dexter now was standing in front of the prisoner, and reaching up, he removed the gag.

A deep, wordless groan came from Slade.

"You've had a chance to rest your body and work your brain," said Dexter. "Will you talk freely now?"

"Yes!" came the thick-tongued, almost inaudible whisper. "Yes, yes—oh ——"

And Dexter cut him down, slashing the rope in two.

He fell, literally, like a lifeless thing, a creature without volition, a being without any power. Slumping upon his side a little, he remained in a heap.

Dexter straightened him out, and then sat him up against the trunk of a tree. He pulled out a flask and pressed it to the lips of the youngster, and Slade Livingston drank deep, groaned, and then caught his breath as though the stimulus of the whisky merely gave him a greater feeling of his own exquisite agony.

"Take a little time," said Dexter cheerfully. "You'll find that the pain grows less, after a time. Will you smoke? No, I don't suppose that you can raise your hand to your face, just now. It will be better later on. Though it may be a month or so before you can throw a saddle on your horse, Slade."

He actually stood there calmly before his victim and lighted a cigarette, and smoked it with careful appreciation. And he asked me:

"Did you ever notice, Dean, that tobacco never tastes by moonlight as it does in the sun?"

I had not spoken since we came there. I could not speak now until he said gently:

"It's about time for you to talk, Livingston."

At this, Livingston said with a groan: "I'll tell you— and God forgive me! I wish that I'd died, sooner!"

"You understand, Dean," said Dexter. "It's to be the whole history of the night ten years ago, as only a Benson or a Livingston could give it. It ought to be worth hearing, eh?"

"What I heard comes from ——" began Slade Living-

135

ston, in a groaning voice which I can still both feel and hear.

But then I could stand it no longer, and the words rushed up from me.

"Dexter," said I, "I'm sorry that I ever laid eyes on your face!"

He turned suddenly toward me. He was so taken by astonishment that the cigarette actually fell from between his fingers.

"Of all the horrible things that I've ever seen, this is a great deal the most horrible!" I went on.

"I understand you," said he "You're a decent fellow, Mr. Dean. I've seen that, of course, before to-night. But you don't realize the whole history that goes behind this. You don't see what I saw, ten years ago, and you don't stand as I stood, to watch your father being murdered. You've not been hounded by the mystery of Scorpio, and the influences behind him. You've not wanted to take your revenge in blood, as a man should, but been too much in the dark to know just where you should strike. But here's the door that will open the whole treasure of knowledge to me. D'you wonder that I wanted to open it, even in this way?"

"Dexter," I said to him, "if you're a human being and not a devil, tell me this: Did Slade Livingston have any part in what was done ten years ago?"

"No, he was only a boy, of course. So was I a boy, but they hunted me for my life!"

"Did this fellow bear a hand?"

"No."

"Then you're utterly beneath contempt if you wring from him a story that he's heard in confidence and that will affect the lives of others."

He began to stare at me. He took out a second cigarette, lighted it, and blew the smoke thoughtfully above his head, where it appeared like milk in the patterning of the moonlight.

He must have stood there for two or three minutes, like that, before he said to me: "You're right. I'm wrong. I'm entirely wrong, and I've done Livingston an injury."

CHAPTER XXV.   THE ORCHARDS

THE grisly picture that I had looked in on was enough of a shock, but I don't think that I was so bewildered by it as I was by the sudden and free admission which Dexter made.

For I dare say that there is nothing which we hold to be more self-evident than that right is obvious, and that we are almost born with a foreknowledge of it. But the understanding of it by Dexter was such a dim thing that he had proceeded blandly on his course of action until what I said pulled him up short.

I had spoken to him without the slightest belief that he would really take my words to heart. I had felt that he must be as far beyond reclamation as any beast of prey that ever hunted after helpless creatures, but it had not needed five minutes to change his mind completely.

He had been a puzzle to me more than once before this. He was ten times more so after this strange event.

He accepted my point so completely that he merely added:

"I'm ten times thankful that I brought you along with me to-night, Dean. I don't know—it seems as though there must have been some controlling force that made me meet you in Monte Verde. About Livingston, I merely thought that ——"

He did not complete the sentence. I suppose he would have said that he had merely looked upon Livingston as an enemy, and therefore one beyond the decent rights of man. Well, I had said enough—far more than I would have had the courage to say, probably, if the impulse had not mastered me in that first moment.

He turned his attention to poor young Livingston now.

The latter was so far gone that, after the interruption, he went on: "On that night, what happened was that ——"

In the torment of his body and mind, he had not understood the effect of my intervention!

"Hold on," said Dexter. "You're not to talk. I've changed my mind about that. It appears that I've been a good deal of a brute, Slade. I'm sorry for that, as you can imagine. But there's to be no more out of you. If it were your father, now, that would be a very different matter, eh, Dean?"

"Would you do the same thing to him?" I asked.

"And why not?" he cried at me. He added, suddenly: "Ah, but I understand your idea. Even when it's wild Indians we're fighting, we have to remain white men. That's your idea, isn't it?"

I told him that it was.

Livingston, now that the strain was ended, now that it suddenly appeared that all the torment had been for nothing, dropped his head back against the tree that propped him up and groaned from the depths of his heart. And my own heart bled for the boy. After all, he had merely been playing follow-the-leader when he rode with Benson or his father against Charlie Dexter.

"What will we do with him?" asked Dexter. "He can't walk—not for a day or two, I dare say. He certainly can't lift his arms for a week. We'll have to get him to his house, I suppose—and give the hornets another chance to sting us. Aye, and *they'll* have no hesitation. Moral scruples won't bother them a whit, because they're beyond being upset by mere trifles. What will we do with this hulk now?"

"Charlie," Livingston said, "if you can get me to the Orchard place, they'll take care of me and cart me home again."

"Are the Orchards still living here in the valley?" asked Dexter, evidently violently surprised.

"Aye, they're still among us."

"I thought that you would have hounded them out, long ago."

"Because they were friends of your father's?" asked Livingston. "Is that why we should have hounded them out?"

"Yes. They stood with us on that night."

"They stood with you, and the others respected them for it," said Slade.

He had mastered his pain in the most manly fashion. Perhaps the relief from the worst of the torment was helping him now.

"And they've been able to keep going?"

"They're poor as mice," said Slade. "But they keep going."

"What made them poor?" demanded Dexter. "They used to have two whole sections of fine land!"

"Of course they did," said Slade. "But—well, they lost a lot of it, I don't know just how."

"And now who has the land they lost?"

"Why, the Dinmonts and the Crowells, I think."

"I thought so," said Dexter. He went on, through his teeth: "Now, God help me to make it up to them! I'd feed them to the fish. Oh, confound them, I'd make the balance swing even for everything that the Orchards have suffered! Tell me honestly, Slade. Have they a friend in the valley?"

"Well," said Slade, "I've seen a good deal of Jenny Orchard. But they're pretty bitter, and the rest of our people don't have much to do with them. They're friends of the Laffitters. Jenny and Claudia are always going back and forth to see one another. If you can get me to the Orchard house, Charlie—it's not more than half a mile from here, I think."

Dexter had dropped on one knee before the other, not in humility, you may be sure, but in order to talk more closely with him.

"I'll tell you what," said he, "I'm going to take care of you, Slade. After you're back on your feet, you'll be after me to get square for to-night's business, and I won't blame you. But now that we're on talking terms for a moment, I want to tell you that I'm sorry about this, Slade. I can't help remembering some of the old days, before—well, I remember the fights and the races that we had together. I'd half wish we could call it square?"

And as I listened, amazed to hear this from the bitter heart of Dexter, Livingston answered:

"Do you think that I blame you much for what you did

139

to-night? Not a bit! I might have done as badly by you. At any rate, I would have shot you down, if I had half a chance, and been glad of it! Charlie, I think that we could call the thing square, so far as I'm concerned!"

"I think you mean it," said Dexter.

"I do."

Dexter stood up.

"There's something coming out of this, after all, and a sight bigger thing than I'd hoped for. Dean, will you give me a hand, and we'll try to get him onto that horse of mine."

We managed it, though it was very difficult, for he was still hardly more than a dead, limp weight. But once we had him in the saddle, with Dexter on one side supporting him, and I on the other, and the second horse led behind us, we made good progress through the wood, and over a hill into sight of a ranch which was now very close to us.

We got into a lane through a set of bars which I lowered while Dexter held up Slade Livingston, and presently there were half a dozen dogs—mongrels all of them, I think—barking and howling about us. Slade called to them, and they seemed to recognize his voice, for they became more quiet.

Then we got to the back door of the house, just as a window screeched up and a man's voice called: "Who's there?"

"Slade Livingston," the youth answered.

"What're you doing around at this time, Slade?" asked the other. "If you're hunting for Charlie Dexter here, you're certainly barking up the wrong tree."

"I've had a fall," said Slade, "and I'm badly done up."

"Hello!" said the other. "I'll be right with you."

When we got our burden off the horse and up to the back door of the house, it was already being opened by a man who had his feet in slippers and was tightly huddling a coat over his shoulders.

He held up a lantern, and something about Livingston's face—its pallor, or the strained look about the eyes, I suppose—made him exclaim loudly:

"Why, you look like you'd been shot! Bring him in,

boys. Easy, now. This way. Stretch him out here on the sofa. Any bones broke, Slade? Wait till I call ma and Jenny!"

And he sent out a whoop that soon brought scurrying sounds through the house.

We had Livingston made as comfortable as we could, with a pillow under his head, and another drink of whisky to raise his stamina. But the moment the lantern light played over his face. I felt a distinct qualm. He looked years older. There were thick wrinkles around his eyes and the corners of his mouth, and the set frown which he wore could not be relaxed. Poor Livingston had been through something a great deal bitterer than death, in the dark of that night.

The women came, then—first little Jenny Orchard, a pretty brown-faced girl, and Mrs. Orchard, bowed with work and trouble, her calico wrapper hanging about her like the feathers around a drowned chicken. And, after these, came a taller girl who commanded one's attention with a sudden force, in spite of the dimness of the light. And this was Claudia Laffitter.

I suppose that I should have been less surprised, having in mind what Livingston had told us not long before, but it was an odd thing to see her there, when I had been picturing her so vividly back there in Monte Verde. She gave us not a glance, but suddenly she was taking charge, and the other two women were obeying her instructions.

Old Orchard drew aside with us. He was as bent and thin as his wife. His shoulders were so pulled down that he always seemed to be supporting a weight in either hand.

"I don't know you boys," said he.

"You knew me ten years ago," said Dexter.

"Hold on," said Orchard. "I knew you? Did you live around here?"

"Yes."

"Where?"

"In Dexter House."

"Hey!" exclaimed Orchard, and snatching the lantern from the table, he raised it high and threw the light full into Charlie's face. His own face was a study worth

141

reading, in the meantime. "Jumping Jehoshaphat! Ma! Jenny!" he exclaimed. "Just look here, will you?"

Dexter, smiling a little, endured the glances which were bent on him, merely nodding to them, and saying: "Hello, Mrs. Orchard. Jenny, it's a long time, isn't it?"

And Jenny was the first to speak.

"It's true!" she whispered. "It's Prince Charlie, and he's come home again!"

CHAPTER XXVI.   A DISTURBANCE

THAT was the beginning of an evening which I shall never forget. It was one of the most impressive things that I ever have seen—the silent reverence and amazement with which the assembled family of the Orchards looked upon Charles Dexter and hailed him, straight off, as Prince Charlie. For the term was an old one in the valley, it appeared, and there had always been a Prince Charlie, of one generation or another, until that fatal night ten years before.

After that first survey of him—of course they had heard before this about his appearance in Monte Verde—they hailed him without any reservation, and I think that this acclaim of theirs sufficed to remove from my mind the last lingering doubts that I entertained about him.

The last? No, I cannot say the last. Throughout, I had in my mind a hazy incredulity, for the young man seemed something less or something more than real, like an actor on a stage, permitted or trained to surpass the normal expectancy.

But on this night, he was to show himself in a light such as I never had seen fall upon him.

I had seen him grave, austere, with something the manner of a cat watching a mouse, and prepared to whirl on a secret enemy that might be stalking from behind. I had seen him hysterically joyous over the sense of danger and of action as he entered into Dexter Valley after that long, ten-year absence.

But now he was like a child in a family—a favored child, let me say, conscious of his position in the affections of all around him, and returning their affection ten-fold. It might be acting, I thought, but certainly it was charming.

There seemed no malice and no bitterness in him.

For instance, when old Orchard drew him aside and, in whispering, strove to pitch his voice so that I might not hear, Dexter reached out and pulled me by the coat sleeve close up to them.

He said, with the happiest of smiles: "This is the best friend I have in the world, though he isn't my oldest. This is the man who has done more for me than any other man. I tell you, I'd be dead and underground by this time, or spinning down the river for the fishes, if it hadn't been for him."

Orchard, of course, looked at me with new eyes, and he said: "I wasn't tryin' to talk behind the back of Mr. Dean. I just wanted to know, Charlie, the right truth of what happened between you and this here Slade Livingston boy?"

"Nothing happened between us," said Dexter, looking Orchard dauntlessly in the eye. "Not a thing. He simply had a bad fall from his horse."

"Livingstons ain't the kind that fall off horses," declared Orchard unabashed by the straight eye of the young man.

"This Livingston took a fall, however," persisted Charlie. "And now, let's forget about it, shall we?"

Orchard, reluctantly, gave over the subject. It had worried him, plainly. No matter how much he detested the other men of the valley, because of the wrongs which he had endured from them, Slade Livingston obviously had a place in his affections. Perhaps Jenny was the key with which Slade had opened the grim old farmer's heart.

In the meantime, however, Jenny had surrendered the care of the injured man to Claudia Laffitter and had hurried out into the kitchen with her mother, where they were bustling about to arrange for some food.

God bless the hospitable heart of the West, which opens

its pantry almost as soon as it opens its door! Go where you will, you will not find surly lip service or a grudging look, no matter how poor a family is your host. So I have always found it, and so I think it must always remain, until the priceless sense of a frontier departs from it under the pressure of multitudes who fill its mountains and its deserts. Even then, perhaps, the old idea and the old ideal will survive. At least, that is my hope.

Claudia made a capable nurse.

She wound a cold, wet towel across the face and the eyes of Livingston, and she put a soothing salve over the abrasions made by the rope around his wrists. The bruised and strained muscles and the drawn ligaments about his shoulders, she massaged.

Her touch, at first, made him grind his teeth at the fresh agony which he was enduring, but presently her skillful manipulation was bringing the blood back, to heal overwearied muscles and to restore tortured nerves.

There is no time for a massage like the earliest moment after a strain, and I suppose that work of the girl's was almost a life-saver for Slade Livingston. Presently, we heard a groan of relief from him.

"You must have hit a rope when you got that fall," said Claudia to him. "These are rope burns on your wrists, I take it."

"I got both my hands twisted in the tie rope, like a fool," he replied.

"And yet your clothes don't look as if ——"

She stopped herself when she was on the point, I suppose, of saying that his clothes did not show that he had been dragged. But, a moment later, she cast over her shoulder, toward Charles Dexter, a most expressive glance.

I thought that poor Livingston would try to keep the secret, but when she had taken the towel from about his eyes, and was massaging, now, with her strong fingers, the aching back of his neck, and the thick, deep muscles at the base of it, he looked straight up into her face and waited for her eye.

When he caught it, I heard him say, distinctly:

"It was Charlie who did it, Claudia. And he had plenty

144

of cause. And I'm not on his trail, either. I'm not even trying to get back at him, no matter what the rest of the people around here may say of him. Now you know, and you can talk as much as you like about it."

She laughed, very softly.

"I wouldn't talk about it for a million dollars," she said. "Not even to Jenny or her father. Slade, I always said that you were the only *man* in the valley!"

She was enormously pleased with the youth, and so was I; and Dexter turned a bright red with satisfaction. I never before had seen him so affected.

Then the meal came in, and of course you can imagine what it was like. It was actually better than most, because the Orchards kept chickens. It is nearly always a sign of a poor rancher or farmer when there are plenty of chickens cackling about the house and barnyard.

But at least the Orchards had eggs, and we got them now, fried, and big, thick strips of bacon, fried Western fashion. That is to say, some of the rankness of the fat remains, and the inside of a specially thick slice may retain a bit of the gristly effect of raw meat. However, for a very hungry man there is nothing in the world to compare with it as a food.

Besides these main dishes, we had slices of new-made bread, cut thick because the loaf was so soft that the pieces cut out of shape. And we ate this bread with pale but sweet butter, newly worked and fresh as daisies, and an apricot marmalade with the flavor of peach pits and some of the pits themselves in it.

This meal may not sound sumptuous in recital, but since I had eaten supper at the house of the judge, I had been through a good deal, and I, for one, can bear witness that troubles of the spirit are worse than mountain climbing for giving an appetite. All through, and at the end, we had quantities of black coffee.

There was only one unusual feature at this table, and that was conversation. It was supplied by a chorus, and Prince Charlie.

The chorus was composed of Jenny Orchard and her father and mother—and a few groaning comments from

145

poor Slade Livingston, who had recovered the use of his hands so wonderfully that, though they trembled a good deal, by managing the coffee cup with both at once, he could bring it up to chatter against his teeth while he took a gulp. I was glad to see that lad recovering so fast. He and the three Orchards kept up a running fire of chatter with Prince Charlie as the victim.

I said nothing. Neither did Claudia. But she was pale with interest, and sat up like a drum major, looking from face to face to see how the story was affecting the various people at the table. Once, when her glance fell upon me, I smiled straight back at her, and she understood so well that she dared not meet my eye again during the entire course of the evening.

They wanted to know everything. And Prince Charlie told them—how he was taken away from Dexter Valley that fatal night ten years before, and how Philip Anson had been like a father to him, and how he had finally returned with Anson, when the latter decided that he might be man enough for the rôle that awaited him, and how his one hope was to avenge his father by killing Manly Crowell, and the massacre of the other members of his family by finding and destroying Scorpio, if that archdevil really still lived.

How they listened to this talk! How their eyes started! How their eyes shone!

"And before the end," said Prince Charlie, "I'm going to get back some of what belongs to my family. And when I get back what is mine, you can be sure that you'll get back what is yours, or else my name is not Dexter!"

Well, he did not need to make promises to any Orchard.

I had a very odd feeling, while I was in that house, watching their attitude toward Dexter. It was as though he were, really, a sort of crown prince, and all their affection and loyalty were naturally due to him as a powerful debt. They did not act foolishly, but with a quiet, deep devotion. There must have been a certain quality in the Dexters of the past, I decided, or else they never could have induced free-born Westerners to have such an attitude toward them.

There was only one disturbance during the course of the evening. That was when the wind, which was still rather high, happened to blow open a shutter.

Dexter got up at once, raised the window, and closed and latched the shutter.

"You did that pretty fast," said Orchard. "You'd almost think that the Crowells and the Dinmounts and the Bensons, and the rest, was all outside of there, ready to jump in on you."

And Prince Charlie made an answer that took my breath.

"Oh, they're out there," he said cheerfully. "They've been there for some time. But they know that I'm not alone in here!"

The current of general gladness was stopped in midcourse, though Dexter exclaimed that everything was all right, that there was no danger to any one, so long as Slade remained with them, and that not a hair of any one's head, including his own, would be harmed.

Jenny Orchard sprang up from the table and ran across the room to the man on the sofa, and stood above him with her fists clenched.

"Slade!" she cried out. "If anything happens to Prince Charlie—I'll never speak to you again!"

And, from the look on Slade's face, I knew that it was a threat sufficient to make him a very miserable lad. But none of the rest of us smiled. We looked at Prince Charlie, and only old Orchard moved from his chair. It was to get his long rifle that hung on two nails against the wall.

CHAPTER XXVII.　　　THE PACK

FOR the first time, I noticed an old grandfather's clock in a corner of the room. It had a long, straight shank of a body and a face as round as the head of an owl, and now that face seemed to be watching us imperturbably, while

147

the clicking of the machinery became audible through the room like a faint strumming upon musical strings. My heart, you may be sure, was running far faster than the ticking of the clock.

Claudia Laffitter spoke first.

"What makes you think that they're outside?" she asked.

"Oh, because this place is so close to the place where I took Livingston, here, and by this time they're sure to have found that spot."

"Then why did you stay here?" she exclaimed impatiently.

I think every one had the same thought, for all heads turned to Dexter, and all attention remained fixed on him.

"Because," said he, with consummate calmness, "the only witness I have that the valley men have been hunting for my life is Mr. Dean, here. And if he's snuffed out along with me, then there would be no one to testify that I ever was down here. Now, however, there's the whole Orchard family, and you'll presently have a chance to see what's waiting outside. Will you stand back from the door?"

We scattered to each side, watching him like school children. He slipped out of his coat and draped it over the foot of a mop, put his high-crowned sombrero above this, and throwing the door wide open, he presented this ridiculous dummy to the outer night, at the same time calling out: "Good-night, every one!"

How could any one be deceived by such a foolish imitation? That thought had barely formed in my mind when half a dozen rifles exploded, and the coat was blown streaming in from the top of the mop, like a flag from its pole. At the same time, with the roar of the guns, there was a hum of bullets, and the crashing of them against the inner wall of the room.

Prince Charlie, laughing a little, slammed the door and locked it.

"All meant for me!" said he, and pointed to the coat.

It was riddled with holes! Every one of the six bullets which we found afterward had bored into the wall inside the house had, in the first place, whipped through the coat

148

of Dexter. It was very good shooting. It was shooting so good that it must have blown him instantly into kingdom come, if he had been inside that coat.

"Yep," said old Orchard, nodding his head. "They couldn't wait—them starved coyotes. They ain't had any raw meat for a long time!"

Without any exception, every soul in that room was calm. I could hardly imagine it. For my part, I was mastering the jumping of my nerves with the greatest effort, but the rest of them were as cool as you please.

Old Mrs. Orchard, I thought, would surely either faint or scream. But not a bit of it! She went and poked the tip of her finger into each of the bullet holes which had already been made in the wall.

"Neater than an auger would've done it," she said, and smiled and nodded to us.

She was a grand old woman, and though time had bent her back, it had not touched her spirit.

Little Jenny Orchard, too, said merely: "We'll have to putty them up. Aren't they a pack of fools to shoot at a dummy like that?"

"I tell you how it be," commented Orchard, rubbing his chin in a contented way. "Your finger gets jumpy on the trigger, when you're hunting big game. The bigger the game, the jumpier the finger. No wonder they was over-anxious to shoot, when it comes to that!"

"It's a dastardly, contemptible thing," said poor Slade Livingston. He got himself up on the sofa on his trembling elbows and exclaimed again: "If I've got a father or a brother out there ——"

"Hold on," said Dexter. "Don't say anything you may trip over later on. I know that it's religion down here in the valley to get rid of me. I don't blame them. They've got so much money at stake that it stops being murder and becomes a war, from their point of view."

Jenny Orchard clasped her hands together and looked at Dexter with worshiping eyes. "I wish that they could hear him talk. I just wish that everybody in the world could hear him talk and *then* doubt that he's Prince Charlie!"

"Well, lad," said Orchard after a moment, "we know

149

that you've been fired on in the night. It makes out a pretty good case, all things considered, agin' *some* people in this valley; but it don't point no finger at no particular one."

"It will, though, before long," said Dexter. "They have a good many young boys, out there, and they're apt to do something foolish, before long—such as shouting a few taunts, or some such thing. I dare say that some of you could recognize the voices?"

As he spoke of the youths, I stared at him; he was hardly more than a boy himself. And yet there was an age in him which was greater than years. He did not seem at all absurd, or talking down.

"We'll find out something about them *now!*" said Claudia Laffitter.

She was at the door as she spoke, and turning the key in the lock, she now jerked it open, as young Dexter had done before, and stood there in her own person, with the lamplight shining upon her! What a target, for marksmen who apparently did not look twice before they fired.

All our tongues were frozen in our throats, except for Dexter. He gave out a terrible, husky cry of "Claudia!" and started for her. But she, with a smile at him over her shoulder, walked straight out into the dark.

I doubled up my hands so that the nails wounded the palms, but there was no crash of musketry to greet her. Hasty as those marksmen were, perhaps they had learned a lesson by the first trick that had drawn their fire.

At any rate, there was Claudia glimmering almost out of sight, for the light of the lamp followed her only dimly. And there was Dexter inside the house, showing more emotion than I ever had seen in him before. He had lost all color. His eyes were as big as a surprised child's when he turned and stared at us.

"What will they do to her? What will they dare to do?"

"Now, you hold on, Charlie," said old Orchard. "You gotta remember that this here is the West. They ain't a thug in all of Dexter Valley that would dare to put a hand on her!" He went on familiarly: "What is it, Charlie? Just general principles, sort of, or are you kind of fond of Claudia?"

Dexter did not answer. He was breathing hard, and passing a handkerchief across his forehead.

Then we could see where Claudia had paused on the outer rim of the light from the house. She was barely distinguishable, standing there. On the whole, I never have seen a woman do a thing so rash, so utterly fearless. And suddenly it illumined the character of the girl for me. There was neither fear nor evil in her, I felt.

Old Orchard, looking out after her, said suddenly: "Ah, she's the pure quill!"

And she was, of course. That was the right word for her.

"She's twenty-four carat and a yard wide," said Livingston. "There's nobody like Claudia Laffitter!"

At this, Jenny gave him rather a hard look, but Livingston was too excited to pay any heed to her.

We were not at such a distance that we could fail to hear what happened now.

The voice of the girl suddenly came back to us rather faintly, strong though it was.

"Who's out here? What cowards are out here, shooting at people in the door of this house? I'm Claudia Laffitter asking!"

I thought that no one would answer. Certainly it appeared an obvious folly to identify oneself as part of a gang of incipient murderers, but almost instantly a familiarly deep voice said in answer—and we heard the words clearly:

"A pack of young fools did that shooting at a hat and coat, Claudia. It didn't mean anything!"

"Didn't it?" she demanded, in scornful anger. "It would have meant a dead man, if Charlie Dexter had been inside that coat!"

"Look here, Claudia," said the voice of Judge Benson in reply. "We don't mean any harm to you or the Orchards, of course. But we have an idea that Slade Livingston is in that house along with Dexter."

"He is," said the girl. "And what of it?"

"Well, we want to know what shape Slade is in."

"Come in and see for yourself."

"Come in there, with that wildcat of a Dexter standing around handy?" echoed the judge.

"Come in and bring your best man with you," said the girl harshly. "There's only two men in there. You know that Mr. Orchard won't attack you unless you attack him or his friends. As for Charlie Dexter—you are not afraid of him, are you? Are two of you afraid of him?"

Her voice rose and rang. Plainly, she was glorying like a young Indian in this chance to taunt the judge. But we heard his voice smoothly answering:

"I only want to know if Slade is badly used up."

"Well, he's not. *Dexter* is no murderer!"

What Dexter's enemies might be, she left easily to be inferred. Imagine the courage and the spunk of that girl, with such a band as the valley men around her! But she did not wince.

"I'm glad to hear it," said the judge.

"And so am I!" exclaimed another man.

I recognized Livingston's voice plainly.

"Now we can write down two of them. We could swear to two of 'em," said Orchard. "Maybe it wouldn't be enough testimony to jail 'em, but it would be enough to take away all the reputation that they ever had. This won't be no country for them to live in, no longer!"

The judge went on:

"We want to disturb nobody in that house, Claudia. I have a friendly feeling for Orchard ——"

"You ought to," snapped that terrible girl, "because you've eaten half of him."

I saw Orchard grin widely. Mrs. Orchard grew red with the memory of the old wrongs.

"All we want," said the judge, "is for Orchard to forbid his house to Dexter. That's all I want."

CHAPTER XXVIII.   BENSON'S OFFER

AT this, Dexter suddenly turned with raised brows toward the host, but Orchard, smiling sardonically, merely stared blankly at the floor.

"That's all you want?" we heard the girl answer. "You only want him to turn out his house guest, who happens to be a Dexter?"

"He's no more of a Dexter than I am," said the judge. "Don't be foolish and sentimental, Claudia. You have better sense than that, if you'll use it! You can tell Orchard from me that there'll be something for him to gain by it."

"Why, what will he gain, except a black name?"

"He'll gain that southwest two hundred and forty that he lost eight year back. That's what he'll gain, for one thing."

"If he'll turn out Dexter to be murdered by you and your men?"

"Who's talking about murder?" said Benson. "Don't be so foolish, my dear Claudia. You ought to know me better. We want to apprehend that young man, because he's dangerous."

"Yes," said Claudia. "I guessed that was why you wanted him. You wouldn't apprehend him with a bullet, I suppose?"

"Certainly not. A formal arrest would ——"

"Have you a warrant?"

"You know that in this part of the world one can't stick on formalities, Claudia."

"I know you can't," said the girl. "My father was murdered by you and your men—and there were no formalities then! There was no formality about that, either. I can understand why you detest formality, judge!"

"In the meantime," said he, "I fear that we're getting nowhere."

"I fear that we're not," she said. "I've only found out that you and Clay Livingston are in this gang. If that's not attempted murder ——"

"My dear girl—my dear child," said he. "When I've come out expressly to bring peace to the valley and to pacify some of the wild youngsters who ——" He checked himself and added: "I'll have a talk to Orchard direct."

Claudia turned and came slowly back toward the house, her head half turned to listen more carefully to the talk between Orchard and the judge.

"Orchard!" called the judge.

"Well, judge?" inquired Orchard.

"I'm coming up there to talk to you, Orchard, if you'll give me a safe conduct."

"I wouldn't trust a safe conduct from you," declared Orchard. "But if you want to trust me, you're free to."

"I'd trust you to the end of the world," said the judge, "because I know that you're an honest man."

"Do you hear that, Lizzie?" said Orchard to his wife.

She grew a brighter red than before. She threw back her shoulders and stood up straight, and the next moment Claudia stepped through the front door, and the judge behind her. Orchard had simply looked at Dexter, and Dexter had nodded his permission.

"Well, well, well!" said the judge as he came inside. "It's a long time since I've seen you folks. How are you, Lizzie?"

He held out his hand. The little old woman simply looked at him earnestly, almost wonderingly, in the face, and kept her own hands folded together before her.

The judge changed face; his smile went out in a mass of wrinkles. I felt almost sorry for him, seeing him so outfaced by the silence of one bent old woman. But, as I was saying, she stood straighter, now, and her flush had taken away some of her years. I could see, dimly, what she must have been in her youth and, also, I could guess what weighted the scales so heavily against the judge. You may be sure that he did not speak any longer with Mrs. Elizabeth Orchard. Instead, he at once gave his attention

154

to the others in the room, though he did not offer his hand to any of them.

One lesson in that direction had been enough for him.

I was amused and seriously interested to see the behavior of this man. He maintained his dignity unshaken from first to last, and I could see that there was little in the world that could embarrass Judge Benson, if he were making his point.

First, as in nature bound, he went across the room to the sofa where Slade Livingston was lying and dropped a hand on his shoulder, as he leaned over the youth.

"My poor lad!" he exclaimed. "It makes my heart ache to see you here, Slade. My heart really aches for you, and your father has been half dead with anxiety!"

Slade, in the meantime, looked up at the judge with a puckered brow. Finally he said:

"If it hadn't been for you and my father, I wouldn't be lying here. I wouldn't have turned myself into a man hunter in the first place, and I wouldn't have been made a fool of, in the second place."

The judge, with wonderful calmness, skipped over the first part of that speech and asked: "My poor lad, what happened to you? What laid you out?"

"Bad advice!" said Slade Livingston firmly.

I was amazed and delighted by his attitude.

"As for what happened, it's between Charlie Dexter and myself," said Slade.

The judge turned purple, and swinging about on his heel, he confronted Dexter silently.

"Slade had a fall," said Dexter, and he looked the judge straight in the eye.

Nothing was to be gained from him.

The baffled judge, repulsed on two fronts, now gave his attention to old Orchard himself.

"I'm sorry," said he, "to see that you're giving shelter to malefactors, and men wanted by the law!"

"What law?" asked Orchard, drawling out the words in his usual tone.

"The law," said the judge pompously, "which forbids

155

men to break into the houses of others by stealth and by force! The law which forbids burglary!"

And he extended his big arm and pointed solemnly at Dexter.

"Tut-tut-tut," clucked Orchard. "You been and robbed the judge, Charlie?"

"Yes," admitted Dexter, to my bewilderment.

"Whacha take from him?" asked Orchard.

"A little of his time," said Dexter.

And suddenly we all laughed. We had to. It was anything to break the tension of the moment.

"What else?" asked Orchard.

"You'd better ask him," said Dexter. "What was it that I stole, judge?"

Like a pouter pigeon, the throat of the judge puffed and swelled with his passion, but he said nothing. And then I saw the point. No wonder that Prince Charlie agreed that he had stolen. For was the judge to admit that he attached such importance to the missing picture? Plainly we could infer that, after the visit of the young man, Benson had guessed why he had come to the house and risked such danger. It was to gain the most convincing proof of his parentage that could be found.

"It's not the matter of the stealing that counts for so much," said the judge, "but those who break into private dwelling houses ——"

"Which really belong to those who break in?" suggested Dexter, with his faint, polite smile. And he gave the judge one of his little bows, something like a fencer who has scored a touch.

It certainly was a touch against the judge, in this instance. He gave the rest of his attention, pointblank, to Orchard.

"Now, Orchard," he said briskly, "things have been running down hill with you for some time. I've been sorry to see it. Very sorry. I give you an easy choice, if you're a man of sense. Get this young rascal out of your house. You've already heard him admit burglary! Get him out of your house, and you'll be rewarded. You understand? Rewarded greatly!"

156

"You said something about the southwest two hundred and forty, didn't you?" remarked Orchard.

My heart sank into my boots. Hunger was in the face of the old rancher—land hunger, I supposed.

"I did!" exclaimed Benson instantly. "Every acre of it will go back to you. I'll arrange that. I'll give you my word for it."

"It's a mighty lot of land," said Orchard. "But I'd have to get my wife's opinion, judge."

"Get any opinion you want," said the judge. "But you ought to be able to see your own way clearly enough, if you have eyes in your head."

"It ain't only my way that counts," said Orchard. "I've had my hard times, in the last ten years, but it's Lizzie that has cooked and sewed and milked cows, and made butter and kept up the kitchen garden, and scrubbed, and laundered and ironed. Her and her girl. They got callouses on their hands, and I reckon that they got a right to answer up for me as much as me to answer up for myself. So I'll just ask her. Lizzie, the judge is offering us two hundred and forty acres."

"I heard him," said Lizzie Orchard quietly, her eyes never leaving the face of the judge as she answered her husband.

"It's more than land that he's offering," went on Orchard deliberately. "He's offering you a chance to dress up Jenny, fine and slick ——"

"Daddy!" burst out the girl.

"You shut up, Jenny," said her father. "I'm talking to your mother. You can get up Jenny to look like the little lady that she was born to be. You can get in plenty of servants. You can set back and rest yourself the rest of your life, and let the vegetables go hang, and just potter around the flower garden, that you hanker after and always have.

"You can have a neat span of hosses and drive to town Sunday morning in a rubber-tired rig, all painted and polished up fine. You can have good, decent clothes, and time to read a paper and a book. That's what the judge is offering, Lizzie, if we'll only consent to turn this boy out of the house—this boy that says he's a Dexter, and we don't know!"

It was a pretty moving argument. The eyes of Mrs. Orchard, however, dwelt as steadily upon the face of the judge as though the words were coming from him.

And the judge nodded, to give emphasis to everything which Orchard was saying.

Finally she said: "There's never been nothing on our hands that soap and water wouldn't take off. I reckon that we'd better keep them that way!"

And I knew that the judge was answered!

CHAPTER XXIX.   A NEW ARRIVAL

THE judge knew his demand had been answered, and if he had any lingering doubts about his power to persuade, they were removed the next moment by Orchard, who said:

"It's a sort of a strange thing, judge, that them that are crooked and take after crooked ways always are figgering that other folks must be the way that they are. But all folks ain't that way. We know that you've tried to murder this here boy more'n once. We know that you've chased after him and hounded him. And now you come in here and ask us to throw him to the dogs. Why don't you ask my Lizzie to throw her own girl over a cliff or to the wolves when they're yammering in the winter?

"You don't have no imagination, it seems, Benson, to come here offering us two hundred and forty acres for the head of Prince Charlie. If his hands was as red as the hands of the Livingstons and the Crowells and the Dinmonts, and the Bensons, still wouldn't you be a fool to come and ask him from us?"

I thought that the judge would burst. He really had worked up high hopes. Now he was stifled, and quite beyond speech.

When he got his breath, he thundered with a force that made things jingle in the room:

"You'll wish that you'd died before ever you come to this day, Orchard!"

"I've wished that before, and you're the one that's made me wish it," said the rancher. "Just open that door, Charlie, will you? Looks like the judge needed a mite more air!"

Dexter glided to the door, while the judge bellowed:

"I've got you in my hand! I've got the lot of you in the hollow of my hand, and I'm going to take my time—and then close the fingers on you! That's what I'm going to do! You're ringed around. There's a fence around you. Let me see how you'll break through, any soul of you!"

And, finally, he turned his back and started for the door. It seemed to me that we were falling into deep and deeper danger, and that this visit from the judge was like a final and irrevocable declaration of war.

Then Dexter opened the door for the judge—and there in the entrance, standing clearly outlined against the velvet background of the night, we saw the small body, the foolish face, and the calf-like eyes of Sheriff Tom Winchell.

The judge was hard hit by that unexpected sight. He grunted as if he had received a body blow and stopped in mid-stride.

The sheriff was perfectly nonchalant.

"Hello, judge," said he. "Going, or coming, are you? Hullo, Orchard! Hullo, Lizzie. How's everything with all you folks in here? I was just stopping along this here way, people, and I seen the light and thought that they might be a cup of coffee setting around and going to waste. Are you folks all up late, or just early started?"

I looked out the window, toward the east, and saw the beginning of the day—a smoky red streak across the horizon.

But I was not tired. I could have prolonged this scene forever. For I did not know which way things would break, or where the sheriff would stand in relation to the troubles that were present in the Orchard house.

The judge recovered himself at once.

159

"I never was so glad to see a man, as I am to see you, Tom!" said he.

"Glad?" responded the sheriff. "You looked more like colic than gladness, when I first seen you."

"It was only surprise," said the judge.

He turned and gestured magnificently toward Dexter. "There you see him!" he said.

"Who?" said the sheriff, blinking his weak eyes.

He actually got out his eternal pocket glass and gave a look at Dexter through it.

"Why, if it ain't Charlie Dexter!" he exclaimed. "I'm sort of surprised to see you together."

"He's a burglar, probably a murderer, certainly a desperado, sheriff," said the judge. "He's violently entered my house this evening. Here before these witnesses he's admitted it all. He's violently entered my house, and I want him arrested at once!"

"You do?" asked the sheriff. "Ain't that kind of hard and sudden on the poor young gent?"

"Tom," exclaimed the judge, "you're a servant of the law, and law is all that I ask for."

"Oh," said the sheriff, "I reckon that you'll get all the law that you want, before long. By the way, ain't those your men that're around in front of this here house?"

The judge, for a moment, was silent, and then he answered that they were people who had come to help him overtake the robber.

"I thought that they was protecting the house from wild Injuns, or something," said the sheriff. "Or maybe, that they was planning a little surprise party for the Orchards. Hullo, Jenny. I didn't see you before. Dog-gone me if you ain't looking right sweet and pretty, these days! Your eyes is getting bluer, Jenny, like I said they would if ever you was to look twice at the same man. Who you been looking at, Jenny?"

This badinage had little effect on Jenny. She was too excited over what was happening around her.

"Besides," exclaimed the judge, "Slade Livingston has been attacked and his life endangered by this young ruffian ——"

160

"It's a lie!" cried Slade Livingston.

"You contemptible young fool!" shouted the judge.

"You crooked old scoundrel!" answered Slade, just as loudly.

"Come, come, come," said the sheriff. "What did Charlie Dexter steal out of his house? Out of your house, I mean to say!"

The question stopped the judge now as it had stopped him before. He could not answer. He could only make a counter-attack, saying: "You've thrown in with this pretender, Tom Winchell. You've chucked the men of Dexter Valley over, and maybe you'll regret it one day."

"I throw in with nobody," said the sheriff. "But I try to make the law run down a straight road. It ain't a straight road, so far as I can see, that you're on now, Benson. It looks like Murder Alley, to me."

This he said without excitement, his mild eyes blinking at the judge as he spoke. And Benson, for the first time, was silenced. Darkly he gathered himself together.

"I see that there's nothing to be done with you," said he.

"Well," said the sheriff, "I dunno. I ain't been offered two hundred and forty acres, yet."

So he had been there at the door, and heard the last part of the conversation which had preceded!

Benson was fairly floored.

"If there's trouble that grows out of this, it's your blame, sheriff," declared the judge.

"If there's trouble comes, I never dodge my share of the blame," replied Winchell.

He turned suddenly upon Dexter and said to him: "Young feller, Dexter you claim to be, and maybe Dexter you are. But whether your name is Dexter or Smith, have you got any charge laid agin' the judge, here?"

Again the judge was floored, and this time more seriously. He actually cast a wild glance toward the door, as though he wished that he never had come through it.

"Hold on," said Orchard. "We give him a safe conduct to come in here, Winchell."

The sheriff shook his head.

"He may have a safe conduct from you, but it ain't

from me," he said. "It looks a powerful lot to me as though they'd been a plot laid and a murder planned around these here parts, and if I was to look around me for the fox, I'd say that the judge was the one for the pack to follow."

I don't suppose that an officer of the law in any other civilized part of the world would have said a thing like that, but this was in the West, and in the days when "Western" meant something. Winchell was the very soul and spirit of frankness.

He turned again to young Dexter.

"Speak up, lad," said he. "Have you got a charge to lay?"

I saw the eyes of Dexter burn.

Obviously the judge was the heart and brain of his enemies. Without him to guide them, the men of Dexter Valley would not be a tithe as formidable. From what I had seen of him, I put him down as an intelligent man without any scruples in the world. For him, the end justified the means absolutely. So I waited for a ringing challenge to come from Dexter's lips.

Instead, I saw an obvious struggle in his face, and then he looked back from Benson to the sheriff.

"He has a safe conduct into the house of a friend of mine," said Dexter. "I'll not say a word against him while he's under this roof—not for you to hear, Sheriff Winchell!"

CHAPTER XXX.   ON A BYPATH

I ALMOST think that the judge would have preferred to go to jail. This was clemency from the last man he had reason to think would extend it.

Old Orchard sang out loudly: "You hear that, Winchell? Now ask me if that's Prince Charlie, or not?"

Winchell was staring at Dexter, with a more halfwitted look than ever. And Benson, without a word, started for the door. He had the look of a beaten dog, I must say, and for a moment, I had another flash of what was almost pity for him. When he was almost across the room, Slade Livingston sang out:

"Charlie, you're a man. I never saw a man before I saw you!"

At this, as though a sword had been driven through his back, the judge whirled about, and he gave young Slade a look that he must have remembered the rest of his days. Yet Benson did not speak, and in another moment he was through the doorway and safe in the night.

I could hardly believe it. He had been there in our hands—better than that, he had been in the rightful hands of the law, and yet he was gone again, unharmed, with no charge laid against him. Winchell, looking toward the door, passed the tip of his tongue across his pale, wind-cracked lips, and it was plain that he felt as a cat does, when a fat mouse has escaped down a hole.

He turned back to Dexter.

"Well, he's gone now," said the sheriff. "And I suppose that you're willing to talk?"

"What good would talk be?" asked Dexter, surprising me again. "Do you really think that plain talk will settle this affair?"

Winchell made himself a cigarette, and sat down with a sigh on the edge of a chair.

"You ain't got an extra bunk here for a tired man, Lizzie, have you?" he asked.

That moment, there was a wide-spread sound of trampling hoofs from about the house. I thought for an instant that the noise was sweeping in upon us, but in another instant I could tell that the hubbub was retreating. They had come up as softly as ghosts, but now their game was played, and they were away.

We looked at one another, without making any comment. Then we made preparations for sleep.

We needed it badly, and in the ramshackle old place they managed to find accommodation for all of us. As I went out, I saw Charlie Dexter pause before Claudia. And I heard him say:

"If it hadn't been for your courage, Claudia, we never could have spotted any of them, really, and the judge would never have been tempted to come in here and betray his hand. I've never seen another woman who could do such a thing, and you make me feel twice the man that I was this morning."

Claudia turned a rosy red; her eyes actually filled with pleasure. But that was the last of what I heard and saw between them, for I had to go through the door that shut them from my view.

I slept in a blanket on a couch in a front room of the house. I did not even take off my shoes, but the instant I was thoroughly wrapped up, my eyes closed, and I was sound asleep. That never had happened to me before, since childhood. I slept, and into my dreams came one continual picture—of a girl walking out into the dark of the night, and stepping on and on, and growing dimmer than a ghost, but still, never lost to my following eyes because of a radiance that did not seem to shine upon her from the outside, but from her own self.

When I wakened, it was past noon in the day. I had a headache which disappeared as soon as I had washed my face and hands in the icy water of the pump, and there I was, more fit than for years, hearty, with an appetite fit for two.

Mrs. Orchard fed me a meal that was half breakfast and half lunch. And when I asked for Dexter, she told me that he had gone off for a ride with Jenny and Claudia, and young Slade Livingston had also gone along with them.

"Good heavens!" I exclaimed. "Do you mean to say that he could sit the saddle, this morning?"

"He groaned a mite," said she, "but he managed it. What happened to him last night, poor boy?"

I shook my head and smiled back at her.

"What would Dexter say if I told?" I asked.

"Aye." She nodded. "There ain't no use telling what kings and princes has got the only right to know! Look at him, the way he went through last evening, with his head up, and his hands clean—and then they doubt that he's Prince Charlie!"

164

I, at least, had ceased doubting, except for that instinctive shadow which, as I have said before, always hung over my mind.

There was still, of course, a good deal of excitement around the house. Now that the Orchards had thrown down the glove and the other people of the valley had picked it up, there was no telling what moment might bring a direct attack upon them.

Orchard himself would not admit that he was actually worried, but his wife pointed out that Judge Benson had never failed before, and he would leave no stone unturned to win his battle now. Men who will not stop at a murder have a frightful advantage over those who play in the open; there was only one main comfort, and that was the fact that the sheriff, though he had not actually stated that he believed Prince Charlie to be what he claimed, was apparently more on his side than on that of the others. And the fear of the law, which the judge never had had against him before, might accomplish a good deal. This I myself pointed out, and the others were inclined to agree.

The sheriff was no longer with them, however. He had ridden off, and all men knew that he had tried to find, again, the trail of Scorpio, or the man who now was playing the rôle of that famous fighter.

Scorpio was the main thing to the sheriff; but Scorpio was also the main thing to Charlie Dexter. He had sworn that he would attempt nothing of great importance on his own behalf until he had avenged Philip Anson, and he was not a man to break his word. The affair at the house of Benson had come on simply because he had gone there to drum up evidence and a new trail that might lead him to the Mexican.

It was two or three in the afternoon when the four young people returned from their ride and reported that the countryside was being watched thoroughly, and scouted by lonely riders who were continually sliding over the edge of the sky, and fading off into the horizon once more. Beyond any question, they were working in the interests of the valley men.

This had decided Dexter on a point that vitally affected

165

me. Now that the hornets were so thoroughly aroused and filling the air with their humming, he thought that he ought to escort me back to Monte Verde. I tried to persuade him that I was quite willing to make the trip alone, but I could not argue against him. I suppose he must have seen that my heart was not in what I said. And in fact, I could not fail to see that now I was too deeply involved in Dexter's interests to be overlooked by the valley crew.

I knew too much; I had seen too much; it would hardly do to let me escape to the calm and safe outer world where I could make talk, at least, and perhaps raise a mighty scandal that would put Benson and Company on a hotbed of trouble. No, from my experience with the lot of them, I was convinced that they really would not hesitate to shoot me down on sight.

This whole affair seemed to lie largely outside of the law. Charlie Dexter did not have a strong enough case for the law courts until he got some sort of a confession from one of the main criminals who understood the events of ten years before. And to prevent this, the Dexter Valley gangs would murder both him and me without a scruple and take their chances with the law afterward. For they would be tried in a county where their own men were sure to form a majority of every jury!

You might say that murder would be easier for them than stealing!

So my arguments had little weight with Dexter, and I was glad of it. We turned over to Orchard the two horses which we had been riding the day before, and he gave us the best animals he possessed. This tough old Westerner clung to the Western ideas about horses—that a horse is not a thing of beauty and wisdom, worthy of affection, but a traveling machine which is not for comfort, but to cover miles of bad ground. The result was that his riding stock consisted entirely of hard-mouthed, ugly-headed, ewe-necked, roach-backed mustangs. They looked like caricatures, with their narrow, sloping quarters, and their pot bellies.

Even the special two he had selected for us looked as like the rest as peas from the same pod, but they had proved their staying qualities long ago. I could not help pointing out to Dexter that, if we were sighted on the way by the men of the judge, we were likely to be gobbled up, but Dexter, though he admitted the danger, assured me that I would find them better than they looked.

Then we said good-by to every one on the ranch except Claudia Laffitter. She had to return to Monte Verde, so she went along with us, riding her own pretty bay mare, which was so full of spirit that it kept dancing and prancing all the way along the trail. But I must say something about that farewell at the ranch, before I go on with the narrative of what was to come.

Orchard and his wife, and Jenny, and Slade Livingston shook hands with me in turn, and every one of them gave me a good grip, and each of them assured me that he or she had been glad to know me, and that I never could come to that house too often. They spoke with a real affection, which puzzled me. It was not until I had reached the road that I understood, but as we were jogging along at a soft trot, it occurred to me that all of this demonstration was because I had espoused the cause of Prince Charlie, and no doubt he had told them that I was not doing it for the sake of a material reward.

Well, I went up the road with Claudia and young Dexter, with my head down and a frown not only on my forehead but in my brain. For I was sorry to think that I was taking my last ride with Dexter and that, in all probability, I never should see him again.

He had advised me—and I knew that he was right—not only to leave Dexter Valley, but to get out of Monte Verde, also, and never stop traveling until I was in the East among my own people. That was the plan which I intended to follow, but as we rode along through the burning brightness of that afternoon, my heart ached, for some I reason I could not tell.

I had not known Dexter long, but when one has rubbed elbows with death, those who have been near by take on a new meaning to one's mind. Certainly he had ridden far into my thoughts. And so had the girl.

As we went up the road toward Monte Verde, I could

not help glancing aside at them, now and again. And what I saw saddened me still more. Their case was obvious at a glance. He loved her. His eyes, when they fell upon her, softened with a wonderful, deep light. They slipped from feature to feature, like a caress. They gathered her to him.

And she, for her part, was as frank and open about her state of mind as a good woman should be, never trying in the least to put on affected airs of indifference, never playing the part of the hunted, for the sake of being pursued, never ogling him, never flirting with voice, eye, or smile. But she looked straight at him, and let her soul stand in her eyes. She was like a brave soldier, unashamed to carry his flag even in hostile country. I admired that girl, I think, more than I ever admired another woman. For she was the strength of a mountain stream, and she was the crystal purity and clearness of it also.

Once, I remember, when he had said something that amused her, she broke into hearty, joyous laughter, and in the midst of it put out her gloved hand and took his, and they rode on for a moment like that, their hands joined together, as their spirits already were joined.

I say that this sight saddened me, for I could not help feeling the cloud that hung over Prince Charlie, and the sudden darkness into which he might disappear even on this very first day of their confessed love.

Well, we left the flat of the valley bottom, and we began to climb the first slopes toward the mountains, but Claudia knew of a bypath which wound across the fields, kept much among the trees, and offered a thousand times better shelter than the main road to Monte Verde. She insisted that we take this way.

"But if you know it, they know it—and they know you know it," said Prince Charlie.

However, he allowed himself to be persuaded, though he insisted that the best way was to do the unexpected thing by taking the plain and open road.

We pushed on into a little steep-sided ravine—not a canyon, but a gully with sharply sloping walls, perhaps ten or twelve feet high. I felt an old presentiment as we entered the mouth of this passage, and we were hardly inside it when a horse neighed suddenly behind us. The neigh, however, was cut short, as though a hand had been clapped over the quivering, distended nostrils.

CHAPTER XXXI.   THE TRAP

THE moment that Dexter heard that sound, he snapped to Claudia: "Quick! Quick! Claudia, get your horse up that bank. They're blocking the two ends of the gulch!"

The words hammered against my brain like the brazen clapper of a bell. They were blocking both ends of the ravine! Yes, and how could they have set a neater trap? Claudia did not argue, or protest, or even cry out in the face of danger, but she sent her mare gallantly at the slope.

It was much too steep to be climbed straight up. But that mare was as active as a cat, and going at the bank on a bias, she clawed and pawed her way slowly up it. Claudia, flinging herself by the bridle reins, began to help the mare along, when, suddenly looking back, she saw that we were not following her.

I would gladly have taken the same exit, but as I swung the head of my mustang to follow her, Dexter caught my bridle rein.

"Where we go, we'll draw bullets after us," he said rapidly. "And we don't want shots to fly in her direction, do we?"

Well, for my part, chivalry was not such an instinct that it cropped up in my mind at the first flash. But, shaky though I was, I was willing to try to play follow the leader as well as I could.

"Down the gulch—straight down! Straight back is our only chance," said Dexter. "They'll hold the upper end twice as strongly as the lower one! Follow me, Dean!"

Whether I wanted to or no, I could not help but follow now. When my mustang saw Dexter's mount turn, it bolted in pursuit with such a jerk that I was nearly flung from

169

the saddle. But I managed to hang on, and now literally we had a message that told us we were riding for our lives, for a bullet cut the air above my head and made me duck and my heart shrink.

I got a good knee hold and bowed low over the neck of the mustang, though there was Dexter before me, sitting jauntily erect, ruling the horse with one hand, and with a heavy Colt balanced in the other. Such courage would have put spirit into a lump of wood, and I felt that we might have a ghost of a chance to pull through. He had hardly started before that first rifleman was echoed by half a dozen others, right behind us.

Wes, whether we tried to climb the bank after Claudia or to push up the slope of the ravine, we were sure to have ridden to our death. Of course they would not fire at the girl; she would be safe enough, slowly struggling up the crumbling slope to the top, and then free to ride on toward Monte Verde.

As for us, the twisting floor of the ravine jerked us out of sight and range of the men at the head of the gulch, with the clamoring echoes of their shots still beating about our ears; the down slope doubled the strides of our horses; we had a gantlet before us, and perhaps we could trust to our speed to get through it safely.

I cannot tell why it was, but at that moment I could think of nothing but Judge Benson. His face appeared before me larger than human, a great crimson vision, with the sign of Scorpio drawn across the forehead. Perhaps I saw, or half saw, that specter because I felt the judge was probably at the bottom of the ambuscade that had been laid for us. Perhaps it was one of those peculiar freaks of mind or telepathy which people often have wondered at, but never can explain. I only know that the thing loomed like a red mist before me, for one moment, and rushed backward with the speed of my horse, and then it suddenly disappeared altogether.

Then I had something more than specters to think of. For the rocks and the brush before us blossomed with gunfire!

I should not give the impression that there were a large

number of men planted there in waiting for us. How many there were I could not estimate then; I cannot guess now, though I imagine that there were far less than seemed to me.

No doubt they were taken much by surprise as we came sweeping down the canyon. The rapid sounds of firing from up the gorge must have made them think that we were trying to break through in that direction; perhaps they were hurrying to get in on the death, for as we turned the lowest bend of the ravine, we saw a man rising from behind a boulder and starting to lunge down the slope as fast as he could go, and another fellow was already in the bottom of the little valley and legging it straight toward us as fast as he could step.

Perhaps the rifle fire up the ravine had drowned the sound of our horses, galloping. At any rate, when those two saw us, they screeched with terror and surprise and leaped for cover.

At the same time, as I've said, several men opened on us.

Dexter fired in return. The muzzle of that poised revolver of his dipped down, and jerked up again with the force of the explosion. He was half standing in the stirrups, I suppose in order to ease the shock of the impacts as the horse struck the earth. And I remember thinking, as I followed on hard behind him, weaponless, frightened to death, both my hands gripping the reins alone, that this man was born in the wrong age. He should have lived in the iron Middle Ages and led knights to battle, and broken ranks.

He fired to the left and was answered with a yelp like the cry of a hurt or frightened coyote.

He fired to the right, and suddenly a tall man stood up from behind a rock and did a strange thing—for he began to walk forward with strides which were made clumsy and gigantic by the sharpness of the slope. His arms he held before him like a man walking in the dark. I, for one, surely thought he was mad.

He looked, in fact, like some maniacal enchanter trying to put a spell upon us. Mountain style, his long hair blew back over his shoulders, for he was facing a steady breeze. And it was a long second before I realized that he simply had been shot and very badly wounded by Dexter's second

171

bullet. He did not know what he was doing; he was walking out to meet his death, one might have said.

I saw him, at last, toppling forward, unbalanced.

Then I saw him no more, for the speed of the racing mustang whipped me past.

The gunfire had died on both sides of the mouth of the gulch. That deadly marksmanship of the quarry was too much for the hunters, I have no doubt, and to this day, I never have seen and never have heard of finer shooting. For his horse was flying at full speed, and yet he was able to pick out with such deadly accuracy every enemy who exposed from behind a bush or a rock so much as a leg or a shoulder.

I say that the speed of the horses snatched us through the mouth of that little canyon; and ten seconds from the moment when we heard the whinny of the horse, we were out again in the safety of the open rolling lands.

Safe? Well, as safe as the running of our horses could make us. But not altogether safe, as we soon had notice. We had slipped from the trap just as it was prepared to close over us securely. If it had not been for the neigh of the horse and the lightning deductions of Dexter, or if he had tried to escape in any direction other than the one he chose—flying straight back toward the sound which had alarmed him—we would have been dead, the pair of us—dead in another sixty seconds at the most.

The sun was strong and bright in that ravine, and yet as I saw the landscape opening to either side, I felt as though I had come out of a dark tunnel of night into a free and beautiful day, and the feel of the wind of the gallop against my face was the most delightful thing, I thought, that I ever had experienced.

We put the first half mile behind us in no time; then, as I looked back, I saw a thing that made me groan. For half a dozen riders were urging their horses down the slope in our direction, and more and more appeared from the background of the trees and streamed off in the same direction. I had an odd feeling that we were two strong magnets drawing iron filings toward us. But if one of the filings touched us, the two magnets would surely be dead forever.

172

Yet they made a beautiful picture, those riders on their fine horses, with the bright slopes flashing beneath them like green fire, and the mountains pouring away behind them. Only, it was a beauty rather hard for me to appreciate; especially, the obvious goodness of their long-legged horses turned my heart cold.

I looked at Dexter. To my amazement, instead of whipping up a great speed, he was reining back his mustang to an easier gait. I did the same thing, of course, because I knew that Dexter's wits were better than mine, at such a time. However, I thought he had gone mad.

He cast several glances behind him, and then nodded.

"I think we'll hold them," said he.

"Then they won't catch us, Dexter?" said I, panting like a frightened child.

"I think they won't," said he. "Those horses have had some hard work to do before ever they saw us to-day."

How could he tell that, at such a distance?

Next, he headed into a stretch of rocky hills where the going was three times as bad as before, and where we were continually dipping up and down like small boats on a choppy sea. But our tough little mustangs—I now began to appreciate the tireless, leathery muscles which drove them along—seemed to run as well uphill as down, and half an hour after we entered this rough grazing land, we could look back from each crest and see the pursuit dropping farther and farther behind us.

This had a peculiar effect upon me. Twice I had given myself up for lost within the last hour—once in the gully and once again when the pursuit began. Now, suddenly, I felt that we were invincible—rather, that Dexter was invincible, and I myself perfectly safe in his company. I think, as the emotion gained hold in me, that I would have entered a den of lions, with Dexter to accompany me.

He himself showed no peculiar exultation. One might have thought that hairbreadth escapes were all in the day's work, for him. At any rate, his color did not change or his eye brighten. But as we came through that broken sea of hills, he merely drew the horses back to a jog trot, which I could sit comfortably enough beside him.

173

"Tell me, Charlie," said I. "How were you able to tell that those horses had had hard work before to-day?"

"Why, that was simple," he told me. "The moment they began to run, they were flashing like swords, those horses, which meant that they were wet with sweat, and that meant that they had had their share of work in getting to the rendezvous where they held us up. No mystery about that, Dean. And you see that they've been run into the ground already?"

I could see that, but I pointed out that I was farther from Monte Verde than before, and that I didn't see how we could return to the road safely.

"We can't," said he. "But we can take a roundabout way and hit into the mountains on the right of Monte Verde. You can see the cleft in the hills from here."

CHAPTER XXXII. THE HORSE TAMER

IT was clearly marked, the higher heads of the mountains standing back a little from a narrow depression, though I never should have judged the place to be a pass. It was not, Dexter explained to me, but merely a place where the mountains were much more accessible. And toward this we now rode.

Since we were swinging to the right, still, we now left the hills and descended into the characteristic landscape. The ground was covered with the finest sort of pasture and dotted by many cows, with groves of fine timber in the depressions and even climbing the hills to the top, here and there. To our right, and lower down, the river flamed too bright for belief, and all the opposite side of the valley was softly under shadow by this time in the day. Blue filled the valleys and ravines, and the heads of the mountains gleamed above them like bright spears.

We went on for a considerable time before we saw a human being except for one ragged lad out herding sheep,

174

with a staff and a wide-brimmed hat that gave him the look of a pastoral creature out of another age. But as we rounded the side of a lofty wood, we saw before us a rider who was having a hard time keeping on the back of a horse.

"There's a green hand!" said I.

The horse was bounding high and, coming down with terrible shocks, threw the rider from side to side. Every instant he seemed about to be flung.

"I suppose you could handle a horse like that without hardly more than a bit of a jounce, here and there," said I to Dexter.

He shook his head.

"That's one of the meanest educated buckers that I ever saw," said he, "and the fellow in the saddle is a remarkable man, I'll bet my money."

I stared at Prince Charlie. I began to feel that his recent successes must have turned his head a little; and after all, he had done enough to addle the wits of a much older man than he.

"What makes you think that he is remarkable?" said I.

"Why, look at him," said the young man.

"That's what I'm doing," I answered rather testily.

"Well," said Charlie, "you're seeing fifty cents' worth of rags on a two-thousand-dollar stallion, aren't you?"

There was something in what he said. The rider seemed, from a distance, as badly clothed as you could ask a man to be. Even from a long distance off, one could distinguish the big dark patch between the shoulders of his tan-colored coat. And the horse was a gleaming beauty which one could see by its own light, so to speak.

"Now, then," said Dexter, "what puts a man like that on such a horse?"

"Stolen, perhaps," said I.

"Horse thieves aren't often found in Dexter Valley," said Prince Charlie. "Besides, who would be stealing horses in broad daylight? And such a stallion as that wouldn't be left to run the range, I don't suppose."

We were coming up fast, for the stallion was bucking in a circle, without getting ahead. Its strength seemed unexhausted, its fury rather increasing. But when we were a rope's throw from the horse, it stopped its efforts and stood perfectly still. The tremor of the light along the silk of its flank told me how it was trembling. Its ears were still flattened along its skull, giving its head a snaky look, and it looked about as much of an equine devil as any I ever had seen. However lovely and dangerous as the horse appeared, no one could have spared it a second glance after seeing the face of its rider.

Every one has seen ugly men. Nearly every one has in mind some case of deformity and hideousness which makes a special appeal to him, like a nightmare. Some hate the aquiline hag, and some hate the monkey-faced brute. But I imagine that if a hundred men and women and children had been allowed to see this fellow at the same moment, each would have chosen him above every imagining as the most competently ugly creature in the world.

He was so excessively hideous that, after a moment, one ceased to be frightened. It was marvelous that he could be so deformed and still be a man.

Yet, after looking at him for a while, it seemed more than clear to me that he was not essentially so bad-looking, but might once have had features as regular as those of any other person. He might actually have been a handsome youth. That thought gave me a shudder, seeing what he was now.

For one could see what had happened. He had been kicked or trampled upon. One could almost indicate just where the hoof of the shod horse had struck him. The toe of the hoof had beaten down over the nose and crushed upon the mouth. It left the nose a twisted thing of cartilage, abbreviated as if by some ghastly disease. The mouth was not a mouth. It was a shapeless, ragged, white-and-purple mark, the lips being thickened here and thinned there with lumps of scar tissue or the pull of it. The heels of the shoe had gone home beside the left eye and under the right. And the blow which had been dealt was still printed deeply into the cheek bones.

I have attempted to describe the mouth and lips as I saw them; I cannot describe the eyes. I will only say that

176

one of them was puckered so that it appeared to open unnaturally wide, and the other had been drawn aslant and almost closed; it looked to me as though there had had to be an operation on the eyelid, after the accident, in order to open the lid. As it was, the sight of that eye glimmered at one vaguely, from time to time.

In other words, a perfect mask had been stamped upon a human face, and the mask had, eventually, taken the place of the flesh. In this heaping up of words, however, I don't feel that I have succeeded in giving the slightest impression of the man as he actually was. The horror of him exceeded belief.

I should add that his hair was white, and one did not have to guess at the cause of that premature whiteness; his own face was enough to age him. More than this, there was the splendid and vital youth of his body. A finer pair of athletic shoulders never were put upon a human body, or a chest with a nobler arch. He carried himself like a statue on horseback; sometimes I swore he was a devil masquerading as a man, and at other times that he was a man masquerading as a devil. In either case, he would have been successful.

Dexter greeted him with a wave of his hand and a word for the stallion which, dripping with sweat, stood in the flare of the sun like a creature made of light.

"That's a grand thing you're riding," said Dexter.

The other shrugged his shoulders.

"A horse is a horse," said he.

"And some horses are ten," said Dexter.

The stranger smiled. That is, he tried to smile, and as a smile one might interpret the wave of disturbance which passed over that frightful face.

"Some horses are ten devils," said he. "This is one, and the son of a devil, and he'll be the father of devils after him."

"The son of a devil? You know his breeding pretty well then?"

"Yes. I owned the sire."

"Thoroughbred, I'd say," said Prince Charlie.

"You'd say wrong," replied the stranger. "There ain't

an ounce of thoroughbred blood in him. He's all mustang, that's what he is. So was his father before him."

"You mean a wild caught one?"

"That's what I mean. No tame rubbish. Blast the things that most cow-punchers call horses!"

He pointed toward our own mounts as he spoke, and I expected Dexter to take immediate offense. Instead, he merely smiled.

"These horses are good enough for us," said Dexter. "But what's the difference between a wild mustang and a tame one?"

"What's the difference between a man in jail and a man out of jail?" asked the stranger savagely.

"Well, there may be something in that," said Dexter.

"There's more than something. There's a mighty lot in it!"

"I'll be willing to admit that, I think."

"Did you ever hunt them, young feller?"

"No. You have, I gather."

"Yeah. You can gather that. I've hunted 'em. I've spent months on the trail behind 'em. I've spent a year and a half after one horse."

"That's not a way to get rich, I suppose?" suggested Dexter.

The temper of the stranger was very short.

"Do I look rich?" said he.

"No," replied Dexter, running his eye deliberately over him. "You don't look rich."

So insultingly cool was that surveying glance that now I expected the stranger to take offense, but a picture of the horse hunt had flashed now upon the eye of his mind and appeared as a flame in his face.

"His tail was the flag that I followed a year and a half. The daddy of that bit of life and fire! I wanted to breed him. I wouldn't mix his blood with common stock. Not me! I wanted the same strain. Where would I get it? I spent six months or so listening to reports, following them up, hunting here and there, riding thousands of miles. Finally I got on the trail of a gray mare. You see, he's her color? Iron in the legs and silver in the body. I worked

178

only a month for her, but I rode five horses to death!"

Suddenly his lips parted, and he laughed.

I am not a sentimental man. I have seen a great deal of misery, and I have endured enough on my own account to make me selfish. But when I saw the horrible distortion of that face with laughter and heard the sound of merriment flowing out, tears sprang suddenly into my eyes, and I had to look down to the ground.

"That's more than two years to get the parent stock," observed Dexter.

"And another year and a half to wait for the foal, while the debt collectors chased me all through the country!"

He snarled as he said it.

But I respected him and began to forget his deformity a little. Every man's heart goes out to another who had followed an enthusiasm with all his might, as this man had followed the ideal beauty of the range.

Well, he was a cartoon of a man, of course, and his clothes were in tatters, and yet I envied him. No matter how ugly the disposition of that brute of a stallion might be, the thing was a treasure, and this wanderer, this man with the one idea, the one creature, had found the source and made the horse.

That was why I envied him and that was why Dexter looked on him with an odd respect. Or, at least, so I thought.

Said Dexter: "We have a need of a good, fast horse, my friend. What do you call this one?"

"Compadre."

"A friendly name for such a mean devil. Is there a price on him?"

"Oh, there's a price on everything in the world," said the stranger. "Bring me a diamond as big as he is, and I'll give him to you!"

CHAPTER XXXIII.
THE STRANGER'S STORY

I SMILED, but Dexter did not. "That's a reasonable price," said he, "if a man has to owe his life to the four feet of a horse. Some day he may get away from you, stranger."

"Some day he may, and then he'll never be caught. He knows too much about men to be caught by them, once he runs wild. You've seen his eyes, eh?"

Dexter nodded. I could see what they meant, by the thing in its eyes. The brute had the look of a hawk. Every time it unhooded its eye or turned it toward one, there was the same unquenchable fire in it.

"He'll buck while he runs," said the stranger.

"But he's never put you off?"

"A hundred times—in the corral. But once I learned his tricks, I've been able to trust myself to him. It takes hand and heel to ride him, though, when he begins his devil's play."

"Yes," said Dexter. "I can see that."

His head was back. He looked at that beautiful fiend of a horse as if at a lovely woman. I never have seen such desire in a face.

"You may hunt wild horses yourself, some day," said the stranger.

Dexter nodded. "Are you living here in the valley?" he asked.

"Bah! Why should I live in a little barnyard like this?" said the other.

"Simply traveling through?"

"Why are *you* here?" asked the ugly face.

"What has that to do with it?" said Dexter rather sharply.

"Simply this: I am here for the same reason that brings you, my friend."

I started. Well, it was enough to make any one start, to hear such a thing—considering that I *knew* why Dexter was there.

"Suppose you tell me that reason?" said Dexter.

"You are Dexter?" said the other.

"You know me, do you?"

"Who else would they be hunting in Dexter Valley?" said the other.

"Well, you've heard about me, but what makes you think that I've been hunted to-day?"

"Your horses are dripping, but you look happy, as though you had won something."

There was a naïve shrewdness about this remark that went deep into my mind.

"You have a pair of eyes," said Dexter, smiling.

"Thank you," said the stranger. And he yawned, as though suddenly he had become weary of the talk, and of us.

"Still you haven't told me why I'm here."

"Scorpio!" said the other.

"Hello!" exclaimed Dexter. "And what have you to do with Scorpio?"

The face of the horseman contorted strangely. It was hard to conceive of that face becoming more ugly, but he achieved that impossibility.

"What have I to do with the devil, you might as well ask!" said he "I've tried to get rid of him. I could not. I have tried to keep away from him, but now here you see me, hunting for his trail, sure to kill him if I find him—yet when we meet, he will smile his handsome smile, and I shall be his slave again."

I wondered if his battles with horses and his pursuits after them might not have addled the brain of this man. He grew very excited. His strange eyes flashed at us, as he went on:

"It will be: 'Tonio, *amigo mio!*' when he sees me again, and then I shall forget murder and stealing and lying and make-believe. I shall trust him once more, and once more he will make a fool of me. Unless I can catch him with a bullet before he has a chance to open his lips!"

181

If I suspected madness before, I was sure of it now. The color of that horrible face changed and became yet more awful, and the eyes still burned at us, as though he asked us to share his misery.

"Yes," said Dexter. "The main reason that I'm here is Scorpio. Some people know it. Others may guess it. How did you come to know?"

"Through Scorpio himself. How else would I know such a thing?"

That seemed obvious enough.

"He knew a long time ago?" asked Dexter. "He knew that I was coming, I mean?"

"Oh, many days. He knew all about it, and where you would go."

"To Monte Verde?"

"Yes."

"That's strange," said Dexter. "I didn't know that myself, until the day before I got there."

"This is what he said, that one! 'He will come to the edge of the valley and look at his land, like a horse hanging his head over a pasture fence. Like a horse standing in a naked road, and looking over a fence at a rich pasture land, amigo. That is what he will do. He will go to Monte Verde, from which one can see the whole of Dexter Valley.'"

"He told you that?"

"Yes, and in those words. And he went off to Monte Verde to get there before you."

Dexter looked sharply and suddenly at me, and I met him with a glance of exactly the same sort. The thing was getting beyond the bonds of common sense and credence. However, here was this man—mad or not—who apparently was talking a sort of sense—and it was about Scorpio!

"Suppose that we ride on a little together?" said Dexter. "Or are you going this way?"

"Oh, all ways are the same to me," said the other. "Why should I leave you? If you want to find Scorpio, you may be sure that Scorpio wants to find you. And if I stay with you, I'll meet him face to face again. Then for a quick hand and a sure shot!"

182

His hand leaped to his holster. Flash-like though the movement was, Dexter with a motion even faster covered him instantly with a steady revolver. But the other did not seem to see. A heavy gun was in his hand, and, exploding, the bullet from it spatted fairly and squarely into the center of a small sapling some ten yards away. It was not a truly wonderful bit of shooting, I suppose, but it was enough to open my eyes. That sapling was not more than three inches across. And the heart of a man is bigger than that!

I was somewhat ashamed of my friend Dexter, who did not put up his weapon until Tonio had sheathed his.

"Well," said Dexter, "I'd be glad to have you with me—particularly glad if I can meet Scorpio while you're along. What's made you hate him so?"

"Listen to me," said the other.

And then, softening his harsh voice a little, and canting back his head, with half-closed eyes, like a practiced narrator, he began to tell us his story.

I grew so interested in it that I think for as much as a mile at a time I failed to look behind me toward the woods and hills from which, at any moment, I expected a line of furious riders to burst out at us.

"You see me, what I am now?" began Tonio. "Well, not so many years ago, I was a man!

"Believe me, señor, I was a man to be looked at twice. I was tall, straight, handsome. Women dropped their eyes on me twice, when I went by. Men liked me, too. I had many friends. I did not drink. I did not gamble more than once a month, on pay day. When people saw me coming, they used to wave their hands and shout: 'Hey! Here comes Tonio! Now things will liven up!' That was the sort of a man I was.

"Well, you see me now?"

He turned to us, and extended both his hands with a peculiar gesture of empty questioning, as though all eyes could see the frightful gulf into which he had fallen out of the old days. And it was true. Even a child could have seen.

"My heart was gentle and soft, in those years, amigos,"

183

went on Tonio. "Now my hand is hard, but my heart is still harder. Because of Scorpio.

"Oh, the fiend and the man together! When he said that he was my friend, how could I help but believe him? I could not help it. When he smiled, I thought he was the best man I ever knew. When he drank with me, the mescal tasted like fire and honey. When he talked with me, I felt that the world was flowing over with friendship. Do you understand?"

"Yes," said I.

But Dexter said nothing. He watched the hideous face of Tonio like a man in a waking dream.

"Even the girl I loved liked me better when Scorpio was with me," continued Tonio.

"Why not? Scorpio was a famous fellow. He had killed men. And he called me his friend. He slapped me on the shoulder and told the girl how much I meant to him. It was a new world, he said, since he had met me. Tears used to come into my eyes when I heard him praise me. And he would be always finding things with his money and ——"

"There was blood on that money," said Dexter dreamily.

Tonio clapped a hand to his face, and I had another pang of shame on account of Dexter's behavior. There was no use in turning the knife in the heart of poor Tonio.

"There was blood on it! There was blood on it!" he exclaimed, with a wail of horror in his voice. "That I know now, but I was a boy and a fool, in those days, and how could I tell? I only saw that he was great and famous and that all eyes trailed after him. 'You are Scorpio's friend,' they used to say to me. 'Have a drink, and tell us something about him!' And I used to drink and swell up my chest and tell them.

"Well, Scorpio would give me a great deal of money. There was nothing he had that I could not have, for the asking. There was no bottom to his purse for me. And he was always suggesting ways of spending it. For the girl, too. I bought her fine mantillas, and little diamonds, and rings, and everything that a girl's heart desires, and every day when I brought her something I would say: 'My love, when are we to be married?'

184

"And she would say: 'When my Uncle Egberto returns from the city.' Or else she would say: 'My poor mother is ill now. I must not talk about such things.' And so she put me off. Oh, what a fool I was! I was blind. Tears of friendship were in my eyes and blinded me. And so it went on. There was everything before my eyes. But I could not see.

"I only knew that she was often silent when I went to her alone. But when I went to her with the grand Scorpio, then she would talk and laugh.

"One day I went, and she was not there. She was gone. Scorpio had taken her. Scorpio had taken her, and I never would see her again. She was struck out of my life. She was stolen out of my heart. She slipped from my hand, and Scorpio caught her, and I never could see her pretty face again!"

And, as he said this, he beat his hands against his ugly face, and the tears poured out of his eyes.

CHAPTER XXXIV.   WILDFIRE

I WOULD rather see a city full of women and children cry than to watch one man break down. I would rather hear a world of women mourning than to listen to the sobbing of one grown man.

And this fellow Tonio seemed to have such an overplus of manliness in him, and he had such an excess of even fierce courage, as it seemed to me, that when that patient tamer of wild horses began to sob, I trembled from head to foot and looked to Dexter, as though to ask him to put a stop to this frightfulness.

But Dexter, upon my word, seemed to find nothing essentially horrible or shocking in what he heard and saw. He still had that dreamy look. He was like some one reading a tale in a book, rather than one who sees frightful reality in flesh and voice.

This upset me a good deal, and my early doubts about the youth returned in a flood. He was too much of iron. I wanted more of a human being. Suddenly I pitied pretty Claudia Laffitter, that fine, womanly girl.

Well, Tonio did master himself. With utter shamelessness, he lost himself in his grief, and it was only when his tears had run out, so to speak, that he finally turned to me and resumed the story.

"You wanted to kill him, of course," said I.

"Yes, yes!" said Tonio. "But when I met him again, I smiled and pretended that it was nothing."

"And the girl? She was still with him?"

"Still with him? How long can a woman live with a fiend? No, no! She was gone. She was gone so far that even Scorpio did not know where she was. Do you see? He had let her fall away from him. He would not lift his hand to save her.

"Well, he seemed glad to meet me again. He said that women were as nothing, compared to the friendship that lives between men and men. I smiled in his face, and I put poison in his food. But the fiend in him caused him to change the dishes. I ate a little, and nearly died. Then I knew that there *was* a devil in Scorpio, and that he was not merely a man, like other men!

"But afterward, I could not help growing fond of him again. He was always with me. And people began to notice me again. For I was Scorpio's friend. Oh, I could tell stories that would last all night, about what Scorpio was and what he had done!"

"Did you ever," said Dexter, "tell the story of what he did in this valley, ten years ago?"

"Ten thousand times!" exclaimed Tonio. "I told how he put the signs on the doors. I told how much money he was given. I told how he met the Dexters and shot them down. Of course I told those things!"

"Very strange," said Dexter. "Now that I think back to Scorpio, I would not dream that he was the kind of a fellow to chatter about his own actions."

"Ha!" cried Tonio. "What do *you* know about him? How long have you lived with him? How many meals have you eaten with him, how many drinks have you had with him, how many songs have you heard him sing?"

Dexter made a gesture of admission, but in his face it seemed to me that there was still a lingering shadow of doubt.

"We used to go gambling together," went on Tonio. "The day while the sun was shining never was long enough for Scorpio, but he had to use the night, also. He would get along very well with two or three hours of sleep. So he used to drag me along. Sometimes my eyes were so heavy that they closed as I sat at the gaming table.

"And I played away everything I had. I played away my land, my horses, my saddles, my clothes.

"Once I said to him: 'Manuel, look how I stand here! I am dressed, but it is in murder. I have money in my pocket, but it is murder, also. For I know how you fill your purse!'

"Always Scorpio gave me more.

"At that, he laughed in my face. 'Drink again, Tonio,' was all that he said. 'Drink to our friendship!'

"I threw the glass down on the floor. It broke into a thousand pieces. I put my face in my hands and wept like a child. But Scorpio put his hand on my shoulder.

" 'If I am not your friend, any longer, who will be a friend to Tonio?' said he.

"Then I started up and looked around me. No man was watching me, except with a sneer. They knew that I had taken the money of a murderer, drunk his drinks, eaten his food, made myself warm in his clothes. I was to them worse than Scorpio. He, at least, was a man, even if his hands were red. The women, most of all, still loved him. The worse he became, the more they loved him. That is the way with women. But I saw, on that day, that I was alone. Scorpio had driven away the rest of the world from me. I was all alone!

"Then I jerked a knife from my belt.

" 'I shall kill you, Scorpio!' I screamed at him, and I leaped on him. He only laughed at my rage and my knife. His hand is harder than iron. With it he beat down my arm, and he stabbed me here, in the throat!"

With this, Tonio pulled open his shirt at the throat, and I saw a great whitish scar—a big lump above the collar bone.

"I should have died, and I should have been glad to die," said Tonio. "But Scorpio would not let me. He used to come and sit for hours at the side of my bed. He made me love life again. He used to talk to me about spring flowers, and the long white windings of the moonlight road, and the tang of tequila, and women, and dancing, and fine horses, fine horses, fine horses! Such horses as he had seen, wild, running over the mountains of Mexico!

"I decided that I would live, and when a man decides that, he cannot die.

"So I lived once more. I was strong. I walked. I went away with Scorpio, and he showed me how to hunt the wild horses.

"Well, in the first corral that we built, I was caught and beaten by a wild beast of a mustang. He smashed in my face. And Scorpio dragged me out of the dust and sat down beside me, and tied up the wounds, and sewed up the ragged flesh, and laughed at me, laughed at me, and laughed. And there was always mirth bubbling in his throat like water in a well."

"Good heavens!" I broke out. "The man really is an incarnate fiend."

"Tush!" said Tonio. "What do you know? Nothing, never having seen him! But I know him. I have had him by my bed all night. I have seen him in the sun and in the shadow, and I know what he is. I know the taste of bitterness, because I know Scorpio. And now I tell you this, that the fever which he put into my blood would not leave me.

"I thought that the blow of the horse would either kill or cure me of my fondness for Scorpio and his ideas, but I was wrong. Yes, I was wrong, and therefore he proved it. He showed me the great stallion. It was dawn, and the morning sun was not as bright as the silver stallion on the top of the hill.

"I saw the horse, and for a year and a half I followed it, as I have told you."

188

"Was Scorpio with you at the time?" I asked.

"Scorpio? Why should he waste his time dragging over the hills, that handsome Scorpio, when there were murders to be done and money to be made and spent on women and drink? No, no! Scorpio was back in a soft bed, and I was starving and freezing and burning on that trail.

"But when I came back with the prize, then you may be sure that Scorpio met me again. He told me the horse was beautiful, and that only I could do the thing. No one else could have remained a year and a half on a trail, not even he. He looked into my face, and told me that I should wear a mask for others, but that for him, my face did not matter. For did he not see my heart?

"Oh, that such a man should have been put on the earth to burn my soul with fire!

"And I went off and caught the mare, because he told me that it would be a good thing, and because he had praised me and called me the greatest horse catcher in the world. So I caught the mare, too, and brought her back, and I spent the patient months until at last this foal was born.

"And Scorpio used to ride the stallion, while I remained in the dust, watching the foal. He would dress himself up like a king, and ride out and smile at the women, and they would tell one another how splendid he was. A rascal, but what a splendid rascal! That is the way that women always have talked about him. One day I had a great quarrel with him. I told him to go away forever. I told him that I wanted to be a free man, and have clean hands. And he laughed at me, but he said that he would go. He would ride down to say good-by to his friends. And he took the stallion.

"He never came back!"

"Hold on," said I. "Did he steal the stallion?"

"They came running to tell me. I hurried down to the plaza. I could not believe it. I could not believe anything they had said to me. Words could not express such a thing. But I came to the plaza, and there was my beautiful silver stallion lying dead. I sat down and took his head in my lap. Even his dead eyes were brighter than the eyes of any other creature, man, or beast."

"And then you swore that you *would* kill Scorpio?" said I.

"Yes," said he. "Then I set out on the son of the old stallion. I set out on his horse, though he was not yet ready for riding. He still has the wild fire in him. You see it in his eyes. Such were the eyes of his father, but the father began to know me and love me, in the end. I have had him come to my hand, and I have had him drop his muzzle on my shoulder."

Tonio looked up, with the face of one who remembers heaven, and my heart bled for the poor, simple, half-mad fellow.

But, when I looked askance at Dexter, his head was canted critically to one side, and he was frowning.

A moment later came trouble, a bolt from the blue for poor Tonio, and the very thing that he had dreaded and prophesied.

The gray stallion was wildfire. No doubt of that. It was wildfire, and now its nature flared suddenly.

It was only a sudden pool of dust that started whirling up the road in the wind, but as it came under the nose of the stallion, the horse bounded to the side farther than most horses could bound forward. Tonio, the eyes of whose mind had been fixed so firmly upon the heaven of a pleasant recollection—how few there were in his starved life—was suddenly sitting in the dust, in a way that would have made people laugh.

But not even a fool could laugh, to see the gray horse bounding away, free, riderless, irreclaimable forever, as Tonio himself had declared!

CHAPTER XXXV. THE PRINCE RIDES

THE very instant that the stallion leaped away, I heard the quick, subdued voice of Dexter at my ear: "Watch Tonio!" And the next moment, he flashed by me with his spurs fastened in the flank of the galloping mustang, and his right hand unshipping his coiled lariat.

I saw Tonio's priceless horse bound over a low hedge of brier. The mustang skimmed it in pursuit, and the long, snaky shadow of the rope darted out from the hand of Dexter. It slid forward right over the head of the stallion, but the latter bounded to the side, the noose fluttered and failed of its mark, and away went Tonio's horse, leaving the mustang hopelessly behind.

It was like watching a train slide away from a man running on foot. I could have laughed again, except that I saw the ghastly importance of the thing to Tonio. The horse was his life, his soul. He had risen from the dust and held in his hand a drawn revolver.

"Look out, Tonio!" I shouted at him. "Don't shoot. The bullet might fly wide and strike Dexter."

Tonio turned his head a little and gave me a fleeting glance which might have meant anything—or nothing. It seemed apparent that he regarded me not at all.

In the meantime, there was a sudden change.

The stallion, bolting gloriously for freedom, had run straight on toward a dense grove of poplars, but as it came near them, it veered away from the trees. It might have been that the trunks were packed together too closely to please the horse; or perhaps there was in its consciousness some buried distrust of woods that now darted into its mind strongly, or perhaps it was the silver flashing of the leaves, as the wind turned them.

At any rate, there the stallion was, turned and rushing at right angles to its former course, while Dexter, who

191

had not flagged in the chase in spite of the way he was being distanced, now swung to the right and cut across the bias to get at the great horse.

How the stallion flew now! I seemed to be seeing it in two places at once, it so lengthened and stretched itself and shot across the face of the wood. But the mustang, running across a short arc, now came momentarily closer, and again the regathered rope shot out from the hand of Dexter.

The mustang, planting its feet, sat down against the pull, and over the head and neck of the great horse dropped the noose. I held my breath. The shock came. The rope leaped taut, disappeared from sight in a humming vibration, and then snapped with a loud report.

Yet there was enough of that shock to send the stallion spinning, head over heels, and to knock the mustang over, as well. Mustang, stallion, and Dexter were all in a trice tumbling on the field. I thought three necks had been broken, but Dexter was up again in a second—and running straight toward the stallion.

The latter heaved itself up; the mustang, also, was struggling to its feet, and I began to think that all the three combatants were made of whalebone and India rubber. As for the stallion, it had plenty of time to get away, but the fall appeared to have stunned it a little. It shook its head, like a hard-hit boxer, and then, seeing the man suddenly beside it, jumped like a cat to one side. But Dexter had the full speed of his sprint still with him, and that feint did not fool him. He swerved, and in a moment he had sprung into the saddle.

He had neither stirrup.

The stallion leaped into the blue of the sky, with Dexter clinging like a long-clawed tiger, his body flinging into the air.

Down came the great horse, and as it landed, by fortune or by consummate skill and strength of arm, Dexter so handled himself that he landed in the saddle.

"A miracle!" cried Tonio, close beside me.

Well, it was a miracle, well enough, from my point of view; but the amazement of the hardy horseman, Tonio, held my attention a little. From that moment my eyes were divided between the fighting horse and the Mexican who owned it. I could remember, now, that Dexter had told me to watch Tonio, and he certainly was worth watching.

The bucking stallion, as it fought and raged, came back closer to us. And again the gun was poised in the hand of Tonio.

"Listen to me, Tonio!" I shouted. "Don't shoot. You may hit Dexter instead of the horse—besides, he'll ride the stallion. You see if he doesn't!"

"The horse will kill him!" scheeched Tonio. "Look! Look!"

For the stallion, beginning to whirl in amazingly swift circles, made the body of Dexter swing far to the side.

I looked to see him hurled to the ground like a stone and then, perhaps, that devil of a horse would pause long enough to trample the youth, before making off to freedom on the heights.

But, gaining a fresh handhold, Dexter drew himself upright again. At that, the stallion reared and toppled backward to crush the persistent rider. It was a horrible sight. The big beast flung backward like a falling mountain, and I looked to see Dexter crushed to pieces.

But he slipped to the side and landed clear, and as the horse pitched rapidly to its feet once more, again Prince Charlie was in the saddle.

It was not, really, like a man fighting a horse, but a tiger battling with some formidable monster. That was how Dexter clung. That was how the stallion raged.

But still I could not watch the horse and man altogether. There was Tonio, who was worth a good deal of attention. He seemed more than half hysterical. There was his treasure, his priceless horse, on the verge of regaining freedom, and only prevented from running free by a man whose skill in the saddle, no matter how great, was, I judged, less than that of Tonio himself. The latter knew the tricks and wiles and ways of the great horse. He could not imagine, it seemed, that another man possibly could sit the saddle on the monster.

Therefore, much as he loved the stallion, he had his revolver still poised. Twice and again I thought that he

193

was about to fire—to save young Dexter from being dismounted and destroyed. Twice I yelled at him, and my yell seemed to give him pause. Again, several times, when the fighters and their dust cloud swept closer to us, Tonio would run out as though he hoped that he could help with his bare hands in the struggle.

But, finally, he burst out into a prayer, invocation, and hymn of praise and advice which ran something as follows:

"Brace yourself, amigo. He will reverse! There! God in Heaven, watch and be kind! Fool of a gringo, he has you off—no! The kind saints hold you up with their strong hands—pull harder. Get in his chin against his breast. Courage! Oh, brave lad! Dog of a Compadre—man-eater! Hi, he has it! No, no! The spur, the spur! Straighten him out. Now he will whirl. Oh, brave lad! What a prince of men! Look, look! It is the end!"

At the last words, he turned to me and, casting out his hands, seemed to ask my admiration of the scene and the accomplishment of young Dexter. At the same time, Tonio dropped his revolver in the dust of the trail and began to dance and shout more like a madman than ever before.

Dexter, in fact, finally seemed to get the stallion under control. I have no doubt that the battle would have ended the other way if the strength and the verve of that big, shining devil had not been half exhausted not long before by the battle with his true master. But, at any rate, there had been enough power remaining to Compadre to make his bucking seem like a series of explosions. Now, he was spent, or rather—for his eye seemed as flashing bright as ever—he had given up for the moment and would bide a better opportunity to unhorse this rider, as he had done the last one.

As the dripping and shining horse came up to us, I thought that I saw a fresh and invincible malice in its expression. For my own part, I would as soon have sat on the back of a Bengal tiger.

But when Dexter came, he dismounted, gave the reins to the Mexican, and soberly went off to catch his own mount, which was easily done. After that, he rejoined us, brushing off the dust and the grass which he had picked up in his fall in the first place.

I could see that he was pale now, and that there was a thin trickle of crimson from his nose—so terrible had been the shocks of that combat. But he made nothing of his exploit. He was as undisturbed as ever and seemed surprised by the praises which Tonio heaped upon him.

The latter was in a new ecstasy as he sat in his saddle once more, restored, one would have said, to the back of an eagle. He patted the wet neck of the horse, swore at it, blessed it, promised it a whipping—and a big feed of oats at the first chance. It was hard to make out whether he were more pleased by regaining the stallion or by the magnificent fight which the animal had put up for freedom.

But even more than the actions of Tonio, my attention was taken by the behavior of young Dexter, who hung back from us even more than before the battle, and somehow seemed to regard Tonio with more suspicion than ever before.

When Tonio turned to him with extravagant praises and called him the one caballero in the world, Dexter merely shrugged his shoulders and continued to look at the Mexican as if at a strange monster. I thought this had to do with the hideousness of the poor fellow's face, and fresh anger against the young man rose in me.

It was now well on into the afternoon, and we could see the cows down at the edge of the river standing belly deep in the water with their images floating dimly before them. The sun was behind a western peak, but it would be a long hour or more before it sank beneath the true horizon, and the upper sky was very brilliant.

Now Dexter paused to tighten his cinches, and while the Mexican drifted a little ahead, I obeyed a small signal from Dexter's hand and lingered beside him.

He talked rapidly as he worked at the straps.

"Dean, I intend to stay down here in the valley this evening. Out of the Mexican I think that I can get the full story of what Scorpio did that night ten years ago. The story will be useful. But I'll need a witness, and you're the man. The trouble is that he won't talk in front of you."

"He has so far," said I.

"Don't argue. Believe me when I tell you that he won't talk about it in front of you. But not far from here there's a shack. When we get to it, I'll suggest to Tonio that we spend the night there. He'll agree. I'll advise you to start off for Monte Verde. You'll go. Then, from a little distance, make a detour, slip up to the shack, and try to get in hearing distance. You have a pencil and plenty of paper. Write down what you hear, if there's still enough evening light left for it."

I gaped at Dexter, but as he remounted, I nodded, and started down the road with him toward the place where Tonio was impatiently waiting for us.

CHAPTER XXXVI.   EAVESDROPPING

COMPLICATED schemes have, on the very face of them, a suggestion which, if it is not crooked, is at least a little shady, and the suggestion of Young Dexter annoyed me a good deal. However, I was so far advanced into his schemes that I felt I had to take them and him more or less for granted. For that reason, I decided that I would do just as he told me to do, no matter how ill at ease I might be.

In a very grumpy mood, I rejoined Tonio, and we three continued on our way until the increasing rose and gold of the sky told us that the sun was setting. In the meantime, I had been turning back and forth in my mind everything that Dexter had said to me, and liking it less and less every minute, you may be sure. Secrecy and spying never had been powers of mine nor ones to which I aspired. I liked people and affairs to be out in the open. I felt that the youth had inveigled me into a wrong situation, and I was increasingly angry.

196

At about this time, we sighted, as Dexter had prophesied, a small shack which stood between two hills, with a darkness of trees behind and a swift little run of water angling about the side of it. Once it had been the beginning of a ranch, I suppose, for there was a scattered wreckage of fencing near by, and the blackened remains of a barn which had burned down. The sense of desolation, however, was ameliorated by the shrubbery which was growing up everywhere. This section was not under cultivation. There were not even many cattle near by. And as a result, the forest was reclaiming its former ground.

When Dexter saw the place, he immediately suggested to the Mexican that they should halt there for the night. Tonio agreed willingly. I suspected that one of his reasons for being so glad of our company was that he himself had not a handful of provisions. We had no sooner dismounted than Dexter told me that I ought to forge ahead and get through the pass into the mountains before the utter darkness set in. Then I could work my way toward Monte Verde.

My safety, he said, would be assured by the fact that he was there in the valley, and there was little doubt that, if the enemy were trailing us, they would prefer hunting him to hunting me. I looked up to the ominous roughness of the mountains—we were now directly under the pass— and, as I had before agreed, consented to go.

So I said good-by to him and Tonio, and put as much emotion into my farewell to Dexter as I could manage to do, and regretted aloud that I was forced to leave him in this manner before his adventures were finished. He, like a handsome young hypocrite, made quite a speech to me about courage, kindness, unforgettable goodness to him, and a lot of other things which almost made me blush for the young rascal.

Then I went off toward the mountains.

Perhaps I need not be ashamed to admit that after I got well on the way, I was more than half tempted to go straight on and make this not a feint but a real maneuver to get me back to Monte Verde. So long as I had felt a straightforward honesty in Dexter, I had not minded so much the various dangers which I had been through for his sake, but now that I suspected him of double-dealing with poor Tonio, I was thoroughly disgusted with the entire business.

Besides, I could not understand what was in his mind, or what there was about poor Tonio that should rouse in one anything more than pity. The unlucky Mexican, nevertheless, seemed to be a mine in which Dexter wanted to work, and I had promised my secret assistance.

It was, in short, a plot; and I loathed my share in it. However, a promise given is a load that must be carried, and when I had gone up through the trees, following the winding trail for nearly half an hour, I turned about and came back to the house.

On the verge of the trees, I tethered my mustang and then started stalking the place. The moment I began to do this, I felt decidedly uneasy. Dexter would protect me if he could, I was sure, but the Mexican had a very nervous way with his gun, as he had proved before this, and if he saw something crawling toward them in the house, he might be apt to split my skull with a bullet just as he had split the slender trunk of the sapling.

There was a good deal of cover to soothe my nerves, however. There were some outcropping rocks behind which I crawled, and several patches of shrubbery that sufficiently veiled me, and so it was that I came right up to the wall of the house, at last.

The two were not in it. They had made a fence of big stones to hide their firelight, and having kindled a blaze within this screen, they were cooking supper. So I crept around the farther side of the house and, at the corner, flattened myself out on the ground. Still obeying the dictates of Dexter, I took out a pencil and the note pad which old habit always kept in my pocket. Thus equipped, I waited here, and noted that there was still enough light remaining for a good many minutes of writing.

But they were not talking of Scorpio, when I came up. It was all about the trail of the mare which, it appeared, though so much shorter had been almost as exciting as the pursuit of the first great stallion. And I remember that the aroma of the coffee, floating toward me made me almost sick with hunger. For another thing, in my position, the rim of my coat collar chafed against the sunburned back of my neck, and often made me grit my teeth with irritation. Yet there I had to wait like an angler for the shadow of a rising fish.

And presently I saw it coming.

"Do you know what you could do?" Dexter asked the Mexican.

"Tell me, my friend," said Tonio.

"Why, you could send the law after him and hang him, if you have enough testimony to use against him."

"Well, the law has been after him long enough, but they never will find him!"

"No?"

"No, no! They never will find Scorpio. He is much too cunning for them. I tell you, señor, that there is no man in the world but myself who can put hands on Scorpio!"

"I'll have to believe you," said Dexter. "But I don't see why another man might not have a pretty good chance, at that!"

"You would not understand," said the Mexican.

He had finished eating, and now he poised a coffee cup in his hand, the tin flashing with the reflected light of the fire, which was now a little stronger, close at hand, than the light of the failing day.

"At any rate," said Dexter, "he was a fool to tell you all of his secrets."

"He could not help it," said Tonio.

"Why not?"

"Because I told him all of mine."

There was a simplicity—if not a weak-mindedness—about this answer that made me pity Tonio and scorn Dexter more than ever.

"So he had to exchange his ideas with yours?" continued Dexter.

"Yes, of course. You cannot get at the heart of a man unless you give him some of your own in exchange."

"Well, that may be, but when it came to talking about

the Dexter murders—you can't persuade me that he told you about them."

"Cannot I persuade you, señor? Señor Dexter, do you wish to make me angry, doubting what I tell you to be true?"

"Come, come," said Dexter, laughing a little. "It may simply be that Scorpio was joking. Who can tell? You know that men don't talk about murders freely—not ones for which their own necks could be stretched."

"As if Scorpio ever were afraid of hanging!" exclaimed Tonio. "But then, it's plain that you never knew him!"

"But I did," said Dexter. "My own belief is that somebody else put the signs on the doors and on the foreheads of the dead men. That fellow Scorpio—why, he was as gentle as a girl, as a matter of fact. He was the gayest young fellow on the ranch, and my father liked him the best of the lot."

"That was why he would not kill your father," said Tonio.

And, at this, I began to write with a furious haste. My business had often caused me to have practice in rapid writing in order to put down minutes swiftly, and though there were frequent pauses in the talk, yet now I was fairly tasked to keep up with the current of it, accurately. However, I started writing, and the white of the page turned gray with the failing light, and the dullness of the evening tarnished the paper and made me strain my eyes until, finally, I was writing more by habit and guesswork than by vision.

It was not mere desire to obey Dexter in what I had promised him to do; after the first few words, I was writing with a furious desire to give the law a document which would enable it to bring justice upon the heads of guilty people—people concerned in the plotting and the execution of a most infernal crime.

CHAPTER XXXVII.

"Of course they wanted him to do that, if they wanted him to do anything," said Dexter.

"Yes, they wanted that. They knew that your father was the greatest of the fighting men on the ranch."

"Well, that's true," said Dexter. "And I begin to think that Scorpio did tell you something of the truth."

"Something? Oh, but he told me the whole truth."

"One thing I'll wager that he did not tell."

"What is that, then?" asked Tonio, his voice rising to meet the challenge that was implied.

"Why, then, he wouldn't tell you why he preferred to murder Marshall and Vincent Dexter rather than my father, Jefferson, when it was my father that had flogged him."

At this, Tonio began to laugh, and the sound sent a chill running quicksilverlike up and down my spine.

"You think that the flogging had anything to do with it?" he asked.

"What other good reason was there, Tonio?"

"A flogging? A murder to pay back for a flogging?"

"Well, but I don't know what else had been done against him."

"Nothing had been done against him," said Tonio. "That devil, that Scorpio, he simply wanted to do something grand and great."

At this, I fairly gaped at the paper to which I was committing the story that I heard. I was horrified, but the very shock of the thing carried with it the thought that the idea must be true.

"You mean," demanded Dexter, his voice lowering, and taking on that strange metallic ringing note which so often indicates the very height of passion, "you mean that the fellow was merely pleasing himself off-hand?"

"Yes. Pleasure and business mixed together. That was what he said to me. 'There is nothing so beautiful, Tonio,' he said to me, 'as a stroke that gives you a dead man and a pocketful of money.' That was why he did the killings. But your father had been very kind to him. He would not touch your father. He told me that they offered him double the amount of money, if he would begin with the murder of Jefferson Dexter."

"Who would give him the money?"

"Why, Don Manly, and the great man—I forget his name, just this moment."

"You mean the judge?"

"Señor Benson. That is the man."

I heard a gasping breath from young Dexter.

"I knew it!" he said. "I guessed it, and I knew it. It was the judge. It was the judge who hired the murderers! Yes, it would be the judge."

"It was he," said the Mexican. "He and Don Manly came to Scorpio and told him that they knew that he had reason to kill the Dexters."

"And they offered him money?"

"Ten thousand dollars."

"He might have had more than that," said Dexter bitterly. "He might have held them up for a great deal more that that."

"Oh, he was no fool to take the first offer that they made," said Tonio. "He talked a great deal about how he loved the Señor Dexter, the famous Don Jefferson. And the next day they came back and reminded him of the flogging he had had. And this time they doubled their price. They offered him twenty thousand dollars, and in hard cash."

"Well, he must have trusted a great deal, if he trusted that they would pay him the money."

"I tell you again: He was not a fool. No, my friend, but immediately he asked for payment down. They offered him a thousand dollars. He asked for five. They made the payment at once."

"Good business," said Dexter savagely. "Ready cash gets the ready profits, I dare say, in this little old world of ours. And then what happened—or rather, what did Scorpio say that he did, because of course he never would tell you the whole truth?"

Tonio exclaimed sharp and high: "You think that I am lying, then?"

"Not a bit. But I know that Scorpio would never tell you the whole thing. Why, he would have been mad to do that."

"Perhaps he was mad, but he told me. You listen, and see if the thing does not sound clear to you, and the truth. Truth has a voice of its own, and presently you will find it, señor, behind the words of Tonio. Ha, señor, to think that I would even repeat a lie to you, after what you have done for me, to-day!"

"Well," said Dexter, "I'll listen to what you have to say. Go on, Tonio. Of course I'm interested, even in seeing how great a lie it can be."

"First of all," said Tonio, "it was agreed that Manly Crowell should try to dispose of your father. And the instant that the gun was fired that killed him, or proposed to kill him, then the rest of the work would be undertaken by the terrible Scorpio. And so they arranged the day when the thing should be done; and for a week before, Scorpio was so happy that he told me he used to wake up in the middle of the night. His own happy dreams and happy laughter used to waken him, when he thought of the dead men and the twenty thousand dollars."

"I understand," said Dexter slowly. "Of course that would be it. Of course that would be the thing. He loved blood for its own sake."

"Not blood," answered Tonio. "You do him wrong. For he hates blood. Yes, yes, the sight of blood even to-day makes him feel sick and faint. But he loves to see things die—strong men—great horses—that is what he loves. That is what he lives for."

"Ah, well," said Dexter, remaining surprisingly calm as he heard this picture of an incarnate fiend, "and what did he actually do, that night, ten years ago?"

"He stood in the hall, until the gunshot sounded, and Marshall Dexter ran out into it. He shot him down. Then he went and found Vincent Dexter. Vincent saw him, and the naked gun in his hand, but he couldn't realize that Scorpio was against him. He called out to Scorpio that he was going in the wrong direction and that the sound of the gunshots had been on the other side of the house. Then he ran down the hall past Scorpio, and when he was fairly by, Scorpio shot him in the back.

"Every one was up, by this time. The place was filled with armed men, but Scorpio went through them safely. They could not realize that he was the killer. Manly Crowell had got out of the way after he had done his share by killing your father. There was only one thing to be done to make the thing complete. That was the murder of young Charles Dexter. Philip Anson, the cow-puncher, had taken him along, and Scorpio got on their trail. He missed finding them, but he hounded them so closely that you did not dare to come back for ten years.

"There were other things that Scorpio did that night. There was the way he killed Laffitter, for instance; that pleased him a great deal. But what you want to know is why and how he killed two of your family, and now I've told you."

I had been writing these words down at a furious rate, my eyes aching with the strain as I glared at the darkening paper through the evening gloom. Now there was a short pause, after which Dexter said:

"Well, Tonio, I must say that Scorpio was a fool."

"To make twenty thousand dollars with two or three bullets? Why was he a fool, señor?"

"To tell the thing to you."

"Because I have told you in turn? Is that what you mean?"

"Yes, I mean that."

Tonio merely laughed, and the sound of his laughter was as ugly as the sight of his face.

"You never will kill Scorpio!" said he.

"I shall not, eh?"

"No. You'll never kill Scorpio, but he'll kill you instead, when he's ready."

"What makes you think so, Tonio?"

"Because he has sold his soul to the devil, and that means that he'll never lose in a fight. Oh, you never could hurt him, señor. He has a charmed life. He laughs at fighters like you."

"And you, Tonio?" asked Dexter. "What are your chances against him?"

"Yes, I can kill him," said Tonio, his tone altering to one of despair. "I am the only man in the world of whom he is afraid."

"You're a good shot, Tonio," said Dexter. "But why should he be so much afraid of you?"

"He always has been afraid. Why else should he have gone to so much trouble to make me his friend?"

"It seems to me that he has not used you as a very good friend, Tonio."

"What do you understand of him?" asked Tonio, very impatiently. "But I tell you this: He is afraid of me, because he knows that I am the man who can kill him."

"In spite of the devil?"

"Do you see?" cried Tonio. "It is because I am willing to die if I can take him away with me. Because I am willing to throw away my life to take his, the devil who helps him could not save him from me. Furthermore, I am not afraid. All the men he has killed—what would they mean to Tonio? I would not care. He knows that, and therefore he always runs away from me; or else he stays and tries to make me happy with his promises and his lies. But he has told almost his last lie. He cannot escape from me. He is no better than dead, I tell you, and you should believe what I say."

"I want to believe it," said Dexter. "I know that you have the right idea. I know that you're not afraid of him, but still, he is said to be a very fast man with a gun, and a beautiful shot. Besides, he'll shoot from behind!"

"He'll never shoot at me from behind," said Tonio, with perfect conviction. "He may murder other people like an Indian, but he'll never murder me in that way. He will have to stand up to me, face to face and hand to hand. He is very good with weapons. Well, that will be all the worse for him when he fights with me. The more skillful he is, the more surely I shall kill him!"

As I wrote down these words, my fingers cramped and numb with speed, I made sure that Tonio was mad as a hatter. But I was wrong. He was not mad at all, but simply telling us a truth which was soon to be made self-evident. Yet, at that moment, if any one had told me that the riddle could be solved, I should have called him a fool.

It was as I finished writing these words, and looked up, easing my eyes, that I saw a form detach itself from the brush near the fire and walk toward the two seated figures of the men.

I was about to shout out; I could swear that this was one of the men of Dexter Valley, coming to attack the enemy. Or else, was it that mysterious fiend, Scorpio himself, whose footfall was as soundless as the falling of a shadow?

But from the approaching figure there now sounded a familiarly drawling voice which said: "Why hello, boys! You ain't drunk up all of that coffee, have you?"

It was the sheriff; and you can imagine the vast relief which I felt. I stopped writing, and sitting up, safe from discovery in the thick of the evening, I enjoyed a pleasant relaxation. How amazing was the trust which I invested in that little giant of the law!

CHAPTER XXXVIII.   A WILD LEAP

AT the sound of the sheriff's voice, both Tonio and Dexter reacted violently, but in an opposite manner. Tonio bounded into the air like a wounded cat, pulling a gun as he leaped, and Dexter, whipping out a weapon, dropped into the shadows along the ground.

But, as they recognized the speaker, each of them put up his gun.

The sheriff, who must have felt a little amusement at the way in which he had taken the pair into the palm of his hand, chuckled a bit as he approached.

"What I was wondering," said he, "as I come up the valley, was whether that was a signal burning, or what. And here I come and find Charlie Dexter warming his hands over it. Who's your friend, Charlie?"

"Tonio," said Dexter, speaking very short, and standing stiff like one full of offended pride. "And—I'll wager that you couldn't have seen the light of this fire a hundred feet away."

"Not of the fire, son," said the sheriff, "but the way that it lighted up the face of the house. That was the thing that made me think there might be some kids up here with a great big bonfire where they could roast apples and potatoes and warm themselves. So I just dropped in and here I find you. Hello, Tonio. Seems like I must've seen you before, somewhere."

"No, señor," said Tonio. "Those who have once seen me, never forget the day or the place."

"Well, I've seen you, all right," said the sheriff. "Might you help me to a drop of that coffee, Charlie?"

A cup was rinsed clean for him, and then filled, and I felt a fresh pang of hunger. Howevever extraordinary the tale which the Mexican had confided to Dexter, I felt that I had paid rather high for it in a certain hollowness of the stomach.

Tom Winchell sat down on his heels like an Indian and sipped at the coffee rather noisily, it was so hot.

"How's things been going, son?" he asked of Dexter.

"Oh, pretty well," said Dexter.

"They ain't tagged you, yet?"

"I've got some fresh holes in my coat," said Dexter. "But that's all."

"It comes," replied the sheriff, "of shooting from a hoss that's running too fast. Bear fever is what they get, when they find that it's a real growed-up man on a hoss that they're shooting at. Their guns begin to go wild, because their hearts is pumping so fast; for otherwise than that, they should've ate you, this day, Charlie."

"Yes, I suppose that they should."

"I'm going to bed," announced Tonio. "I've ridden a long distance to-day."

"How far you rode, Tonio?" asked the sheriff, in his drawling, friendly voice.

"Eight hours in the saddle," said Tonio.

"That's a long ride—eight steady hours. It'd take a good hoss to stand it."

"I have a good horse," said Tonio. "Good-night, my friends!"

"Just a minute," said the sheriff. "I'd like to talk to you for a minute, if you don't mind, Tonio."

"I never waste time gossiping," said Tonio.

I was surprised at his harshness. There had been nothing offensive in the sheriff's manner.

"But I was going to tell you," went on Winchell, "that I'd been nine hours in the saddle myself, this little old day. That was what I wanted to talk to you about."

"What is there to say?" asked Tonio.

"Why, we might talk about the ground where we've been riding," said the sheriff.

"I never talk of ground that's behind me," said Tonio, as rudely as before.

"Well, that's a mistake, son," answered Winchell. "You oughta figger out that what your back trail has been, your front trail is likely to be. There ain't really a better way of plotting what your course will be, than sighting back along where you been yesterday and the days before."

"I don't understand," said the Mexican. "I am sleepy, señor."

"Well, Tonio, I could wake you up," said the sheriff.

"How, señor?"

"I could tell you the trail which I have been following."

"You have a friend here who will listen," said Tonio. "How could it interest me?"

"Because it's Scorpio that I've been after," said the sheriff. "I reckon that you've heard his name, a good while before this?"

Tonio was silent for a moment.

"Yes," he said. "I have heard his name—curse him!"

"Oh, he's accursed, right enough," said the sheriff. "But he ain't hanged, yet, and a sheriff like me has gotta take a good deal of interest in him."

"You will never hang him," said Tonio, still more slowly. "You never will hang him, sheriff."

"That's what other folks have told me," said the sheriff, while I rather wondered to hear him so garrulous about his work to a stranger like Tonio. "But you know that a trail is a trail, for an old hunter like me. You're a hunter yourself, Tonio, I take it?"

"Yes, I have been a hunter."

"Deer, and such?"

"Yes," said Tonio.

"Ay, and hosses, I reckon."

Tonio started a little.

"Who has told you that?" he asked.

"Why, I guessed it, only. By the look of your clothes you wouldn't 'a' *bought* a hoss like that one that's shining in the dark, over yonder. You wouldn't 'a' bought it, and likely then you would 'a' hunted it or raised it."

"And why shouldn't I have raised it, señor?" asked Tonio, coming a little closer, so that I could see the hideousness of his face more clearly by the firelight.

"Ah, yes, you might 'a' raised it," admitted Winchell. "Only, that ain't the sort of a thing that I would 'a' expected you to raise, Tonio."

"And what would you have expected me to raise?" asked Tonio, in a very ugly voice, indeed.

"Cain!" said the sheriff, drawling, and pleasant as ever.

Tonio said not a word, for a moment or so. Then he shrugged his shoulders.

"You are an old man, señor," said he, "and you talk in an old way. Shall I go, now?"

"Oh," said Winchell, "I wouldn't hold you here, Tonio. Only, while we was talking about trails, I thought that they was a little more that we could say about that, old son."

"And what of it?" asked the Mexican, raising his voice.

And I hardly wondered that he should be excited, there was something so persistently annoying in the manner of Winchell.

"Why, you was a hunter of deer, of horses, and such," said the sheriff, "and so've I been. And so I wondered might you likely have been a trailer of men, too—like me?"

"What should I have had to do with that?" said the Mexican. "Why should I have been a hunter after men?"

"Well, I was asking," said the sheriff.

Here Dexter put in: "I'll tell you what, Winchell. That is one of the best men you and I could have met, because he's after Scorpio, just as we are!"

"Hello!" said the sheriff. "After Scorpio, like us?"

"Yes," said Dexter.

"Well," said the sheriff, "I'd put a bet on him that he'll find Scorpio before us."

"Do you think that I shall, señor?" asked Tonio. "Even before you know what I can do on the trail?"

"Oh, but I know what you can do on the trail," said the sheriff, putting the cup down on the ground beside him.

"You know what I can do?" exclaimed Tonio, justly amazed.

"Yes, I understand. You see, I've been following and learning a good deal about you. I've been following you for ten years—Scorpio!"

That name knocked at my brain like a heavy hand.

And then I saw that instead of a coffee cup, the sheriff was holding a long Colt trained carefully and steadily upon the Mexican!

Scorpio!

He stood frozen in place, regarding that gun, and letting his hands slowly creep up and up until they were level with his breast, and shoulder high, and then up to his head. The slow motion of those hands was more than the most stirring words to give me a picture of the storm which was going on inside the brain of the Mexican. Every inch he moved them, he surrendered another chance of drawing a weapon.

"Scorpio!" exclaimed young Dexter. "Oh, by the eternal, and I guessed at it, I guessed at it! I saw it like land on the horizon, Winchell, and couldn't tell whether it was real or a dream."

I remembered the thoughtful, abstracted manner in

which Dexter had accompanied us down the road, that day, and I could realize that he had been struggling with something that had to do with the personality of the Mexican. Was it this? Had some echo of the truth remained with him, some recollection out of his boyhood of the personality, or the voice which belonged to Scorpio?

But my mind was whirling fast and leaving me in a cloud. I could not keep up with these men before me. They were leagues ahead.

"Why do you draw a gun on me?" demanded Tonio. "Why do you call me Scorpio? I ask you why, señor? This friend of mine will tell you that I am not Scorpio. My name is Tonio. I hate Scorpio. I hate him worse than I hate any one in the world."

"Of course you do," said Dexter, answering in the place of the sheriff. "Of course you hate him, because you're the only one who knows the real truth about him. And of course you're the only friend he ever had, and of course you let him tempt you into trouble, and then let him be your comforter.

"Of course you would find him before any one else could. Of course you were sure that one day you would kill him. Why, with the memories that are inside you, Scorpio, it's a wonder that you haven't poisoned yourself. You've already tried to cut your own throat, as you explained in your little allegory."

"What's this all about?" asked the sheriff.

"He's been telling us some stories about a fiend called Scorpio—a man who sold himself to the devil, d'you see? quite true, Scorpio. You're his friend, because you're a friend to yourself. You hate him, because you know yourself. D'you see, Winchell? He's divided himself into two parts. One is honest Tonio, who loves horses and tames them and never has done wrong—except in associating with the murderer, Scorpio, and spending the murderer's money. The other self is the great Scorpio himself. It's a rare thing!"

"Rare?" exclaimed the sheriff. "Yes, it's rare, well enough. He would have showed you Scorpio some time this night, Charlie. He would have cut your throat for you!"

211

"Of course he would." Dexter nodded. "That was his plan. Only, I wondered why he didn't shoot me out of the saddle, when I was riding and catching his horse for him, to-day. Will you tell me why, Scorpio? Was it because of my friend, Dean? I'd a dream of a suspicion of you before, and told Dean to keep an eye on you!"

"Because of him?" responded Scorpio, sneering. "That feeble fool? He would break up like dead leaves, at the first touch of the hand. No, no, it was not because of him. It was because of the horse."

"You were afraid that you'd nick the horse, while you were shooting me, Scorpio? Or that he'd run free, after you'd blown me out of the saddle? Didn't you put any more trust in your marksmanship than that?"

"It was neither," said Scorpio, who seemed to admit his identity, now." It was because I loved the horse, and admired the man who could ride him. The time that you hung from the pommel with both hands"—here he stretched his hands out before him—"and Compadre jumped into the middle of the sky ——"

With that, the Mexican leaped straight forward in a single gigantic bound. Straight forward mind you, at the crouching sheriff, and over him!

CHAPTER XXXIX.   SCORPIO'S HOPE

THE sheriff fired, taken completely by surprise as he must have been. But I suppose that he had felt the situation was so entirely in his hands that for a fraction of a second he had allowed the perfect concentration of his wits to dissolve a little, and the criminal had taken advantage of the thinnest gap.

Straight over the sheriff he sprang, then, with the roar of the gun beating at my ears.

I saw young Dexter flick out a weapon and start shooting, but by that time, the Mexican was running like a snipe, dodging from side to side, and sprinting with a wonderful speed.

Dexter, ceasing fire, raced after him—the sheriff made for a horse—and then Scorpio turned in his flight and came straight toward me!

I could hardly realize that the danger was suddenly mine, and that I was no longer to be a mere onlooker. No, he was lurching straight toward me, and though Dexter came veritably like the wind behind him, he could not overtake the Mexican before Scorpio had reached me. He needed, in passing, merely to pull the trigger of the gun he carried once, and I would lie there with a broken back or a splintered skull.

In a cold frenzy of terror, I leaped up.

I should say, that I would have leaped, but I was stiff and cramped from long remaining in one position, and I only succeeded in lurching half to my feet when the swift body of Scorpio struck me.

Down I went as though I had been clubbed and he tumbling over me. My yell might have raised the dead, it went so shrieking and whistling down the wind. And then I saw Dexter spin around the corner of the shack and dive at the body of the Mexican like a swimmer into water.

They rolled over and over.

I, stumbling to my feet, shaking like a leaf, half sick with fear, saw the pale gleam of a gun lying on the ground and reached for it. I raised it up, and gripped it hard by the barrel, intending to bring the heavy butt down on the head of Scorpio when the chance offered. But if you ever have seen two wild cats spring at one another and writhe and tumble over and over, that was how the pair of men I was watching were now fighting. Besides, it was utterly dark, now, and I hardly knew which was which.

The sheriff, in response to my frantic yells, was already rounding the corner of the shack, when I heard the voice of Dexter say:

"That has you, Scorpio, I think. Try to move, now, and I break every bone in this shoulder."

He was perfectly calm.

213

So was Scorpio, as he answered: "I will not move. You have me, all right, Charlie."

That name struck horribly upon me. "Charlie!" In the old days on the ranch, before the murders had been bought and paid for, he must have called the boy by that familiar name.

"Get a light," said Dexter. "I don't want to budge until we've made pretty sure of him, this time."

The sheriff lighted a match, saying as he did so: "Well, boys, you never would guess that I'd ever took after a man, or handled a fighting man before in all my days. I set there and chattered like a fool of a guinea hen, and while I was a-setting, he walked over and stepped in my face and sashays off into the night. And we have to have folks grow up out of the ground to stop him, eh? How are you, Mr. Dean? I sure hope that you didn't get your neck busted, when he went slam into you!"

This casual chatter of the sheriff went on while he supplied Dexter with several bits of tie rope such as cattlemen use for tying the feet of cattle. With these, Dexter firmly secured the hands of the Mexican behind his back. Then he was allowed to get up, brought back to the fire, and by the light of it he was searched.

They found on him a good deal that was of interest.

Item: A stiletto with a blade hardly wider than a darning needle and a handle of pearl, very delicately worked with gold inlay. This devilish thing looked as though the force of a breath would thrust it through a man's heart.

Item: Another knife, which I believe they referred to as a bowie knife. It had a long blade, curving back. Furthermore, it was very heavy, and the grip was roughened to make sure of the hold. I never saw a more businesslike weapon. He wore it in a thin sheath just inside the band of his trousers.

Item: A revolver hanging under the pit of his left arm. In the handles of this were worked five notches.

Item: A smaller weapon, which I believe they called a derringer. It had two barrels not longer than my little finger, but the caliber was large. The sheriff said that the balls would stop a man and kill him as well as a bullet from a Colt, in case the discharge took place at very short range. This gun was slipped into a pocket or pouch inside the front flap of the coat. I suppose so that it could be used for a surprise attack, when he seemed to be fumbling for a match, or some such thing.

Item: A tobacco pouch made of soft, strong, chamois leather, closing with a ring. The patient sheriff, looking through the pouch and pinching it, discovered within the store of tobacco a little metal capsule which he opened, the two halves of it fitting neatly and strongly together. Inside, there was a small quantity of a white powder, which he examined carefully, almost timidly.

Then he looked up at the Mexican.

"Headache powder, Scorpio, eh?"

And Scorpio smiled that hideous grimace of a smile of his.

Item: A wallet of very good and strong pigskin in which there was contained a small needle case with several needles of various sizes, a little awl which I suppose would have been useful in repairing broken harness or in soling shoes, a picture of an astonishingly pretty Mexican girl with a rose in her mouth, and languishing eyes; and, finally, a thick wad of bills, which the sheriff counted on the spot. It contained thirty-seven hundred and eighty-five dollars.

Besides these things there were odds and ends, such as a big bandanna handkerchief of a good quality of silk, and cigarette papers, matches in a steel, waterproof match box, and a good pocket-knife with three blades.

I have been particular in writing down a list of these things, not that they were important, all of them, in themselves, but because at the time all that was produced from Scorpio's pockets seemed to me new parts of his character which were revealed to us. Besides, there was a peculiar solemnity about this occasion. It was the end of a ten-year trail for more than one person. It was the door of death for Scorpio himself. And the matter-of-fact way in which the people concerned were talking was not able to cover up the significance which, I knew, they all attached to it.

For my part, I think that I cast more glances at the black of the shrubbery and the rocks around us than at the central trio. I half expected that at any moment people might spring out at us—the Bensons and their crew.

"Tell me, Scorpio," said Dexter, who showed in his voice and manner not the slightest animus against the man he had hunted down. "Tell why you described so fully what you did on that night?"

"Because," said the Mexican, "I saw that you were suspecting me when we were riding on the road. I wanted to give you something which would take your mind away from me and fasten it on the Scorpio of ten years ago. And I succeeded!"

"And this money," went on the youth, "was given you as part payment for hunting me down?"

The Mexican shrugged his shoulders.

"Why should I talk any more?" said he. "It may be that you will cut my throat. It may be that you'll let the sheriff take me off to prison. In either case, there's no reason why I should talk. If the case comes to the law, then I'll have a better chance if my mouth has remained closed."

"Scorpio," said Dexter, "do you really in your heart keep the slightest hope that you'll save your life?"

"Hope is the cheapest stuff to fill a barn," said the Mexican. "Hope has brought many a man through a naked winter. Well, why shouldn't I hope, then?"

"Because we have your own word against you."

"What word? What have I told you? Merely fiction! I've told stories, and you've listened. You cannot prove that I am Scorpio. You swear that I have admitted it. I swear that I have not. There we are. The jury may believe your oaths. It may believe my face. Besides, I shall have friends to help from the outside."

"The Bensons, Crowells, and the rest, of course," said Dexter. "Well, that's one thing to trust to. But what will you say to this? You have something written, Dean, I hope?"

216

The interest flashed to me, for a moment, and I was glad of it. I pulled out my notebook, and turning back the pages to the beginning, I read off by the firelight everything that I had written down, though I had to pause several times toward the end, where the darkness had made the scribbling a matter of guesswork.

When I closed the book, young Dexter said:

"There you are, Scorpio. I don't think that you can get away from that confession."

"Can't I?" answered Scorpio. "Why, I tell you the stuff isn't worth a hang, without my signature."

I could not help saying: "I see the point in that."

"You might ask him to sign it, Dexter?" said the sheriff.

And Dexter, his face suddenly convulsed, answered: "If you'll leave me alone with him for ten minutes, I may be able to get that signature, sheriff, in spite of your smiling."

The sheriff shook his head.

"Tut, tut, son," said he. "This man is my prisoner. Leave him alone with you? I'd rather leave him alone with a hungry tiger! No, no. I'll look out for Scorpio."

Young Dexter began to walk up and down. I could see that Scorpio had made a very good point. He would have to be tried in the valley, and there the influence of his friends would almost undoubtedly hang the jury. In a sense, it was almost as though the capture had not been made. Not altogether, of course, for once his identity was proved, and the written report I had made out was reasonable proof, it appeared, then there was the possibility of a lynching—and a most excellent possibility, at that.

However, the triumph of Dexter seemed blocked, in spite of the fact that the man was in his hands. It was the presence of the sheriff that blurred the victory. I could see other viewpoints, as well, and I could not help saying:

"It's a time for a compromise, Charles."

He jerked about at me.

"Don't I know it?" he exclaimed. "Don't you see that that is what's eating my heart out?"

217

CHAPTER XL. A NEW PLAN

IT was about as odd a scene as any one could imagine—the four of us sitting there in the dark of the night, with only the very dull red of the fire glowing in front of us. It did not light our faces. It merely showed us to one another as blurred and bulky outlines. But stranger than the picture was the talk. Stranger than the talk was the emotion behind it.

We had taken a famous murderer. He was helpless in our hands. The law was with us. But that same law kept us from laying hands upon him. If we brought him to trial, the corrupt jury would let him go. In a sense we had gained from our possession of Scorpio nothing but the truth. So, for a time, we sat in idleness, talking of things about which we really did not care at all.

We asked the sheriff how he had got on Scorpio's trail, for one thing. And Scorpio, you may be sure, was interested in this. But the sheriff would only chuckle a little, and say nothing at all until suddenly young Dexter cried out:

"Why, Winchell, the way you found Scorpio was by following *me!*"

The sheriff laughed and admitted it.

What had seemed most miraculously clever now was turned into a simple thing. He had followed Dexter, feeling sure that sooner or later Scorpio would try to do to Dexter what he already had accomplished on Philip Anson.

We asked Scorpio, then, what inspired him to make his famous mark upon the foreheads of his victims, but Scorpio now had fallen into a silence. His head hung down. He seemed to be lost in his thoughts.

And what a wilderness in which to lose oneself, what a hideous and stark world!

Yes, I could realize how such a man would divide himself, for his own contemplation, into two beings, a sort of Jekyll and Hyde, one good but weak, one all evil and terribly strong.

Seeing how we had the man in our power, I became suddenly furious because we were able to get no real good out of him. Not even when we held him with the blood money on him! This exasperation spurred into my mind a new thought, which was that we might make use of Scorpio in spite of himself.

I took Charlie Dexter to one side.

"Charles," said I, "I think that I'll make another trip back to the house of Judge Benson."

Dexter chuckled. "That sounds like a sensible thing." said he. "Do you want to leave behind you any messages for your friends?"

"You mean that he'd murder me, in cold blood?"

"Have you any doubt about that, man?" asked Dexter. "Don't you see what he is?"

"Well," I said, "I only need one thing to make him helpless."

"What is that?" asked Dexter.

"The signature of Manuel Scorpio at the bottom of this confession."

"Is that all you want?" said Dexter. "Well, Dean, I congratulate you on getting down to the solution of our trouble."

"Thank you," said I. "But don't sneer yet, Charlie."

"I'm not really sneering, old fellow."

"I said the signature of Manuel Scorpio," said I. "I didn't say his real handwriting."

He understood me then. "You mean, a sham to impose on the judge?"

"That's it."

Dexter leaped at the idea.

"If we could only get a sample of his writing!" said Dexter.

And we tried to wheedle one out of him; but Scorpio, by this time, was a thousand miles away, lost in the forest of his mind. He would not come out to meet us. He merely looked at us with his dreadful eyes, red-stained from the firelight, and made no reply at all.

"When you used to talk to Scorpio in the old days," said I," did he ever tell you how long he was in school?"

"I don't remember that he ever said a word about school," answered Dexter. "Maybe he never went there at all—hold on, Dean. He may not even know how to write his name. A lot of them don't, you know."

Suddenly he asked to see the notebook. We freshened the fire a little, and by the light of that, using a fountain pen and writing on the last page of the notebook, Dexter carefully spelled out a name.

He showed it to me and I saw, with amazement, that he had not attempted to produce a flowing signature, but that he had written laboriously, letter by letter, with a rather wavering and uncertain line, the name of Manuel Scorpio. It was like a schoolboy's work, so square and foolish were the letters.

"Do you think they'll swallow this second-grade writing?" I asked him.

"Not if they've ever seen Scorpio's hand," said he. "But if they haven't, they'll say that it must really be his writing. And, if he has signed anything for us, it means that his spirit is broken, and that he'll sign other things—that he's our witness—that he's ready to turn State's evidence. That's what you had in mind in the first place, isn't it?"

"Yes," said I. "That will be worse than a gun held at the head of the honest judge, I take it. And we can easily bluff him into making the right terms."

Dexter groaned. "For ten years," he said, "I've sworn to wipe out the murders which Scorpio performed, and to get even with the men who hired him. Now you talk to me about compromise?"

"Well," I said, "is there any real revenge in getting yourself hanged for murder? And that's what surely will happen if you kill Benson and Manly Crowell. Scorpio? No, they couldn't very well touch you for that, but how to get at Scorpio, now that the sheriff has him? After all, I think that Benson would almost rather be killed than give up half his property. Here you stand without any real proof

220

of your identity except information which they'll claim you could have picked up from other people, and in addition, a faded old family portrait. They may say that Anson picked you up on account of the likeness and then taught you everything that you know about Dexter Valley. I don't think that you have a good case to bring before the law."

After this, he remained for a time brooding on the fire.

"Tell me, Dean," said he at last. "Did you feel that way about me, at first? Did you have those suspicions?"

"Yes," I told him frankly.

This made up his mind. He stood up and pressed a hand on my shoulder when I rose in turn.

"Would you really walk into that lion's den again, on my account?" he asked.

I told him that I would.

However, it was not altogether on his account. I had been bullied, hunted like a dog, and browbeaten by Benson, and I had a cold hatred for him such as I think I never have felt for any other man. I wanted to go back there as an emissary in a position to make him crawl.

"If by any chance," said Dexter, "they are familiar with the true writing of Scorpio, then what might they do to you when they see that your document is a sham?"

I could not help a shudder, at this thought, but I shrugged the possibility away.

"There's not much likelihood that letters were ever exchanged between them. The judge wouldn't be fool enough to commit himself in writing to a known murderer, and neither would the murderer be apt to write to the fellow who hired him. I don't think that there's a chance."

That was the way I argued.

In fact, I was feverishly anxious to get back at the judge. I would not even wait until the morning. By cutting across to the river road, I could wind up at the house of the judge in less than an hour of riding. I only had to settle with Dexter what terms he would ask.

"Mind you," said Dexter, "that I say nothing about burying the hatchet. As for what happens between me and the judge and Manly Crowell, that's a thing for me to decide with my conscience for judge. But if I can wring my rights from the valley farmers, I'd be a fool to let the chance slip. I agree not to bring Scorpio into court against them. I agree to turn Scorpio loose—or rather, to let the sheriff take him to jail. I can imagine how long any jail in Dexter Valley will hold him, once the judge starts moving his levers!

"Very well. There's the case. I get half of the land of Dexter Valley, acre for acre. The alternate quarter sections go to me. But outside of Dexter House, I don't claim the buildings or the stock or the implements. I get only the land, the acreage. They've had this valley so long that they'll howl like sick cats when they hear the terms. They know how bad my case is to bring up in the courts, too. But they'd rather pay up than hang, I suppose."

Surely nothing could be clearer than that.

I saddled my tired little mustang. Well, he was no longer half so tired as when we dismounted at the end of the day's ride, and certainly he never broke from his steady, gently rocking lope from the moment I put foot in stirrup to the time I got to Dexter House.

It was a pleasant night, I remember, and as I rode up the side of the swinging river, I would glance now and again through the cloudy masses of the trees which overhung the way and see the stars moving like bright hosts of bees. There was a soft wind, with the green smell of the fields in it, and a rich sense of growing things in the darkness about me.

I wondered if it had been on such a night as this that Scorpio and the armed men fell on the Dexters and slaughtered them; and the fugitives and their defenders and the enemies who followed them swept down the riverside to the place where, legend said, both Scorpio and Prince Charlie had been killed and lost in the stream.

These were not very cheerful thoughts, and the beauty of the night was a dead thing for me by the time I had reached the house of the judge.

I went up the driveway with a good deal less courage than I had had at the start, and at the door of the house I hesitated for a long moment before I used the knocker.

The door was pulled open a moment later by the great

lout of a Benson boy. He gaped at me, and then reached out and got me by the collar and pulled me into the room.

"Hey, look what I found out in the dark!" said he.

CHAPTER XLI.   THE LIONS' DEN

THAT big room had in it a number of men, all armed to the teeth. Several had rifles leaning against their chairs or balanced across their knees, and all were belted about with cartridges. A rougher or more efficient-looking crew of fighting men I never have seen in all my days.

Manly Crowell was there, and Steven Dinmont, and Clay Livingston, besides the judge. They represented the four dominant families in the valley, and besides them and young Benson, there were several others, of whom I recognized only Dandy Bullen.

Mrs. Benson had just brought in a bucket of coffee and she was going about ladling out portions in huge tin cups. Some took it black. Some had a trickle of condensed milk run in afterward, and nearly all joined a spoonful or two of sugar to their ration.

My coming made a good deal of an impression upon them, I saw, but the work of sharing the coffee was carried on without interruption. Mrs. Benson only paused to scowl at me over her shoulder and resumed the ladling.

Of the men, not a single one rose, though at the first instant I thought the judge would leap to his feet. One hears a good deal of faces changing color and swelling with passion, but one seldom sees as I did then a dark purple flush and veins suddenly standing out in the forehead. It was a passion of good, thoroughgoing hatred and the infinite satisfaction of having the object of the hatred at hand and apparently helpless.

I think that the judge loathed me even more than he did Dexter, though why his hate should have been so great

I don't know; it was as inexplicable as mine for him, and I suppose that we merely were possessed by an instinctive rage at one another. We were simply opposite natures.

The judge, with that livid face turned toward me, finally settled himself back in his chair.

"Fetch him here," he said to his son. "But don't choke him—yet!"

The boy actually had stopped my breathing by the violence of his grip which was twisted into my coat collar. Now he relaxed it, and showed the authority of his strength by sending me before him with a jerk that almost knocked me sprawling on the floor.

You will imagine that this reception, and the savage grins with which those ruffians watched the process of the bullying did not serve to soothe my nerves. As a matter of fact I felt the opposite of fear.

In the first place, I had been among them under difficult conditions before this. In the second place, though it was possible, as Dexter had suggested, that they would see through the sham signature, yet I was inclined to trust in it, and in the reality of the document which I had scribbled.

If I could convince them that the thing was real, and that Scorpio actually had been tormented to the point of surrender, I felt that I would have them in my hands. Weak as I was, and single before so many, still I had that hope, and the tingling anticipation went thrilling and leaping along my veins in the most amazing way.

I rearranged my coat and stood there before them, panting a little, but amazed by the steadiness of my nerves. I waited for them to speak, and the judge, of course, was the first to open his mouth.

"Here's the messenger boy again," he said. "What does the fake Dexter want out of us now?"

I made myself smile on the judge. Almost with affection I smiled on that brutal man and saw his upper lip lift with the hate he felt when he saw me smile.

"He's sent me to give you his lowest terms."

"*His* lowest terms!" snorted the judge. "And what makes you think that we want to hear any terms from him? You fool, you ——"

He stopped himself, for rage was swelling his voice to too big a note for the room, and for such an early moment in the interview. But then he added: "Dexter sent you in, eh? Well, tell us what he wants. Tell it quick!"

"He'll take half the land, alternate sections through the entire valley."

The judge lifted his head and laughed. It sounded like the baying of a wolf.

"He'll take half the land, will he! The fool's crazy. You hear that, boys, do you! He'll take half the land!"

Clay Livingston watched me with a ghastly grin. His hands were working, where he kept them folded together over one knee.

"He'll take half the land," said I. "That's final."

"And you really rode in here to tell us that," said the judge.

"Yes," said I, "I really rode in here to tell you that, and a few other things that may interest you."

"What other things? Tell us what other things before we start telling you something you may be very much interested in."

"No," said I, rejoicing in a sudden savage triumph. "I'll do the talking, this evening. I believe that I'll do most of the talking, and the rest of you will simply sit about and listen—like dogs when they see the whip."

How they started! They could not believe their ears. I saw young Benson turn on me with his fist raised, but he held back the blow. He could not realize that he had heard the thing. It turned little Oliver Dean into a mystery, as though a bird should flirt its wings under the very nose of a snake.

"Go on!" said the judge. "Whatever's coming to you will wait, till you've had your little say. Go on, Dean!"

"I don't come from Dexter alone, in the first place," said I.

"Who else, then?"

"Scorpio."

Ah, that had them where they lived!

Clay Livingston shouted out: "You dunderhead, Scorpio has been dead for ten years! It was only some fool of a joker that used his sign up in Monte Verde!".

"You may be simple enough to believe that Scorpio is dead," I told him. "But first look at the judge and see what *he* believes."

In fact, that sudden bringing out of the name of Scorpio had struck the judge under the fifth rib. I suppose he had been so utterly sure of himself, what with the lapse of ten years, and the frightful alteration in the face of the murderer, that he could not dream the identity of the man would ever be discovered.

And the judge showed the shock. The purple had not entirely left his face, but it was patched with white, and his eyes were those of a man who sees a ghost.

So it made a very good effect for me, as I stood there pointing at him melodramatically, with outstretched arms.

"What in blazes is the meaning of it, judge?" asked Clay Livingston.

"Yes, what?" said Steven Dinmont, standing up.

The judge moistened his pale lips. They seemed stiff with cold, and speech came slowly.

"It's all a lie," said he.

But his voice was dead. He had power to make it loud, but he could not put any ring of sincerity into it.

I think he knew it. He glanced quickly from side to side, to read the expressions of the others. They were staring back at him partly in horror and partly in bewilderment.

Only one man shouted: "It's a fool's idea. Scorpio! Bah! He's been dead ten years!"

This came from a wide-shouldered man with a head that jutted well forward, so that it gave him a very aggressive look. He had the battered face of a prize fighter, but one could see that it was not simply blows of a fist that he had endured.

He got up and came from his chair toward me, as he shouted the words.

And something suddenly spoke in me.

"I suppose that you're Manly Crowell?"

This stopped him like a blow in the face.

"Why ——" he began. Then he stopped, reaching for a word, amazed.

"You and the judge," said I, "have good reasons for not wanting it to be known. But both of you know that Scorpio's not dead. The kick of a horse wasn't enough to kill him, though it changed him enough to make him serve your turn, or to start to serve it."

This was a settler for Manly Crowell.

He muttered something about "blasted nonsense" but he came no nearer to me. The heart was out of him. And as for the judge, he was rallying himself only slowly.

Some of those people knew about Scorpio from the first, it was plain. Others were ignorant. The ignorant ones should not be left longer in the dark, I felt.

So I pulled out my notebook and began to read. From the first they were fascinated. From the first they were amazed, and every time the word Scorpio appeared, and each time there was a mention of some name known in the valley, I could feel the stir of heads and eyes before me.

Well, the thing sounded as real as daylight. When I got to the end, the judge, who had been gathering breath as the words flowed along, the judge whose reputation had been receiving a blow from which it never could recover even in the eyes of his own followers, broke out:

"It's a plot. It's a faked up document. It's a lie from beginning to end. Even if Scorpio hadn't been killed ten years ago, he's the sort of a man who never would have told such things as this. Wild horses never could have torn such a thing from him, even if it were not a lie. Without Scorpio's signature under it, everything that you've heard read out of that scoundrel's paper is not worth a hang. Dean, you contemptible rat, let me see it!"

"The signature?" said I. "Oh, certainly."

And I held up the notebook at the last page. The lamplight fell flush upon it, and the big, scrawling handwriting which Dexter had assumed for the nonce was plainly visible. In its very childishness there was conviction. For one moment I dreaded lest the judge would see that it was a sham, but the look of him convinced me instantly that I was wrong.

"Merciful Heaven!" breathed the judge.

227

And he slumped back in his chair so hard that the chair creaked under him.

Well, he had received his blow all right, and it just about sunk him on the spot.

I added a final touch.

"He's in our hands, judge. He's ours, body and soul. We can get any testimony out of him. He's turning State's evidence, and so I've dropped in here to see if we couldn't arrange a little compromise. Or do you really wish to hang, Judge Benson?"

CHAPTER XLII.   SURRENDER

IT isn't a pleasant thing to see a man go down with such a crash as that. The judge sat with his chin on his breast, one arm dangling toward the floor, and his eyes rolled up at me. He looked as though he were overcome by the fumes of liquor.

Steven Dinmont stood up in his place.

He walked straight up to the judge and said: "What I've always known about the night when the Dexters were killed is bad enough. What we all know is bad enough. But to think that Scorpio was hired! I've known that you were a hard man, Benson. I didn't know that you were a professional murderer!"

He turned on his heel.

"Hal and Red, come along with me," said he.

At once two fine boys got up and tiptoed after their father out of the room. They got their horses, and rode away.

I had split the enemy into two camps, at last!

The judge felt this defection, of course. The blow of it gradually brought back his wits, and he got to his feet. The others watched him in amazement and in terror. They could see that they were involved in his fall.

"Suppose that Scorpio is back. Suppose that Scorpio

is in the valley," he said, "and suppose that Dexter *got* what he wants—a deed to half the acreage—then what?"

"Then Scorpio is turned loose to go where he pleases. He has enough of your money left to get him out of the country."

Clay Livingston, gripping both sides of his chair, leaned forward and groaned: "Judge, judge, you ain't turning us down! You ain't going to try to get our land out of us? You can do what you want for the others, but my land is mine, and is going to stay mine, no matter ——"

The judge looked at him, and there was that in his eyes which silenced all the violence of Livingston, and put out the fire of revolt that was kindling in all of the faces around the room.

"You can talk, Livingston," said the judge, "some other day and some other place. Now you'll listen to me. Dexter has us on the hip. He's got his teeth in us. He can hang me, for one thing, if he's got the mouth of that blasted Scorpio open. I'm not here to defend what I've done. If I've done more than the rest to make the valley land ours, I haven't taken more than my fair share, have I?"

He did not continue in this line, half of confession and half of justification. He dared not. The sick look of those in the room stopped him.

He went on: "Scorpio can hang me. He can hang others. You know who he can hang. Every one of you knows, or can guess. I say that Dexter has us on the hip. I say that we're going to make out a joint deed. I've got the papers upstairs. I've got the blanks, and I'm going to fill them out, and every man of you is going to sign. Pete, ride after Steve Dinmont and get him back here. The fool forgets that *his* neck is inside of the noose."

He turned to me.

"You sit down and wait," he said.

His words were simple. His loathing was immense.

Not one word of protest further came from that guilty crew. The sense of the old crime was leaden in their brains, now.

Only Manly Crowell said: "Hold on, judge. Suppose

229

that you give that multiple deed to this here boy messenger—what are we going to trust to that they'll fill their side of the bargain?"

"The judge will tell you," said I, "that you can trust in Dexter's honor."

I answered Crowell, but I looked straight at the judge, and he looked straight back at me. It was a hard cut and with a poisoned edge.

I thought he would strike me down. But he merely said:

"Confound you!" through his teeth, and went out from the room, and we heard his heavy footfall climb the stairs.

At the same time, there was a tap at the front door, and then the knob turned, it was pushed open, and Claudia Laffitter stood there against the outer dark, brilliant and shining with her flushed youth and the wind of hard riding.

She waved her hand around the room and came in.

"Looks like Quakers' meeting," said she. "Hello, Mrs. Benson. What's the matter? You look sick, all of you!"

Mrs. Benson looked at me, and Claudia's eyes ran down that glance as if along a wire until she found me. Then she gave a shout and came to me.

Mind you, up to this time there had been no actual talk of marriage between that extraordinary girl and Charlie Dexter. But she cried out to me, before them all:

"Oh, I've ridden like mad all over the valley—all afternoon—all evening—and I couldn't find a trace of you. Tell me—tell me—is he all right? Is Charlie safe and sound?"

She got hold of me as she finished the last words, grasping me by both arms.

I smiled back at her.

"He's as safe and sound as a bell," said I. "He's found Scorpio, made the fellow talk, and forced these people to their knees. Half of Dexter Valley is his, and the deed goes into his hands inside this hour. His friend, the judge, is upstairs fixing the thing, right now."

It was a good deal of news to cram into a few words, and Claudia could hardly swallow it down, but when she did, she controlled her enthusiasm. She did not want to insult all the others in the room by rejoicing in their faces.

I suggested that she and I had better go outside and take a walk until the judge called us to receive his message.

That was what we did.

We walked out of the stunned atmosphere of that room, where all that man power and all that supply of weapons had been rendered useless by five minutes' talk, and we walked up and down through the woods in front of the house, following a well-beaten path. All those woods would come back to Charlie Dexter, now. I told the girl that, and she looked about her, and hugged my arm in a childish transport, but said not a word.

Then she wanted to know the story of everything that had happened. Then she changed her mind and would hear it only from Charlie.

"But is it really true? Did that—that man-killing Scorpio—did he talk, at last? Has he really consented to turn State's evidence?"

"Not a bit," said I. "We got some testimony which he'll deny. We faked a signature. And we've bluffed the judge with it. Criminal? Mildly so, perhaps. But the bluff has worked, and Judge Benson is in our pockets!"

"And *you* worked the bluff!" said the girl, after a moment.

The emphasis showed that she had not had an entirely complimentary opinion of me, before, but I hardly cared about that. The triumph was ours, now. Let the past take care of itself.

And the girl said no more. She just walked up and down beside me, and now and then she gave my arm a hug. She was a grand girl, was Claudia. The size of her mind was a man's size, and something more.

We heard Steven Dinmont returning. We heard him go again. Other men trooped out of the house and got their horses. Then the judge called me and we went in.

He looked like a very sick man, but he had set his jaw and there was still fire in his eyes.

I shall never forget the tone of his voice, or the final words that I heard him speak.

"I've been beaten, Dean, so far," said he. "How much

231

of a share you've had in it, I don't know. But I advise you to get out of this section of the country. Too many men are thinking hard thoughts about you."

"Thanks," said I, and took the thick wad of folded papers which he held out to me.

"It's a transfer of acreage, all legally water-tight," said he. "You can look it over, before you turn loose Scorpio."

I smiled and said that we probably would look it over, but that I was inclined to trust his word.

Then he turned to the girl.

He actually put his hand on her shoulder and looked almost kindly into her face.

"Claudia," said he, "are you going to take a step in the dark?"

She said nothing at all. Her opinion of the judge was not particularly a gentle one, at that moment; but both she and I guessed that there was a double meaning. Claudia showed it when she got outside of the house. For then she insisted that she go back with me to Charlie.

"You'd better go home," I advised her. "No, that's too far to go, but you can stop at any of these houses for the night. It's no time for you to be gadding about."

She chuckled a little, deep in her throat.

"D'you think that I could close my eyes, this night of all nights?" she asked.

I knew it was useless to argue, and we started together to get back to the shack.

CHAPTER XLIII.   AMBUSHED

WE came back under the brightest moon I've ever seen. I felt pretty contented. Altogether, it was about the best night's work I'd ever done, and it made me feel more a man than ever before. What with the brightness of the moon, and the sweet air, and the great tree shadows on

232

the white of the road, it was like riding through Elysium, to me. I was almost drowsily content, in fact, but Claudia was nervous as a cat.

She kept asking me what the judge could have meant by her "taking a step in the dark," though of course he must have referred to her apparent affair with Charlie Dexter. Once or twice she pulled up in the middle of the road and told me she was sure that she had heard hoofbeats behind us. Suppose that they were following us to the shack, where they could gather in Charlie Dexter, and close Scorpio's lips with a .45-caliber bullet?

This hung in her mind so long that at length I consented to leave the straightaway, and we made a detour through the fields—a roundabout trail with which she was familiar, for she knew the valley like a book and recognized the shack the instant that I spoke of it.

I remember that the grass was wet with dew, and where the blades were long, they bent under the weight of it and flashed like steel in that keen moonshine. And all the world was holding its breath, it seemed to me, with only the whisper of the striding feet of the horses through the grass.

When we got near to the shack, on the face of which the moon was now shining full, Claudia held back a little. She wanted me to go in and tell Charlie that she was there, and I, laughing a little at her embarrassment, rode on ahead.

I had barely left the trees and come into the clearing, when I saw Scorpio, his hands still tied behind his back, step into the open doorway. He was looking toward beautiful Compadre, and the stallion, as though recognizing its master, lifted its head and whinnied. It seemed a stroke of affection, though I knew how little love there was in that brute for any man.

But the odd thing about this view of the Mexican was that the shadow of the eaves cut across his face, and for the moment he appeared to me not the cadaverous mask which I had seen before, but another being, handsome—almost femininely handsome.

He spoke to me, and his harsh voice, even, seemed a little softened, and to have a gentler ring in it.

And just on the heels of his words, just as I was swinging down from the saddle, a rifle report rang out on the rim of the clearing, and I saw Scorpio drop as though he had been struck down from behind by a club. He fell straight on his face.

I could not understand it. My mind was in a blur. Instead of dropping to the ground, or trying to bolt through the doorway to safety inside, I merely stood there like a clod, though I could hear Claudia screeching something on the horizon of my senses.

Then came a second thunderclap that in an instant ripped across my scalp with a finger of tearing fire, and also flattened me on the ground.

I lay there semi-conscious. My mind was not out. It was merely frozen still. I lay there and looked straight up at the big, dazzling shield of the moon and tried to blink my eyes, and could not.

Then some one leaned over me. A hand jerked the wad of papers from my inside coat pocket, and the voice of the judge growled:

"You've got your hire at last, you cur!"

I've often wondered, since, what could have convinced him that I was dead. It could not have been the mere blood on my face. It must have been the open, blank eyes. Actually, I did not see him. I merely knew him by his voice.

At the same time, it seemed as though the whole heavens was filled with shouting and the noise of firearms exploding. I heard the judge curse, his voice diminishing so that it showed he was sprinting away very fast.

And then I got back some of my muscular control and pushed myself up on both hands.

Scorpio had not stirred. He lay on his face.

And to my right, I saw the sheriff charging brilliantly across the clearing on the mustang from which I had just dismounted, and firing at the line of trees ahead of him, his revolver extended far before him with a stiff arm. It looked like a dashing illustration for a battle scene—some heroic charge against great odds.

But the enemy was not standing to receive the charge. I could hear the crash of their horses, retreating.

And then another rider went past me like a blinding flash. It was Dexter, who had mounted himself on Compadre. The stallion was not running. It was flying, literally, only flicking the earth now and again with its toes, as it made the ground slide away behind it. I told myself that the horse was too big to dodge through that line of trees. I gathered myself and waited to hear and see the crash. But instead, Compadre faded out among the shadows, and I heard the long rhythm of his gallop in the distance.

My mind went wool-gathering again, after that.

When I came to a bit, a little later, it was to find Claudia washing the blood from my face.

I said to her: "Move that lamp, Claudia, will you? It's shining right in my eyes."

It was the moon, mind you.

Claudia began to laugh, but she had been crying, too. She told me that she had thought I was dead.

"I'm never going to die, Claudia," said I. "I'm going to live to get better sense. Of course they were following us, long enough to get our direction, and when we turned off the trail, they were not deceived. Not a whit! They simply kept straight on, and so they got here before us and waited. What made them run, though? Surely they wanted to get Charlie more than they wanted to get me!"

"They didn't want you. They wanted the stuff in your pocket," she said. "And as for running, when they had a glimpse of the sheriff and Charlie at the same time, I suppose that it was too much for them. It's the judge, and Manly Crowell. I saw them both. If they get away to-night, I can swear that I saw them both, clearly, in the moonlight!"

"I hope they get away," said I. "I hope that Charlie doesn't corner them. They'll fight like rats. They're too dangerous, Claudia!"

Well, she was a Western girl, and I suppose that I should not have been so surprised and rather shocked by her answer.

"If there's a God in heaven," said Claudia, "He'll give them justice out of Charlie's hand!"

That was how she felt about it. She had no more doubt

235

about Charlie's overtaking them, than she had about his victory in the fight that would follow.

In the meantime, there was a faint groan from Scorpio. And both of us went to him, amazed. My head was a bit giddy, when I sat up, for I had lost a good deal of blood before Claudia got the bandage on. The bullet had ripped straight down my scalp, from front to back, and that sort of a wide surface wound is always sure to bleed freely.

We got to Scorpio, and I helped to turn him on his back.

He had been shot straight through the body, under the heart. I knew very little about wounds, but I could guess from the position of this one that he was no better than a dead man. Claudia gave me a nod, to say that my silent guess was right.

Well, we worked to make him die a little happier. We gave him a drink of brandy out of a little metal flask which I always have carried since my health grew weak, and in another moment he had opened those frightful eyes and was looking up to us.

"Hello, Claudia," said he. "You ought to give a horse his head in the middle of a jump."

I thought it was the wandering brain of a dying man, but Claudia gave a little half cry, half sob. His memory, I learned afterward, had jumped back to the old days on the Dexter ranch, when Manuel was cow-puncher there, and had given little Claudia Laffitter riding lessons across the range.

"Well, I remember, now," said he. And he put his hand to his wound, and then nodded.

No one had to tell him what a bullet in that place meant.

"Claudia," said he, "suppose that you sit there where I can see you?"

She sat, without stirring, right beside him. I gave him another drink of the brandy, and he gave me a glance out of those slitted eyes of his.

It was hard strain on Claudia, sitting there to make a pleasant picture for the man who had murdered her father, but to a noble soul like hers a time comes when forgiveness is made easy. She began to tremble,

236

and I knew it was heart-breaking pity that moved her.

Once he remarked: "Do you remember the day we put the new weathercock on the barn?"

"Yes," she said, "and you stood up on the ridge of the barn and waved your hand to me."

He smiled, and continued to stare at her until the end, which came presently. There was a short convulsion. He sat up and gripped at his throat with both hands. That strange fantasy of the dual soul came back on him, and he gasped out: "Scorpio, Scorpio, you are choking me—devil!" And twisting over, he fell on his side and died.

We sat there through a long silence.

My mind was out there galloping after the fugitives and their two pursuers. There would not be two pursuers when the battle started, I knew. The mustang never could keep the sheriff up with the race, and Dexter would fly ahead on the wild stallion to close on the enemy.

So I waited, saying nothing of this, but leaning my chin in my hand until I heard the sound of horses in the trees.

Was it Dexter and the sheriff, or had the other two come back?

"Charlie! Charlie!" cried Claudia.

And there he rode out from the woods alone, and took off his hat and waved it to her, and passed from the shadow of the trees into the brightness of the moonlight. And his gesture reminded me of a prince indeed—some painting I had seen, of Henry IV at Ivry.

He dismounted, and the stallion stood like a lamp behind him.

Suddenly it struck me that that was poor Scorpio's life work—all the good that ever he had done, standing there at the back of Dexter, subdued and gentle.

"Tom Winchell?" gasped Claudia, losing her courage now that her hero was returned to us safely.

"He stayed behind—to arrange things," said Prince Charlie. "He thought I'd better come back to tell you. And Scorpio?"

We pointed, and Charlie Dexter went and stood for a

long time looking down at the covered face, with his hat still in his hand. And his bowed head gave him a certain air of reverence which I myself had felt for the better half of Scorpio's soul.

"THE KING OF THE WESTERN NOVEL" IS MAX BRAND

THE BIG TRAIL	(C94-333, $1.75)
BROTHERS ON THE TRAIL	(C90-302, $1.95)
DRIFTER'S VENGEANCE	(C84-783, $1.75)
FIRE BRAIN	(C88-629, $1.50)
FLAMING IRONS	(C98-019, $1.50)
FRONTIER FEUD	(C98-002, $1.50)
GALLOPING BRONCOS	(C94-265, $1.75)
THE GAMBLER	(C94-328, $1.75)
GARDEN OF EDEN	(C94-290, $1.75)
THE GENTLE GUNMAN	(C94-291, $1.75)
GUNMAN'S GOLD	(C90-619, $1.95)
GUNS OF DORKING HOLLOW	(C94-204, $1.75)
HAPPY JACK	(C90-303, $1.95)
HAPPY VALLEY	(C90-304, $1.95)
THE INVISIBLE OUTLAW	(C94-343, $1.75)
THE KING BIRD RIDES	(C90-305, $1.95)
THE LONG CHASE	(C94-266, $1.75)
LUCKY LARRIBEE	(C94-456, $1.75)
THE MAN FROM SAVAGE CREEK	(C90-815, $1.95)
MARBLEFACE	(C90-307, $1.95)